A Faithful Following

A McNulty Brothers Novel

CAMELLIA CANN

For my Muncas.

Idaho Code § 18-1504(4)

"The practice of a parent or guardian who chooses for his child treatment by prayer or spiritual means alone shall not for that reason alone be construed to have violated the duty of care to such child."

By mid-2022, only two children in Idaho had died due to COVID-19 related factors.

To date, more than 200 children in Idaho have died due to faith-healing practices.

According to medical experts, 90 percent of them would have lived if treated with modern medicine.

ONE.

"Hey all, Brit here," the sprite-like, gamine woman announced playfully. "Who wants to see what we've done with the new digs?"

Britlyn Robbins grinned into the webcam, pushing a glossy, brunette strand behind her right ear. The ring light mounted on her laptop danced in her eyes, illuminating their warm, cocoa color.

"This isn't just farmhouse style, this is *legit farmhouse*," Britlyn assured her audience, gesturing towards the old-fashioned apron sink. "We literally can't even wait to like, grow stuff. Maybe get some farm animals. Who wants to see me milk a cow? Okay, seriously, 'like' this video if you want me to milk a cow. I could totally milk a cow."

Britlyn flashed another winning smile at her laptop, walking backwards as she showcased the home.

"The sweetest part is that we are RIGHT on the river," she gushed, sharing the view of the blue ribbon slinking through the property. "Can I tell you something? I am so going to lay out there with a floatie. Someone find me the best river floatie ever, like right now. Seriously, hashtag, #summerfun. Hashtag, #no-tan-lines." Britlyn winked at the camera, letting the dark red strap on her tank top fall loosely over her shoulder.

Britlyn ended the stream, then clicked off the ring light. The kitchen suddenly grew quiet, and she released the heavy breath she'd held tightly in her chest. Her signature bubbly energy could be grueling to maintain when she wasn't feeling well. She closed her eyes for a minute, allowing the sound of spring rain dancing on the rooftop above to reset her mind and calm her nausea. In furry, white slippers, she padded to the cabinet, grabbing a saltine cracker and strolling to the dining room window.

Outside, the Palouse River roared past the quaint home. Britlyn had been telling the truth — it was indeed an old farmhouse. However, the previous owners had modernized the dated residence, updating the electrical and plumbing. After they bought it, the Robbinses had gone a step further, elevating the vintage house by infusing modern conveniences. Stylish and efficient lighting was provided free of charge from a blog sponsor; an up-and-coming design firm had furnished the home with stunning, midcentury modern furniture; and a major tech website had fully outfitted the home with smart technology in exchange for Brit advertising their devices on her platform.

Just as she'd promised her husband, they were making the old house into a dream home with the money earned from her online persona alone. Before they moved in, she'd worked with local contractors to demolish some of the walls, opening up the smaller spaces. Appointed with minimalist, gold tone hardware and Carrara marble, the now-expansive kitchen was clean and bright, ripe for entertaining guests. The plain, sliding door in the walk-out basement was replaced with a full wall of glass for panoramic views of the rolling landscape. The east bedroom was converted to an office, complete with a custom, built-in desk tucked under that bay window overlooking the water.

Finally, the last bedroom had been painted a delicate shade of shell pink, and a chandelier made from subdued, wooden beads replaced the basic, flush mount lighting. In the coming weeks, Britlyn would complete the floral, DIY Roman shades for the windows, then she'd chalk paint the ornately carved armoire. She'd finish by flanking the room with two driftwood-inspired cribs, both gifted to her from a high-end store. Then, she'd debut the perfect nursery to her fans when she made the big announcement: she was pregnant with twin girls.

* * *

THREE MONTHS LATER

At 3:30 P.M., Agent Shawn Robbins started his walk across the parking lot over an hour before the other desk jockeys normally left.

Before he even reached his vehicle, a sleek, midnight-hued German sports car, he had yanked the knot from his tie and crumpled the paisley patterned, silk noose in his hand. He slid into the driver's position, tossing everything onto the buttery, soft leather of his passenger seat. Rummaging in the glove box, he located an orange plastic bottle and popped its white lid. Crunching on two of the small, powdery tablets, he closed his eyes and tipped his head back against the rest. As he chewed, his jaw ached from a day's worth of clenching. He rubbed his fingertips over his clean-shaven face, massaging the muscles beneath.

Often, he'd find relief at the local gym, pounding the treadmill's rubber track until his lungs burned and sweat soaked through his shirt. Other times, he'd hit the basketball court for a pick-up game with the guys. Or find a buddy to spot him while he lifted a few sets. Strolling into his satellite office at the local police department this morning, however, he'd been greeted by the sight of his desk piled high with hard drives, dark repositories ready for a careful, forensic analysis of the most perverse and graphic child pornography that could be produced. Some 4,000 images later, the last thing he wanted to see was any more skin.

Ascending Fox Trot Ridge, he could almost taste the sweet tang of crisp juniper as he pictured the freshly made gin and tonic he knew would be waiting for him next to their well-stocked, stylish bar cart. Sure, by the time Brit took a million photographs from as many angles, the drink would be sweating. But he'd grown accustomed to it, and besides — his job with ICAC, or Internet Crimes Against Children, wasn't footing the bill for either the sexy coupe or the upscale home. *Or even the good gin*, he admitted to himself, picturing the plastic bottles of lesser spirits of years past. No, Brit had made good on her promise to turn being beautiful into a business, and her rising social media success was the only thing that made this luxurious new life possible. Within eighteen months, they had left their one-bedroom Seattle apartment for forty acres of charming countryside in Cattail, Idaho. After a short training, Shawn was able to transfer to the Idaho State Police, which allowed him to work remotely from the local police department or from his new home, an upgraded farmhouse located on a hillside overlooking the Palouse River.

Their property included water frontage, and Shawn had hoped the couple would be spending long summer days soaking up sun on their very own bank, maybe playing some games in the yard. That's how he'd met Britlyn, after all — a volleyball tournament one unusually warm weekend at Alki Beach. She was about five feet, two inches of perfectly tanned yoga body, and he had wanted her instantly. Now, she was all belly and swollen ankles, hardly the picture of provocation he'd married two years prior. He was admittedly grateful that her inflated income would allow them to hire a full-time nanny so Brit could get back to her old self.

Still, though his sex-on-the-beach dreams were shattered for this summer at least, he loved his wife. She was disciplined, enterprising, and insightful enough to realize that her looks were the number one thing she could leverage. As Shawn pulled into the circular, brick driveway approaching their handsome home, he was grateful the day was over.

Shawn touched the handle on the coupe, automatically locking the vehicle. He ascended the front steps to the grand entry, a set of knotty alder double doors with exquisite wrought iron accents.

"Honey, I'm home," he announced.

The smart system quickly assessed his biometric data, and he heard the deadbolt unlatch.

"Welcome home, Shawn," the system greeted him as he strode in, hanging his tie in the entry. Before he had even reached the kitchen, hip, indie tunes began streaming from the speakers placed throughout the home.

"No," he snapped at the automated assistant. "Turn that shit off."

He walked to the bar cart, dismayed to see it was not already in use. Shawn reached past the gin for the Patrón, pouring himself a hefty tequila shot and throwing it back, then refilling it.

Contemporary beats continued to play.

Yeah, it was gonna be that kind of night.

"Music off. Turn it off," he commanded irritably.

The volume increased.

"Off, off. Not up. Stupid, fuck!" Shawn screamed, chucking the dimpled rocks glass and spraying glass throughout the kitchen.

Now you've done it, he told himself. Brit would come down any second, furious about the mess.

Taking a deep breath, he poured himself another drink in a fresh glass, then fumbled through the drawers for the vacuum's remote. The disc-like device whirred into action, pivoting around the massive island with a low purr that softened the incessant melodies that were still playing. The job was finished in mere minutes.

But Brit didn't come.

Shawn finished his cocktail with one swallow, then set the new vessel gently on the marble counter.

"Hey, Brit?" he yelled for her.

No answer.

Shawn walked to the foyer, stopping at the base of a shapely, curved staircase. He leaned against the railing.

"Brit?" he called out again, concerned.

As he climbed the stairs, he suddenly froze. Four steps up, a single scarlet spot stood out against the plush, silver runner. About the size of a dime, it sat atop the carpet fibers, as shiny and bright as if it had just fallen. Dumbfounded, Shawn thumbed his own nostrils, checking for a bloody nose. He quickened his pace, racing to the top.

"Britlyn!" he shouted now.

Reaching her office, he realized he didn't have his gun. With his hand against the door, he paused for a moment, thinking about its location. Sure, he rode a desk, but he had a duty weapon — he was a real cop, POST-certified and all — but he never really *needed* it.

He could picture it now, in a case under his driver's seat. Too far away — Brit could be in trouble.

Shawn pushed open the door, gasping at the disarray. The carefully curated items that normally adorned the antique white desk and shelves littered the floor, and an elegant, cantilevered floor lamp had crashed over, crumpling the shade. Worse, Shawn spotted more blood: the door jamb bore a crimson smudge, and the wall had also been hit with a long, narrow splash.

He had to get help.

"Call 911," he instructed.

Abruptly, the music stopped, and the system began to dial. As Shawn waited for dispatch to answer, he was suddenly aware of the melted marshmallow sensation of benzodiazepines swimming in booze.

"Wait, stop. . .hang up!" he shouted, slurring slightly. "Call. . ."

His mind was gummy as he struggled to recall the Chief's name.

"I'm sorry, I'm having some trouble understanding you. Who do you want me to call?" the A.I. asked.

"McNulty," Shawn finished.

* * *

Chief Jack McNulty's cruiser squealed into the circular driveway, coming to an abrupt halt in front of the double entry doors. Beside them, Shawn frantically paced the porch. Jack got out, then reached up, snugging down his brown cowboy hat. He wore a matching leather vest over a crisp white shirt and dark jeans, a casual but classic combination that reflected the rural atmosphere but fit well enough to look sharp. Over his heart, a star-shaped badge gleamed in the late afternoon sun.

Jack was trim and long-legged, with salt-and-pepper hair and narrow, dark brown eyes that suited his careful, pensive temperament. At the moment, they were hidden behind reflective, aviator sunglasses. Shawn wished they weren't; he was worried enough that his demeanor would raise concern, and now he'd be unable to read Jack's expression.

Shawn smiled and waved as the man drew nearer. "Chief," he greeted him.

Jack continued his approach, finally stopping a few feet from the steps. He said nothing.

You idiot, Shawn berated himself. He cleared his throat and the smirk from his face.

"Thank you for coming," he tried again in a more serious tone. The words were mushy as he spit them from his mouth.

"Given your state by the time you called, I guess it's safe to assume you got a little head start before you got home," Jack remarked pointedly.

"You know how difficult my job is," Shawn explained, looking over at the cotton candy geraniums blooming in their window boxes. "The photographs today, the Nelson case—"

"Bullshit," Jack interrupted. "I've got a tow truck driver who's been sitting in on his DUI for two weeks because he can't afford bail. Know what he does for a living? Peels dead kids off the road. He's not combing through pictures from the comfort of his office chair with a soy latte in his hand. We're happy to have your help, Agent Robbins, but if you get caught driving like this again, you'll get grace. Not a pass."

Shawn hung his head. "Yes, sir," he responded.

Jack ascended the steps. He noted the elegant seating arrangement and directed Shawn to sit. Jack eased into the adjacent wicker chair, removing his sunglasses and tucking them into his pocket. The porch was immaculately decorated in shades of cornflower and cream, and the ceiling had been refinished with white planks. Had Britlyn Robbins been home, he imagined she would offer him a glass of sun tea, then bring it out on a crystal tray with sterling silver bowls of sugar cubes and lemon wheels.

"Now," Jack began. "Any idea who would do this?"

"None whatsoever," Shawn answered.

Jack's stare was penetrating, and Shawn almost wished he'd put the sunglasses back on.

"Bad blood?" Jack continued.

Shawn huffed. "She plays fucking dress-up on the internet, Chief. . .who's she gonna beef with?"

Jack raised an eyebrow, then tilted his head in agreement.

"Alright. What about stalkers?" he continued. "Anybody around town been clinging too closely?"

"She doesn't even leave the house," Shawn replied.

Jack frowned. "And that's not concerning for you?"

Shawn shrugged.

Jack crossed his arms over his chest, sitting back against the seersucker cushion.

"You two been fightin'?" he asked.

"What's that supposed to mean?" Shawn exclaimed, straightening his posture. "You think *I* did this?"

"I'd like to rule you out. Want me to Mirandize you first?" Jack flashed a wide, white smile, but Shawn knew he wasn't kidding.

"No," he sighed finally. "No fighting. We never fight, actually." Shawn's voice never failed to carry a note of arrogance, but his answer did sound sincere.

Jack stood, adjusting his belt. "Alright, then. Let's get your statement to Buchanan, and I'll get Camden and Corbin up here to start piecing things together."

"Great — Tweedle Dee and Tweedle Dum," Shawn complained.

"I know you're relatively new here, Agent Robbins," Jack cautioned. "So, in case you somehow forgot, Tweedle Dee and Tweedle Dum are my nephews. They're young, sure. But they're bright boys. And professional."

Shawn stifled a groan, choosing instead to nod in agreement.

The Chief gestured towards his vehicle. "Hop in, Robbins. Seems like you could use a designated driver."

* * *

Jack quickly disposed of Agent Robbins at the station for his interview with the other officers, then stopped to grab a cold can of Pepsi on the way out. Though the man had been gone from his cruiser for several minutes now, his overpowering, musky cologne hung so thickly in the air that Jack worried it may never fade. He rolled the windows down and sped up, hoping to flush the scent from the hot cab.

He barreled along, passing the Grange Hall and a wrecking yard on his way out of town. The wind churned the wheat fields of the Palouse like a golden, magic carpet, sending ripples in every direction. The road snaked alongside them, gradually fluctuating with the gentle, rolling hills. The rise and fall of the highway, the same route he traveled home, usually soothed his soul; the day's troubles were swept from him like they, too, were prairie grass. Today, however, he worriedly plucked the soda pop's aluminum tab, his mind cruelly shuffling the horrible outcomes for the young woman and her unborn babies. Even if she escaped her captor, the endless prairie could be cruel and confusing, and cougars and wolves roamed the grassland at night, preying on the lost. Especially for city folks, the odds were slim.

Jack refocused, speeding faster towards the farm. *Agent Robbins was an asshat,* he acknowledged to himself, *but his wife was apparently smart enough to amass an empire without even leaving the house.* Hopefully, that would translate into the smarts to stay safe long enough for them to find her.

As Jack neared the large parcel the family shared, his mother's cistern came into view. When it came time to fly the coop, his daughter Cayla had volunteered to stay with her; Nan's vertigo had become concerning, but her mental health was really what made living alone too risky. Corbin found a spot at Nan's, too, converting the loft above the barn into a one-bedroom apartment. Camden put his trailer on a far corner of the property, but he checked on his grandma morning and night, often joining Nan and Cayla for dinner. Having briefly inquired at the office and learning that the boys were out for the day, Jack expected to find them at the farm enjoying one of their first days off this summer.

They were good boys, the best he could have ever prayed for. *Oh, and he did pray.* Indeed, he hadn't stopped since the moment they fell into his lap over twenty years ago. His older sister Molly was chasing fame in Hollywood, emphysema and cirrhosis were nearing the end of their decades-long contest to kill his dad, and his mom was crazy. Yes, Jack won by default — but he wasn't going to let his brother's sons grow up in the shadow of what happened to their parents. Jack pushed through his withdrawals, the boys pushed through the night terrors, and they all made it through the shitty spaghetti together. A couple years in, he met Sandy, and it was like God had turned on the sun again. TV tray dinners and awkward, doorway "g'nites" gave way to wholesome, home-cooked meals, bubble baths, and story time. Boo-boos got kisses, homework got finished, and holidays became magical gatherings. By the time Sandy gave birth to their daughter, Cayla, the boys didn't think twice about calling her their baby sister instead of just their cousin.

A buzzing sound cut into Jack's thoughts. He followed the noise, finally landing on an object cutting tight figure-eights in the tall, yellow fields. It grew louder as he approached. Then, another trail appeared. As the objects grew closer, they began to run parallel paths, and the buzz became a mechanical chorus roaring towards the edge of the pasture.

"What in the hell???" he muttered aloud.

Jack punched the pedal in hot pursuit.

* * *

"Gentlemen, start your engines."

Camden McNulty's low, smooth voice gave way to the roar beneath him as the shiny, green machine rumbled to life. He hit the throttle and it jolted forward, its broad, square nose quickly pushing a track through the tall, yellow stalks. Over the noise of the racing engine, Camden could just barely hear his brother's uproarious laughter. On his own red machine, Corbin flipped Camden the bird and a cheesy smile as he blazed past.

Camden went faster, blurring the field around him. His tee flapped in the breeze, a welcome sensation on the sultry afternoon; since around eight that morning, they'd baked in the sun while mending the north fence. Camden could feel the resulting sunburn forming on his cheeks just where his goggles rested. Luckily, though his father's Irish heritage bestowed upon Camden his light hair and blue eyes, he and his brother both shared their mother's olive skin tone; he knew the pink tint would quickly resolve to match the bronzed coloring of the rest of his face and arms. Camden caught up to his similarly suntanned little brother, and the duo plugged forward, beginning the last leg of their race. The final stretch would end at the barn near the entry to their grandmother's portion of the 100-acre farm shared between the boys, Nan, their aunt and uncle, and their sister. The long driveway — like Uncle Jack's, a gravel road flanked by grass — was just in sight. He could hear Corbin revving the engine, urging his red steed towards the finish line. Camden matched him, accelerating faster and faster.

Suddenly, the unmistakable contrast of a black and white cruiser zipped into view.

Shit.

Camden spotted it immediately, reflexively braking and slowing the mower to a crawl right as he reached the grass. Corbin braked too late, and the final rotations of his thick, rubber tires sprayed gravel down the body of the car. Camden grit his teeth, waiting for the sound of chipping glass. Miraculously, the sedan appeared unscathed.

His uncle was another matter. Jack leapt from the car, shaking his head.

"What kind of jackassery is this?" he began, slamming the driver's door.

"Uncle Jack—" Corbin began.

"Don't 'Uncle Jack' me, Corb," Jack interrupted. "You want to catch the whole county on fire?"

"We're being careful." Per usual, Cam began to take responsibility. As he said the words, he caught his reflection in his uncle's mirrored lenses. In them, Lieutenant Camden McNulty could see the picture of two adult men in comical, plastic goggles, balancing their muscular frames atop souped-up lawnmowers like circus bears.

"Careful?" Jack questioned incredulously.

Cam's sunburn was suddenly not the only thing turning his cheeks pink.

Corb shrugged. "Come on. . .we're s'posed to have today off, then Cayla had us fix the damn fence all morning. What's the harm in blowing off a little steam?" He grinned at his uncle, predictably softening the older man's expression. Jack sighed.

"I doubt that Nan wants you spinnin' donuts in her wheat fields. Party time's over," Jack instructed. "Listen up: I'm here with official business. A kidnapping."

"Whose kid?" Corb asked.

"Kidnapping's not just for kids, Corb," Cam pointed out.

"I know that," he scoffed. "But it usually is. Somebody didn't get the kids this holiday, or that one, then one parent's dragging out their court order and calling the cops on the other. . ."

"True. I had three of them just last Christmas," Cam acknowledged.

"It ain't that kind," Jack stated solemnly.

"Who then?" Cam asked.

"A lady. From the internet," Jack responded.

"*From* the internet? What does that even mean?" Cam asked, furrowing his brow.

"Like a mail-order bride?" Corb chimed in.

"No, not that. Damnit, I can't keep up with all this new-age shit. She's famous on the internet. Inter-gram, something-something. . ." Jack trailed off, shaking his head.

"Ah," Corb uttered. "You mean she's an influencer."

Uncle Jack pointed his index finger at his nephew. "That. Bingo."

Cam crossed his thick forearms. His shirt was covered in wisps of wheat and grass. "I didn't know we had anyone famous in Cattail."

"They haven't lived here all that long. I believe you know her husband, Agent Robbins."

Cam tried to disguise his eyeroll.

"Like Shawn Robbins?" Corb chimed in, his voice dripping with disgust.

"You got a problem with Agent Robbins?" Jack asked.

"No, sir," Cam respectfully replied.

"Hell yeah, I do. He's a tool from the city," Corb snorted.

"Well, that tool's wife is missing. . .his pregnant wife. . .and I promised him I could trust you two to not fuck it all up. You gonna make me a liar?"

Corb slid his rubbery goggles up his forehead, leaving red rings around his olive-green eyes and pushing his sweaty, sand-colored hair up in a dozen spikes that stuck out like a damp crown. "No, sir."

"Then let's go find her."

T W O .

Britlyn sat at the milky white executive desk, tapping her long, gel-lacquered nails on the surface. She gazed out the large window, taking in the vibrant, green grass and cloudless, blue sky. Last year, she would have been frolicking through the field and enjoying the hot, sunny day, camera in hand. Instead, beside her, a cup of chamomile tea was getting cold. She took another careful drink, wrinkling her nose as she felt it trickle down her esophagus and into her queasy stomach. As soon as she finished her sip, the reflux returned, searing through her chest as if she'd swallowed a lump of coal. Despite what she portrayed to her followers, pregnancy was far from glamorous. Much to Shawn's chagrin, once the camera was off, Brit slipped out of the ruffled, designer maternity dresses and into a pair of his old basketball shorts, which she paired today with a threadbare Hard Rock T-shirt that clung tightly to her growing belly.

She cleared her throat, trying to ignore the heartburn. At 28 weeks, she was grateful to be over the halfway point but still dreading the next few months. Some of her internet friends were trying to convince her to just schedule an early C-section to spare herself the worst of the stretch marks, but even she had a limit to her vanity. She was aiming to carry the twins in her womb as long as she could.

She returned her attention to her keyboard, clacking away. From outside, the familiar buzz of the gardener employing a weed eater around the property served as white noise, helping her focus.

A sudden creak caught her attention. Though the Robbinses had masterfully updated the home, the original hardwood floors still complained underfoot in a few places. She had become accustomed to hearing the noise as she lay in bed each morning, trying to find a comfortable position against her pregnancy pillow while she listened to Shawn get ready for work.

But Shawn wasn't home, a difference that distinguished this particular creak and gave her pause as her brain tried to rationalize her suspicions. Her doctor hadn't required it, but she did discontinue her anxiety medication for the duration of her pregnancy. She was pleasantly surprised that her illness was mostly manageable, save for instances like this where her increased clarity and perceptiveness lent itself to paranoia. She recalled a few other times she had felt the distinct sense that she was being watched: once, in the girls' room, she swore the newly installed video baby monitor was tracking her as she moved. Even during intimate moments with her husband, she felt a troubling lack of privacy she'd never experienced before. Shawn chalked it up to the big windows, and she hadn't thought much about it since.

Suddenly, in the darkest corner of her laptop screen, a figure appeared behind her.

Her heart thudded as she stealthily turned her brightness down, enhancing the reflectiveness of the surface before her.

Not just a figure, she realized. *A man.*

A man crouched in the doorway, and he was growing closer.

Even as her mind questioned her eyes, her body naturally prepared her for the worst. Her pulse quickened, and she made a mental list of every item she had to protect herself. *Knives in the kitchen. Shawn's golf clubs in the garage.* Nothing accessible came to mind. Then, she remembered.

As a housewarming gift, another successful fashion blogger had recently sent her a chic, sterling silver, designer letter opener. Obscuring her hands from the doorway, she slid open the center desk drawer. There it was, nestled inside the signature, Robin's-egg blue box. She withdrew it, clutching it tightly in her shaking right hand. With her left hand, she held her belly. The air suddenly felt heavy, and Britlyn fought the urge to look at the man's reflection. Choked with fear, she couldn't resist allowing herself to watch the man approach.

He was much closer now, and his dark clothing and black gloves triggered violent images in her mind. Though a balaclava obscured most of his face, she could see his eyes, pale blue and wrinkled at the corners. In the blackness of the screen, they met hers. For a moment, he paused. *Was he smiling?*

She exhaled.

Suddenly, he leapt forward, and Britlyn sprung from the chair. He cornered her, stretching his arms around her body as if he were giving her a bear hug. Britlyn reached back, slashing her letter opener until she hit something solid, then twisted it in deep. The man yelped in pain. As they rolled down the wall, glass frames fell from their places and shattered on the hardwood below. She continued to stab behind her, frantically clawing at his arms with her other hand. On her third attempt, she sunk the tool in flesh again — this time, something softer. He loosened his grip. Britlyn squirmed, managing to slip from his grasp.

As she turned to run, he regathered his strength, reaching out and tightly grabbing her by the loop of her messy bun.

The searing pain caused her to drop her makeshift weapon. Panicking, she began to shout for help.

Outside, the weed eater stopped.

Yanking her hair back, the man pulled her to the floor, then pulled her towards him.

"Help me, someone please!" she screamed louder, attempting to crawl towards the door. *"¡Ayúdeme!"*

Then, she felt the sharp prick of a needle. It embedded deep into the muscle of her buttocks.

"There you go," the man soothed her. "Shhhh."

As he withdrew the syringe, Britlyn could feel the room shrinking down on her, its edges becoming fuzzy. Exhausted, she rolled onto her back, laying her head against her intricately patterned, Persian area rug. Her eyes felt heavy, and she struggled to keep them open. Outside, the weed eater resumed. Its dull buzz filled the room, resonating off the walls as if she were laying inside a bustling beehive. The man leaned over her and gently wiped her hair out of her eyes.

"How—" she stuttered, her groggy voice barely above a whisper. "How did you get in?"

He pushed up on his mask, revealing his face and the sly smile she suspected. "Oh, honey. . .you invited me."

* * *

In the back of Jack's cruiser, Detective Corbin McNulty listened as his uncle briefed them on specifics. He calmly and methodically reviewed the missing woman's appearance, daily agenda, and other pertinent information, stopping only to sip his soda pop every minute or so. Whatever minor irritation their lawnmower races had caused, he was over it now.

But then, Corb had only really seen Uncle Jack mad a couple of times. The Pontiac came to mind. He remembered the night he'd crashed the cherry-red, classic car into the willow tree at the bottom of Uncle Jack's gravel driveway.

As kids, Jack would let them perch on his lap while he drove to Nan's. When they got older, sometimes he'd let them sit in the driver's seat and start it. The V8 would rumble, shaking Corb to the bone. Jack only had one rule: they were never, ever allowed to drive it. Still, the Pontiac beckoned Corb from the dusty, old barn like a ruby locked in a vault. . .and Corb knew where to find the key. What he didn't know was what would happen when it turned over, or when he harnessed over 300 horses under his bare foot.

At the sound of shrieking metal, Jack had flown from the house, dressed in only a ribbed, white undershirt and plaid boxer shorts.

Once he was sure Corb was alright, his uncle's mood had quickly changed. The damage to the front end wasn't terribly extensive, but it wouldn't be cheap to fix.

"What is going on in your head, boy? You been drinkin'?" Jack had asked sharply.

Corb had scowled, ignoring him. He liked his Uncle Jack, but he was embarrassed, and at thirteen, it was an emotion he didn't process well.

"Answer me," Jack demanded.

Corb looked away, continuing to glower.

"God damnit, Corbin!" Jack shouted, catching the boy's attention.

Corb mumbled something under his breath.

"What's that?" Jack asked.

"I *said*," Corb rudely responded, "maybe YOU should lighten up and have a drink."

The impact of calloused fingers across his dewy, young cheek startled Corb, and against his will, tears started to well in his eyes.

It was the only time Jack had hit him. The tap was light, but it had wounded Corb's pride.

The pained look on Jack's face told Corb that his uncle felt the sting of the blow worst of all.

"I ain't been drinkin', my foot just slipped," Corb explained. "I promise."

Jack eased backwards, burying his face in his hands.

"I'm sorry," Corb added.

"Go find your brother," Jack had whispered, his words heavy with regret.

Quickly wiping his tears with his palms, Corb squeezed his narrow hips from the car and skittered up the stairs into the house.

Like his brother, Camden was supposed to be asleep. Instead, Corb could see the cool glow from the screen of Cam's handheld game emanating from under his knotted, navy and white quilt. Sandy had made the boys matching blankets soon after Uncle Jack had proposed to her, and Corb always saw it as her way of asking to be their aunt. Of course, they had loved her from the day she was introduced as Uncle Jack's "friend." She was bright-eyed and full of laughter, and her easy, gentle manner balanced Uncle Jack's stern, no-nonsense approach to rearing the brothers. Sometimes she would ruffle through Corb's hair with her fingernails, or present him with a freshly baked chocolate chip cookie, and he wondered if the love he had for her was how it felt to have a mother.

Undoubtedly, she would be awake; she would have heard the crash and sent Jack to investigate. Corb could have stopped at the master bedroom for maternal consolation — it wouldn't have been the first time he ran to Aunt Sandy for an injury, though they were usually of the type that required a heap of cotton balls and bandages, something to bite down on, and that big, brown bottle of hydrogen peroxide. No, this time, he tip-toed on by: he had questions that only Cam could answer.

As he drew closer to the foot of Cam's bed, the light quickly shut off.

"It's just me," Corb whispered to his brother.

Cam popped out of the blankets, relieved. "What do you want?" he asked, returning to his game. "You break something big this time?"

Ignoring him, Corb flopped down on the bed, propping himself on one elbow.

"Why doesn't Uncle Jack drink?" he asked.

Cam blinked, continuing to play. Corb could see him tumbling the answer around in his mind. When he was done, he'd furnish the response, a gleaming, polished version of reality, but with all the rough edges smoothed off. Corb figured it was Cam's way of protecting his little brother.

"The truth," Corb demanded.

Cam sighed. "He used to. Uncle Jack and dad went out drinkin' all the time. Came home stupid. . . sometimes didn't come home at all. Mom used to cry about it a lot."

An uneasy feeling washed over Corb as a strange, new memory jostled loose from his brain. It was their mother, cross-legged on the floor with her back against the washing machine, teardrops falling from her splotchy face to the scratched linoleum below. Her sadness alarmed him, and he had climbed onto her lap, hoisting his chubby legs over hers and offering her his stuffed bear.

"Dad killed Mom, didn't he?" Corb suddenly asked.

Cam set the game down. His face wrenched with anguish, he looked at Corb with sorrowful eyes. Behind them, he wasn't polishing.

"Yeah, Corb," he answered quietly. "He did."

THREE.

Hugging the hillside, the trio continued the last leg of their climb to the Robbins residence. The house was painted in a meticulous, crisp white, which served as the perfect contrast for the wooden double doors and matching columns supporting the grand front porch. Next to Shawn's pretentious sports car, Britlyn's white Range Rover was similarly parked at an angle, spotless and shining in the sun. Glossy, green boxwoods formed a natural border, while flowers of every size and color sprouted from the beds hugging the home. The centerpiece, a large, three-tiered fountain, graced the courtyard in the middle of the home's circular driveway. As they parked, its peaceful babbles were audible from the cruiser's open windows.

"Being famous on the internet pays good," Cam observed.

"I'd say so. Think it's too late to change my job to influencer?" Corb exclaimed.

"How about you influence your way into that house already," Jack sternly redirected the brothers. "And don't come out until you have an idea where to find Mrs. Robbins."

"What about Shawn?" Corb asked.

"Leave him to me. He won't be on the case, of course. . .he's too close to it." Jack looked down at his watch. "He's still down at the PD talking with officers. He'll be out of your hair for a while, anyhow."

"Just us then?" Cam added. "Or should we get some guys from County?"

"Not yet. I'm working with the FBI to get some outside help on this one. I'm worried there might be some special motivation we might not have experience with," Jack responded.

"And it's gonna be high profile," Cam pointed out.

"Get ready for an influx of obnoxious journalists," Jack confirmed. With that, he rounded the driveway and headed back down the hill.

Inside the Robbins' residence, Camden and Corbin were greeted by a heady perfume bearing hints of wood and musk. As he cautiously stepped onto the polished hickory floor, Corb flared his nostrils, intently sniffing the air. It reminded him of the few times he'd set foot in a department store.

"Candle?" he asked his brother.

"Maybe some sort of diffuser?" Cam posited.

"Fan-cy," Corb whistled. He stopped and took a picture of the foyer and the landing. A few stairs up, he noticed the spot of blood that Uncle Jack mentioned.

The scarlet drop that Shawn first saw when he climbed the stairs had settled in and stained the carpet, darkening as it dried. Corb snapped another photo. He scanned the adjacent banister and wall, carefully inspecting them for any additional spatter. He nodded at his brother, and Cam began to cut around the stain, collecting a small square of the runner and underlying pad. They'd send the scrap for rush processing at the state's forensics lab; hopefully, they'd have a match by morning. The brothers slowly continued their ascent, noting additional droplets every few steps.

At the top, Corb paused as he observed the entry to Mrs. Robbins' office. From his vantage point, he could see blood on the door frame and various wall hangings knocked askew. He captured the necessary photos, then approached the threshold. After examining the light switch for a moment, he turned it on.

Inside, the room was as Shawn had described — in complete disarray. Broken glass had been crunched into the plush, oriental rug, and additional blood smeared the walls in long, messy stripes. What appeared to be coffee or tea dripped from an otherwise pristine, white desk, and a sleek laptop had toppled to the floor in an open position.

Click. Click. Click. Corb added to their growing collection of photographs.

"This might take me a while," he relayed back to Cam. "Want to do a check of downstairs?"

"I'm on it," Cam confirmed.

Corb carefully advanced, studying every surface of the room. The bay window was intact, but the curtain rod above was bent as if from the pull of body weight, and the ivory, linen-like fabric cascading from it was speckled with blood. Corb drew closer, noticing the center drawer of the desk was ajar. He photographed it, then pulled it further open. A blue box featuring an upscale brand had been hastily torn open but was now empty.

Jewelry? he wondered.

Suddenly, something bright caught his eye.

Click, click.

He crouched, examining the small, orange pen cap tucked beside the rear wheel of the rolling, leather office chair.

No, he suddenly realized, examining its tiny crevice.

A syringe cap.

He removed his cowboy hat and lowered himself to the floor, peering under the desk. Amber liquid had collected in a puddle on the exposed wooden planks just beyond the rug. He got closer, inhaling the scent he recognized to be herbal tea.

From that perspective, Corb continued to scan the floor, glancing under a fallen lamp and the overturned laptop. He then followed the perpendicular lines of the area rug. Where they met, they pointed to an object beneath one of the matching, carved bookcases. It reflected the beam of his flashlight.

Holding his light in his mouth, he photographed the item, then carefully pulled it out into view.

The knife, an elegant, heavy, silver piece, was coated in blood.

* * *

"Cam," Corb shouted down. "Got somethin'."

"Me, too," Cam responded. Corb could hear his footsteps drawing closer.

"You first," Corb insisted as his brother appeared in the doorway.

"Broken glass," Cam revealed.

"Tracked from up here?"

"No. A drinking glass."

"What kind?"

"Can't tell yet. It's busted to smithereens. Guessing it was thrown," Cam deduced. "Found some pieces of it in their robot vacuum — smells like tequila."

"Hm. Well, Uncle Jack said Shawn was all fucked up when he got here," Corb reasoned.

"Yeah, booze and pills," Cam remembered.

"Any reason to think he's an IV user?" Corb asked.

Cam raised his eyebrows. "That's pretty heavy. I'd be surprised. Why?"

"Found a syringe cap," Corb mentioned. "But more importantly, I found this."

With a click, he brought his flashlight to life and pointed it at the shining blade that was still tucked halfway under the bookshelf.

"That's covered," Cam observed quietly. "Could be from bloody hands."

"Yeah. Or sinking it in real deep," Corb rebutted. They stood in silence for a minute.

Finally, Cam cleared his throat. "Only one way to find out. I'll collect a few more samples while you finish up. Then we'll get the techs up here to start processing some of this, pull some prints, and gather the rest. We'll see if we get a match on that DNA. . .and that will give us a better idea."

"Sounds good," Corb acknowledged as his brother left the room.

He thought of the pregnant woman fighting against her captor. *Was it her blood?* he wondered. He closed his eyes, struggling to put the violent image out of his mind.

He turned his thoughts to the kitchen. *What was Shawn's issue?* The man's tantrum was shocking, but that didn't necessarily entangle him with his wife's disappearance; a person couldn't know what was going on behind closed doors, even the doors to a country castle such as this. Begrudgingly, he admitted to himself that he had thrown many a liquor-filled glass, albeit never at a living target.

Corb left the office behind, ducking down the hall towards the bedrooms. On the left, the smaller room had been painted pink. Inside, matching cribs were arranged against the far wall, and a modern rocker was tucked into the corner. Above it, a shelf held a small camera that was angled to capture the twins' movements.

Making a mental note of the camera, he cautiously walked the nursery, examining its surfaces. From there, he scanned the guest room, master bedroom, and master bathroom. Noticing nothing awry, he returned to the office. Corb picked up the laptop and inspected it for damage. The device was high-end and well-built, and it appeared to have survived its fall to the plush rug without a scratch. Tucking his boots under his jean-clad knees, he sat cross-legged on the floor, positioning the computer upright on the carpet. He pushed the power button, awakening the operating system.

Britlyn Robbins' computer was locked but not password protected. That wasn't surprising — typically, adults without children didn't feel the need to secure their personal computers at home. Unless someone was having an affair, of course. *Doubtful in her current state,* Corb noted, remembering the scent of the spilled, stomach-soothing chamomile tea. Her browser was open, and it looked as if she was in the middle of composing her newest blog post. Below her draft, a faint, gray line of text notified him of the last auto-save:

2:20 P.M.

He snapped a picture, then perused the device's other programs. He quickly located the smart hub and instantly accessed over a dozen cameras planted in and around the home.

Under the "Kitchen" option, he found a small microphone icon and clicked it. "Hey, can you hear me?" he called out.

"Son of a—" Cam shouted, startled. "Yeah, I can hear you." On the screen, Corb watched as Cam searched for the device. After a moment, he located it. The large touchscreen was cleverly disguised as a framed piece of art on the kitchen wall, given away only by the tiny, circular camera lens at the top.

"Hey, how many fingers am I holding up?" Cam joked, flashing Corb his middle digit.

"Forget fingers," Corb replied. "I can practically see your prints. These things are no joke," he exclaimed. "Really high def."

"Who would do this to their own home?" Cam shook his head. "I mean, being constantly on camera? It's like living under a microscope."

"Beats me," Corb agreed. "But I think it gives us some clues about our kidnapper."

"You think he accessed the cameras?"

"It would be an easy way to learn their routine. Know who's going to be home and when."

"Our guy should be on there too, then."

"And yet, I'm not finding him," Corb answered, chewing his bottom lip. He had minimized Cam's video feed and was scrolling through earlier footage. "By default, motion should trigger the system to record, but it's nothing but the wife."

"Even outside?"

Corb navigated to the outdoor cameras, then scrolled down. "Looks like some sort of labor worker showed up around 11:00 A.M. Drove a white pickup truck."

Cam stayed silent while Corb skimmed the videos.

After a moment, Corb sighed. "Just a landscaper. He never came inside."

"Is it a company truck?"

"Unmarked. I've seen this fella around town, actually. He's got a lady clown tattoo on his shoulder." Corb toggled through various windows, digging deeper into Britlyn's PC. "She's got him on her agenda here. Even a phone number. I'll follow up, but I'm thinking he's probably not our guy."

Corb could see Cam rubbing his temples, frustrated.

"The longer she's gone. . ." Cam began.

"Hold up," Corb suddenly interrupted. "They're on a loop!"

Cradling the laptop in his arms, Corb made his way down to the kitchen, where he set the computer down on the marble island.

"Look at this." Corb pointed at the screen. Cam hunched over his shoulder.

"The time stamp keeps changing but the video stays the same. Until suddenly. . ." Corb fast-forwarded through the clip. "It jumps ahead."

Cam studied the footage.

"Look at the entryway. Through the windows on either side of the doors here, you can see shadows from the hanging flower baskets on the porch. First, they're here. But instead of gradually shifting across the floor. . ."

Corb clicked ahead, advancing the video.

"There it is," Cam gasped as the shadows jumped across the screen. "How big of a chunk is missing?"

"Based on just the shadows? Couple hours, I'd say."

"Some sort of backdoor in the network?"

Corb swiveled toward the entry, studying the bronze-finished smart lock and knob. "Maybe. And then someone walked right through the front."

* * *

Soon, other officers in the department arrived at the Robbins home, and Cam directed their analysis of the scene and collection of evidence. Meanwhile, Corb focused on the videos captured by the many cameras posted throughout the property. They knew from the bloody display that a scuffle had ensued which resulted in Mrs. Robbins' absence from the residence, but that interaction and her departure were not anywhere to be seen on the footage he'd reviewed.

The cameras did catch Agent Shawn Robbins, however. As Uncle Jack suspected, Shawn swayed as he trekked from his car to the front door. Once inside, he started taking shots of liquor, then grew cross with the home's smart technology and virtual assistant. He'd chucked his glass in frustration, confirming Cam's assessment that it had been thrown.

Corb felt a pang of sympathy as he watched Shawn tightly shut his eyes and put another tequila to his lips. Having been in the field nearly ten years now, Corb was no stranger to the ritual of cleansing disturbing images from his mind with the sting of hard liquor. Though he'd investigated a handful of crimes against minors, he was grateful that most of his assignments featured adult victims; while it was no treat discovering a days-old body of a drug user or playing referee between sparring spouses, only a handful of his cases each year centered around kids. On the other hand, Shawn's entire job involved viewing wide-eyed, innocent children in various stages of undress, often mid sex act. Corb knew the content could sometimes be violent, and he'd even heard of victims as young as infants. It was an unenviable position.

On the video, Shawn and the robot vacuum cleaned up his mess before he ascended the stairs. Soon after, Chief Jack McNulty could be seen pulling into the home's driveway, then planting his hands on his hips and conversing with Shawn.

Looks like an ass-chewing, Corb thought. The receiving end of Uncle Jack's reprimand was yet another unenviable position that he knew all too well.

Corb placed the laptop on the coffee table before him and studied his surroundings. While techs examined the upstairs, he'd taken up residence on the couch to scour the remaining surveillance footage. The Robbinses had remodeled the dwelling to conform with an open concept design, and this room was now connected to the kitchen to form one large living space. It was defined by the seating arrangement, which included matching armless chairs with modern, lollipop legs, and the regal Chesterfield sofa on which he currently sat. Its tufted, pristine, oatmeal upholstery threatened to suck the grass stains right from his jeans. Across the room, a vintage window frame had been repurposed into a stylish mirror, flanked by old shutters and crowned by a soft, green wreath affixed at its center.

Discouraged, Corb took a deep breath. Thanks to the ample sunlight streaming into the home and the resulting shadows, he had discovered that the cameras covering the driveway, entry, stairway, and second floor hallway had been placed on a loop, creating a concealed pathway by which the intruder could enter and exit the home. The remaining devices in the house were fixed on the empty kitchen and living room, and the baby monitor in the nursery simply faced its closed door. Outside, the cameras tucked under the eaves captured the movement of the property's sole laborer, along with the various visiting wildlife and the light breeze that played through the ornamental grasses surrounding the residence and down to the pasture below.

The brothers figured that their suspect was banking on the live feeds to help camouflage the unchanging stillness of the looped channels. Luckily, they'd caught onto the trick quickly, which helped with profiling the kidnapper: clearly, this person was highly skilled with computers, or they had help from someone who was. Still, Corb had hoped he might also catch a glimpse of the intruder through one of the home's many lenses. Corb tapped a cheap, stick pen against the sparse notes on the pad at his knee, watching the techs in the mirror as they scurried up and down the stairs behind him.

In the mirror, he suddenly realized.

Pulling the computer onto his lap, he shuffled through the system's various feeds, locating the stream from the living area. As he dragged the mouse backwards, this time he watched in the mirror as the techs descended again, followed by Corb and his brother. Then, Uncle Jack and Shawn Robbins. Reaching the afternoon, he saw Shawn stop on the step to examine the bloodstain.

Finally, just a short while prior, a pair of figures appeared on the staircase. One was a man clad in dark clothing and a fabric covering that obscured his face.

In his arms, he carried the other: a petite, brunette woman with slender limbs and a protruding belly.

Her body was limp.

FOUR.

Cam leaned over the screen on his brother's lap as he watched the footage for the third time.

"Good catch," Cam lauded Corb, patting his back.

"I'd feel better if she was at least kicking and screaming," Corb admitted, exiting out of the video player. He closed the laptop and set it on the coffee table once again, then got to his feet. "But the way she was just hanging in his arms. . .that ain't good."

"He might have just knocked her out cold," Cam offered. "Or else, what's the point of taking her with him?"

"Pregnant lady with a concussion," Corb shook his head. "That doesn't really put me at ease. Although. . ." he squinted his eyes.

"What?" Cam prodded.

"Maybe he injected her with something. That could explain the syringe cap," Corb considered.

"Well, we should start putting together some ideas about our suspect," Cam recommended. "Prosecutor's heading this way."

"Big Rob?" Corb asked.

"Baby Rob."

"Fucking Baby Rob?" Corb groaned.

"Big Rob's in trial," Cam explained. "That Lewd Conduct case."

"With the bus driver?"

"Uh-huh," Cam confirmed.

Corb could picture Big Rob's booming voice reciting the evidence of that case, then guiding the jury to a guilty verdict. The Cattail Prosecuting Attorney was a bear of a man, with almost enough fur to pass for one. Easily six-foot-five, he wore his thick, brown hair swept to one side, where it fell smoothly until it joined with the wiry tufts of his long beard. He was broad-shouldered but also big-bellied, so much so that he would use his stomach as a shelf for his computer during court appearances, chatting up prosecution witnesses while clumsily jabbing the keys with his fat fingers like some giant playing with a toy. Despite his gruff appearance, he was unwavering, competent, and effective; though he often made out-of-town defense attorneys huffy or tearful, for the most part, he had a reputation as a fair and reasonable man with an excellent grasp on the law and an eagerness to see justice served. He shared Uncle Jack's practical, no-nonsense attitude, and the men were longtime friends.

"I thought Baby Rob was just an intern?" Corb frowned.

"Not anymore. He passed the bar exam. Been working on his own since he was sworn in," Cam informed his brother.

"I don't have time to explain all this shit to him," Corb continued to gripe.

"Better figure it out. That's his car right there."

The men watched the burgundy, mid-size SUV creep into the driveway, then carefully park alongside one of the police cruisers. As the driver got out, he skimmed the scene for the two brothers, then smiled broadly as he located them, driving the round apples of his smooth cheeks up into his small, green eyes. Without any of his father's strapping appearance, and all the finesse of an emperor penguin, Robert Howard II waddled towards them, the cuffs of his pants dragging on the smooth asphalt. He wore a navy, three-piece suit that appeared custom tailored to his squat, rotund physique, along with a matching tie. An Albert chain stretched across his plump middle.

Corb sighed, covering his eyes with his hand. "Why is he dressed like a train conductor?" he said under his breath.

"Just give him a shot. He's been doing this for a couple months now," Cam insisted. With that, he elbowed his younger brother, causing Corb to drop his hand from his brow and stand upright.

Cam greeted the man with an outstretched palm. "How are you, Mr. Howard?"

43

"Lieutenant, nice to see you again," the younger Rob responded, shaking Cam's hand. His voice was high-pitched and jovial. He nodded at Corb in acknowledgement. "Detective."

"What's up, Rob," Corb casually muttered.

Rob brushed off Corb's cold and informal welcome, continuing to speak cheerfully. "Not much. Hoping you might fill me in. What are we working with here?"

"Our abductee is a female in her 20's. Pregnant. Some kind of internet celebrity, hence the digs," Corb gestured to the stately residence.

"Sure, sure. Okay," Rob processed, rubbing his hairless chin emphatically.

Corb fought the urge to roll his eyes. *It was like he'd learned his body language from cartoons. He WAS a cartoon.*

"I hear her husband is a cop, right?" Rob asked.

"Sort of," Cam took over responding. "He's a state employee, but he's assigned to the Palouse region, so he works out of our office. Name's Agent Robbins."

"Agent Robbins," Rob repeated, shifting uncomfortably.

"You work with him much?"

"We did some warrants together. Unfortunately," Rob replied. "I had to clean up a couple of his probable cause affidavits. One was so overbroad, it didn't even include an apartment number. Anyhow, he didn't take the criticism very well."

The mutual dislike for Shawn Robbins caught Corb's interest. *Maybe Baby Rob was alright, after all.*

"Any reason to think he's involved?" Rob continued.

"I think we can rule him out. He has an alibi during the time she was abducted — he was at the office — plus, their cameras support his story," Cam explained.

"That's good at least. We don't need to foster any more hostility towards law enforcement," Rob opined. "God knows you guys catch enough flak. So, what other theories are you working with?"

Corb cleared his throat, gaining the young prosecutor's attention. "She appears to have been unconscious when she was carried out. We thought maybe she got knocked out, but anyone who knew she was pregnant and wanted to keep her alive probably wouldn't risk causing a serious head injury."

"You think she was drugged," Rob deduced.

"Yes — I think she was injected with something," Corb clarified. "And any general anesthetic is going to be Schedule III, at least. So, maybe someone in the medical profession? They'd need easy access to sedatives. Or a script."

Rob half-smiled. "That's not as hard as you might think, Detective. The pandemic relaxed regulations for in-person prescriptions. These days, it's almost as easy as just ordering it online. Plus, there's always the chance it was street drugs."

Corb tilted his head, considering the possibility. "Yeah. Maybe."

"Did anyone show up on video who might have criminal history?" Rob prodded. "Landscapers, housekeepers, food delivery drivers. . ."

"Just one worker here today," Corb confirmed. "He's accounted for on surveillance pretty much the whole day, though. I can see if he's got a record, but I get the feeling that we're dealing with someone a little more slick. The video loop trick, the timing. . .this is not your average burglar."

"I agree," Cam chimed in. "No sign of forced entry. This was precise, up until you get to the office. Then. . ." he trailed off.

"He surprised her on the computer," Corb began to piece the scene together. "She was in the middle of writing, then he popped up out of nowhere. That's when they started to struggle."

"The Chief mentioned you'd found blood," Rob said quietly. "A lot of blood."

"Yeah," Corb confirmed. "But right now, we don't know whose."

"Seems like a whole lot of trouble to carry a dead body out the door," Rob stated, echoing Cam's earlier reasoning. "I'm holding onto the hope you two find her alive. And her kidnapper, too. I'll nail that asshole to the cross. I'm not having the folks in this town worry they aren't safe in their own homes."

The brothers' eyebrows jumped as Rob swore.

"Anyhow, I'm not trying to make myself a witness, so I'm outta here. You just say the word if you need anything, okay? Dad. . .er. . .Robert and I are here to answer your questions, or draft documents, or whatever," Rob assured them. "Just keep us in the know."

"Will do," Cam agreed. "How's his trial going?" he added.

"It's about done. You guys got kids?" Rob asked.

The brothers shook their heads.

"Well, that defense attorney didn't do his homework or something, 'cause that entire jury is made up of moms and grandmas. Angry moms and grandmas, now. I'd be surprised if they deliberate more than ten minutes," the young prosecutor said confidently. "Plus, the guy had a prior complaint. A different kid on a different bus."

"They didn't try to get that excluded?" Cam asked.

"Oh, they tried," Rob revealed. "But the judge denied it. We were able to show it was part of his larger plan. . .using his employment to get to these kids. I'd say he's driven his last bus."

With that, Baby Rob spun on his heels back towards his car. As he rolled away, he offered a polite wave to the officers, then disappeared behind his rising tinted window.

"You know, I used to wonder if Mrs. Big Rob had an affair with some chubby, little postman, but now. . ." Corb observed aloud, "I think Baby Rob's just a chip off the ol' block!"

"I told you," Cam chuckled. "He's sharper than he looks. And a pretty decent dude."

"I have to admit, I am pleasantly surprised," Corb replied. "Plus, he thinks Shawn is a loser. That alone earns him some points."

"What's your beef with Shawn?" Cam asked, shaking his head.

"I don't like his face," Corb quickly shot back.

Cam frowned. "Seriously? Don't be childish. What's the real reason?"

Corb rolled his eyes, then sighed. "He's lazy as shit. He throws files on my desk without any summary, any conversation whatsoever. Like I'm his fucking subordinate. He's condescending. Rude."

"You're rude," Cam pointed out.

"I'm not rude; I'm brusque," Corb corrected. "Shawn is rude. Lazy and rude, AND entitled, which is exactly what I'd expect from some yuppie out-of-towner who thinks Idaho is some unoccupied land that only money can conquer."

Cam half-smiled. "Can I get you a soapbox?"

"You asked," Corb snarled.

* * *

While the brothers discussed their opinions of the victim's husband, another vehicle crested the hill.

As a courtesy, a colleague had volunteered to take Shawn back to his residence after his interview at the station. The patrol car paused to unload its passenger, and he flung open the star-clad door of the aging sedan, jumping out and striding quickly towards the brothers.

The nostrils of Shawn's slender, aquiline nose flared as he watched Camden and Corbin casually conversing on his immaculately manicured, lush lawn.

"What's with the standing around? You boys think you can get back on task?" Shawn demanded. "And who the fuck said you could stand on my grass?"

Cam frowned. "We're on task. Just comparing notes, is all," he explained in a slow, smooth tone.

"In plain clothes, huh? Thought you'd come up here in your blue jeans and just drag your filthy cowboy boots all over my home, all over this crime scene. What a joke," Shawn spit. He pulled polished, designer shades from his face and folded them neatly, hanging them on the buttoned neckline of his pressed dress shirt and smoothing his gelled, black waves back into shape.

Cam shrugged. "Time is of the essence, Agent Robbins. If you'd kindly give us some space, we do have a lot to review here."

Shawn ignored him, suddenly shifting his attention to the younger brother.

"Wait. . .is that *chewing tobacco*?" Shawn angrily shouted, eyeing Corbin's lower lip.

"What of it?" Corb responded, smiling widely enough for Shawn to see the brown shreds stuck in between his bottom teeth.

"I was hoping your uncle might wise up and send in some real police officers for this job," Shawn hissed. "Instead of the gool-ol'-boys club."

"That a fact, city slicker?" Corb smirked nonchalantly. He stepped towards the well-dressed man.

"You'd never make it outside Cattail," Shawn answered, clenching his fists. He inched closer towards Corb, fire burning in his dark brown eyes.

"Hey, Agent," Cam interrupted, slipping between Shawn and Corb. "We got a problem?" He crossed his arms over his broad chest, which pulled his T-shirt taut and revealed a farmer's tan line beneath the stretched collar.

"We *will* have a problem if your brother doesn't get his ratty, redneck beard out of my face," Shawn responded. "Unprofessional, white trash—"

"Like I said," Cam interrupted, increasing his volume. "We're trying to work quickly to find your wife, and stopping for uniforms would have slowed us down. And as far as the scruff goes, Chief lets him keep it to cover the scars. Take it easy."

Shawn glanced back at Corb, noticing for the first time the gnarled skin in the hollows of his cheeks.

"Shot in the face my third day in the field. Can you believe that?" Corb laughed out loud. "You should see the other guy," he added in a menacing whisper.

Cam flashed his brother a look of disapproval.

"Yet here we are, years later, and you're still a shitty cop," Shawn growled at Corb, becoming agitated again. "I'm only sorry that shot wasn't about four inches higher. Could have saved everyone the trouble of dealing with you."

Cam drew closer to Shawn. The larger of the two brothers, his stature and sculpted arms typically commanded authority without him saying a word. Shawn was apparently the rare exception. Though Cam's eyes were a hazy blue instead of brown, they shared the same piercing quality as his uncle's. He set his jaw and squinted down at Shawn, stabbing a rigid finger into his chest.

"That's enough," Cam demanded firmly. "We're all on the same team."

Shawn looked up at Cam. The combination of their size disparity, Cam's threatening glare, and the hard poke to his sternum appeared to finally pierce Shawn's ego and deflate it slightly.

Cam then turned to address his brother. "And *you*. Take a walk."

Corb spit a long string of tobacco on the pristine lawn, then spun on his heels.

He only lasted a few paces.

"Hey Shawn, speaking of shitty cops, I got a question," Corb began, walking back towards the men.

"Drop it, Detective. That's an order," Cam reprimanded.

Corb ignored him. "How does the guy whose one and only job is being good at the internet get his house hacked in the middle of the day?" Corb asked aloud, his eyes twinkling.

"What in the hell are you talking about?" Shawn snorted.

"See, at first, I saw Ramón on the video and thought he might have a hand in things," Corb began.

Shawn looked at him blankly.

"You know, Ramón?" Corb pressed.

"No, I don't. Indulge me," Shawn said flatly.

"C'mon, Ramón? Gets here every day about 11:00?" Corb quizzed him, clearly enjoying the man's confusion. He walked closer.

"Brit has people coming and going. I don't know." Shawn's cheeks flushed slightly.

"Well buddy, Ramón is your landscaper. Turns out he was here today, and I know that because he's all over the cameras on the outside. So, I thought, this will be easy, Ramón is going to get caught up in this, right?" Corb gestured upwards with his palms.

"I guess—" Shawn began.

"Wrong," Corb interrupted. "Ramón was outside the entire time. He probably didn't even know your wife was gone. Then I'm looking at her computer, referencing the cameras, checking out your video doorbell, your digital lock, all these smart security features. . ."

"Get to the point," Shawn insisted through gritted teeth.

"And I put together a timeline," Corb continued. "According to your system's history, at 2:10 P.M., your front door was unlocked. So, I go back to watch your video doorbell and see who it is, and guess what? Nobody's there. Then, your cameras go haywire — the doorbell, entry, and all the second-floor cameras cut to a looped feed at 2:12 P.M. Meanwhile, the missus is on her laptop at 2:20 P.M. I know that because the draft of her blog post autosaved within seconds of her last key stroke. Your intruder didn't account for us catching his escape, but thanks to y'all's love of mirrors, he's on a reflection captured by another camera unit, which is how I know Britlyn was carried out the front door at 2:26 P.M. The remaining cameras are restored at 2:30 P.M. Ramón leaves at 3:00 P.M. You show up at 3:40."

Corb cocked his head. "You want me to get to the point, Shawn? I'm guessing we have an extremely sophisticated kidnapper, someone who can control your system remotely before he even gets here. Someone who has been watching your wife for a very long time. A person who can compromise even the smartest of homes, especially when they belong to someone who ain't. You wanna pick a bone with me. . .with my family? In my town? You're so busy spending your wife's money, you don't even know the name of the fucking guy who cuts your grass."

Shawn's face and smug facade dropped.

"You saw someone carrying her?" he whispered, his tan complexion growing pale. "Was she alright?"

"Can't tell," Corb offered in a somewhat softer tone. "Frankly, it didn't look good."

Shawn covered his eyes with his hand, flashing a two-toned Rolex that stood out like a sore thumb against the soft, natural lines of the prairie backdrop. Suddenly, he cupped his mouth, and his upper body jerked forward. Doubling over, he hurled vomit onto the lawn. After a moment, he stood, wiping his mouth on the back of his sleeve.

"She told me a couple months ago she thought the baby monitor was watching her, following her around the girls' room when she was singing," Shawn's voice faltered. "I thought maybe it was just hormones or anxiety making her paranoid. Oh Jesus, Brit," he trailed off, clasping his hand over his face again.

Suddenly, the sound of the Chief closing his cruiser's door rang through the air. Stiff-legged, he made his way around the vehicle to address the group. He'd snuck up during their quarrel and had apparently overheard the entire interaction.

"Don't beat yourself up. But Detective McNulty is right: you're blinded in all this. Too close to the case. You're on leave until further notice, and I want you to stay out of this investigation," Jack directed.

"I mean technically, if we're talking suspension, I come under the State's department, not the local police department," Shawn began. "I'm not sure you have the authority. . ."

Jack raised an eyebrow.

Shawn closed his mouth.

"You boys done here?" Jack asked his nephews.

"Deputies are just finishing bagging a couple things. They'll be done tonight," Cam responded.

"Find a place to stay tonight, Agent Robbins," Jack advised. "We'll keep you posted."

* * *

From the back of his uncle's sedan, Corb finger-waved at Shawn through the window. Shawn pulled his mouth into a tight line, almost managing a smile. The car's tires squealed slightly as they pulled off the tightly looped driveway and onto the main road.

"Rich asshole," Corb muttered.

"Looked like two assholes to me," Jack snorted, addressing Corbin. "Your brother's trying to keep a lid on this guy, and you keep lighting a fire under him."

"I don't know, Uncle Jack. I almost let Corb take him down a peg or two," Cam posited. "That cocky, little—"

"But you didn't. That's why you're a good team," Jack interrupted. "Anyhow, you two did exactly what I hoped you would: you got us a trail to follow, and you weeded out Agent Robbins. Sure, he's a little. . .cosmopolitan. . . but I don't see him being a kidnapper. Or a killer," he reasoned.

"Killer?" Corb nearly choked on the word. "You don't think she's. . ." he trailed off. The men sat in silence for a minute, watching the fields of long grass outside sway in the light, summer breeze.

"Hopefully not. Not sure what sort of sicko we're dealing with here," Jack answered, turning back into the parking lot at the PD. "I'm hoping we can get some answers from someone who does."

"Who?" Cam asked.

"An agent with a grip on this internet stuff," Jack responded.

"I can figure it out," Corb insisted. "We don't need 'em."

"We do. FBI's sending someone from Cyber Crimes. Already flew out of Salt Lake."

"Oh, good. Think we'll get another winner like Shawn?" Corb quipped. "Maybe he and Shawn can sit around and trade stories about how many awards they've gotten without leaving a desk. A big circle jerk."

Jack ignored him. "You boys will be on your best behavior. Agent's landing in Pullman in just a few hours. I'm gonna grab a late supper, then head to the airport. Finish your workup from the scene tonight, then we'll meet back here early tomorrow morning. I want to see you at five sharp. And boys?"

They returned his gaze in the rearview mirror.

"Take a shower, will ya?"

The Chief let the brothers out of the back of the patrol car, then plopped back into his seat, speeding away.

Cam gazed up at the sky. This close to the solstice, it still glowed in tones of pink and blue, and it felt like darkness never fully arrived. He glanced at his watch.

"It's almost 9:00," he informed Corb. "What's your plan?"

"I might know where to find the landscaper," Corb responded. "I'd like to surprise him. Might spook otherwise."

"Good thinking. Maybe he knows of someone she's had trouble with," Cam agreed. "Someone who worked on the house or something."

"Yeah, I'm wondering if maybe a cable installer or repair person is where we should start looking," Corb suggested.

"Would help explain the computer skills," Cam nodded. "I'll get some calls out to her family and friends. She might have mentioned this baby monitor paranoia to someone else."

"These are pretty modern folks. You might have to bust out your computer and make a few of those calls emails instead," Corb teased. "Maybe text messages. Do they make a kidnapping emoji?"

"Ah, screw all that stuff," Cam rolled his eyes.

Corb glanced at their surroundings, then adjusted his hat. "Indeed. Welp, if you need me, I'll be at the Coop."

Cam frowned. "You said you were interviewing Ramón."

"What I said was, I thought I knew where to find him," Corb clarified, grinning. "Two birds, one stone. Catch you tomorrow, brother."

With that, Corb tucked a hand in his pocket and began the short walk to the bar.

FIVE.

Underneath a gaudy neon sign that glowed against the darkening sky, the Cattail Coop was housed in a corrugated metal building with an asymmetrical roofline and grungy, warped vents near the gable. Iron bars obscured advertisements and posters hanging in the windows, and the powder-blue entry door was black with smudges from dirty hands over the years. On top, a comical, colorful rooster as tall as Corbin interrupted the otherwise unobstructed view of the rolling hills beyond. In the next week or so, the cock would be fitted with a patriotic top hat. For now, a deep-cupped, fraying lace bra hung from his orange beak.

Inside, a stale tobacco cloud hung against the low ceiling, and the sound of billiards filled the air. Scanning the tall tables by the dart boards in the back, Corb spotted the young Hispanic man amongst a group of males similar in age and appearance. They all exhibited the tell-tale signs of day laborers — some were caked in drywall, while others, like the man with the clown tattoo, wore tanks and tees still covered in grass clippings. Corb caught the man's eye. Apparently uneasy, he backed away from the table, scanning the bar for a way out.

Corb wagged his finger, then tapped the badge he wore around his neck. He grabbed a barstool, then gestured for the man to join him.

Reluctantly, the landscaper approached. He looked to be in his younger twenties, with a shaved head and dark eyes. Though his tattoos told Corbin the young man had seen his share of hard times, he was betrayed by his fearful expression.

Probably undocumented, Corb thought.

"Cerveza?" Corb asked, pointing at the cooler of beer behind the counter.

The man paused, then nodded.

"That's pretty much the limit to my Spanish, friend. You speak English?" Corb inquired.

"Only a little," Ramón answered cautiously. Corb could tell from the ease with which the words flowed off Ramón's tongue that he was downplaying his fluency in case he needed to play dumb later.

"I'll keep it simple, then. Have we met before?" Corb asked pointedly.

"Big storm. You gave me a ride," the man refreshed his memory.

"That's right," Corb snapped his fingers. "I knew it. Ramón?"

"Sí," the man confirmed, seemingly surprised by Corb's recollection.

Corb laid down a ten-dollar bill for the two bottles of golden liquid, waving the bartender away when she tried to make change. The slight and sallow woman thanked him, then stuffed the cash into her faded black apron. He handed one of the beers to Ramón.

"Well, Ramón, relax. . .I'm not here to fuck with you," Corb insisted, taking a long drink. "Or your amigos." From the back of the bar, the group had been observing the interaction with the wariness of a watchful dog. Corb hoped they wouldn't feel the need to bare teeth.

"How do I know you aren't lying?" Ramón asked skeptically.

"Guess you don't," Corb smiled. "How about you take this seat here, I start talking, and then you can decide for yourself?"

The man looked back at his posse, but otherwise remained frozen.

"I'm gonna drink this beer either way," Corb shrugged with another swallow.

After a minute, Ramón sat.

"Good," Corb praised him. "Now, in case it's not abundantly clear from the circumstances, you're not in custody. You want to leave, go right ahead. But I do want to ask you some questions about Britlyn Robbins, if you're willing."

"Is she okay?" Ramón asked worriedly. He sounded genuine.

"I was hoping you might be able to tell me," Corb responded.

"My buddy saw a cop car at the house today. Flashing lights were on," Ramón revealed. "That's all I know."

"After you left for the day?"

"Uh-huh," Ramón replied, taking a sip.

"What do you think the car was doing there?"

"Señor Robbins is police. Maybe a friend of his?" Ramón guessed.

Corb shook his head. "Nope. First, because I really don't think Agent Robbins has any friends. . ."

Ramón smirked, nodding in agreement.

"And second," Corb continued, "they were there investigating."

"Oh," Ramón said quietly. He took another drink of his beer.

"What do you think they were investigating, if you had to guess?"

Ramón shrugged.

"Guess," Corb insisted.

Ramón shook his head. "Maybe a theft? Someone stealing their things?"

"So, you would think they are the victims. . .not the suspects?" Corb cocked his head.

"Señora Robbins is a good lady. She is honest and fair," Ramón reasoned.

"And Shawn?" Corb pressed.

"Hm," Ramón thought for a moment. "No. He just drinks. Pops a lot of pills, too. But most gringos are crazy in the head, no?"

"That is true," Corb laughed. "No illegal drugs though?"

"I don't see any. Don't smell any."

"How about violence? They ever fight?"

"No," Ramón answered. "He is. . .not so great of a guy, right? But fight with her, no."

"What do you mean, 'not so great'"?

"*Engreído.* He won't talk to me or the others. We are shit on his shoes."

Corb snorted. "Ha! Me too, pal. I know the feeling. You want another?" he asked, pointing at Ramón's empty bottle.

"Please," Ramón answered. He rested his elbows on the bar top, and his band of friends appeared to collectively exhale. "But why are you asking me these things? What happened?"

"It isn't something that was stolen," Corb whispered. "It's someone."

"She is missing," Ramón deduced.

Corb nodded. "And if we're gonna find her, I need you to tell me everything you can about today."

* * *

Cam pulled into the parking lot of Spud's, a brick-sided saloon with a flashing, neon sign hanging just below the rickety fire escape for the handful of second-story apartments above. The historic bar was wedged in between an ice cream shop and a law office, and just down the road from the Coop. Cam selected the spot nearest the front door, where a skinny young man with a greasy mullet and a tattoo of a Chevy symbol on his bare shoulder attempted to perform security.

In his wire frame eyeglasses and sensible, blue pickup truck, Cam looked like an angry father picking up his teenage daughter from some unauthorized party. Shortly after his arrival, the bar manager cracked the door, then walked with a hobbling Corb to the passenger side.

"What the hell, Don?" Cam seethed. "Figured you'd call me long before he got this hammered."

Don scratched the back of his neck. The man was in his sixties and wore his hair and handlebar mustache in their natural, white state. He was average sized, save for a slight beer belly that hung over his belt. Tonight, he was dressed in his typical bartending uniform, which consisted of cowboy boots and jeans paired with a black T-shirt adorned with a liquor brand on the front.

"I'm not —" Corb hiccupped loudly, then covered his mouth.

"If you puke in my truck, so help me God. . ." Cam began.

Corb removed his hand from his face, letting it fall to his lap. "I'm not hammered," he finished.

"What do you call this?" Cam asked his brother angrily, gesturing to Corb's disheveled state.

Corb shrugged, drooping into the passenger seat.

Don shoved him off, then quickly closed the truck's door. Through the open window, Cam addressed him again. "Well?"

63

"I'm down a cocktail waitress, so we were slammed. Besides, I didn't know he was on one," Don apologized. "Then he started shooting whiskey, then tequila, then. . ." he trailed off. "Well, I think the tequila's what did it."

"You think?" Cam replied sarcastically. "Who was he with?"

"Just Rabble Anderson, at first. Then a bunch of Mexicans came in, and he said he was gonna buy 'em a round," Don explained. "That's when the tequila started."

"Young guys, look like field workers and such?" Cam asked.

Don nodded.

"Damnit, Corb. How helpful is it for you to interview our witness if you don't remember anything he says?" Cam scolded him.

Corb opened his eyes. "I remember," he argued. "Plus, I wrote it all down."

"On what? Cocktail napkins?" Cam scoffed.

"I did. It's back in my truck," Corb insisted. "At the PD."

"Where are your keys?" Cam asked irritably.

Don reached into the cab, handing them over.

"Thank you," Cam said, slightly softening his tone as he pocketed them. "You fight him for these?"

Don shook his head. "He gave 'em to me when he opened his tab."

Cam frowned at his brother. "So, you knew you were gettin' shitfaced tonight."

Corb sighed heavily, considering his options. He was too drunk to lie, especially to Cam. "Yup."

"Tomorrow is a real big day for us. I don't understand what on Earth possessed you to—"

"Lizzie," Corb explained.

"Lizzie?" Cam repeated, surprised.

"I saw Lizzie," Corb confirmed.

"Here?" Cam asked.

Corb blinked rapidly, attempting to improve his blurred vision, then adjusted himself in his seat. He hoped sitting up straight might increase his sobriety, but it only added pressure on his stomach, which was feeling queasy and weak. He hunched over again, burying his head in his hands.

"I did my interview with whats-his-face. . .Ramón. . . over at the Coop, just like I said. Only had a few beers. Then I heard Sam was playing over at Spud's, and I just popped over real quick," Corb explained. "Sorry, man."

Sam Lang, an old buddy from high school, had recently returned from Nashville, where he'd earned backing from a major country music label after years of singing and songwriting. Long ago, he'd regaled the McNulty brothers and other friends around many a campfire with his soulful voice and hand-me-down acoustic guitar.

"I understand going to see Sam," Cam conceded. "But I am still failing to see how shit went completely sideways."

"Huh?"

"*Lizzie*," Cam emphasized, reminding him.

"She was here watching Sam, too," Don explained.

"By herself?" Cam asked, wincing as he waited for the answer. He wondered if an unlucky new boyfriend was going to be part of tonight's collateral damage.

Don nodded. "Just herself. She bolted when this one walked in the door." He gestured to Corb. "But it was too late, I guess."

"I wasn't gonna drink," Corb chimed in. "Shit, I wasn't hardly gonna stay. But I just walked in and saw her, and I. . .I wasn't ready for it," he apologized.

"You're alright," Cam sighed, forgiving his brother. "And thank you, Don. What do I owe ya?"

"A drywall patch for the bathroom," Don rolled his eyes. "I ain't sure it was him, but the timing seems right. And the height." He mimed a punch.

Corb looked down at the knuckles on his right hand, which were red and bore traces of white powder. *He'd forgotten about that.*

"I'll get it fixed. Did he settle his tab, at least?" Cam asked.

"For himself and his amigos. With a generous tip, I might add." Don winked.

"Good. Thanks again," Cam replied.

As he reversed out of the parking space in front of Spud's and began to roll down the road, Cam looked over at his brother.

"Thanks for calling me, at least," Cam offered.

"Yeah," Corb acknowledged. "I know Uncle Jack would kill me if I drove."

"As would I," Cam pointed out.

The soft scent of nearby mint fields trickled into the car with the night air, which was tepid but still pleasant, especially in comparison to the sweltering daytime temperatures that particular June. The aroma seemed to soothe Corb's troubled mind, and he rested his head against the door frame once more. The truck passed downtown, then turned towards the McNulty property. As the streetlights faded behind him, Cam became aware of the sun's efforts to wake, embodied by the cornflower blue stripe that was beginning to inch over the prairie's edge and replace the night sky.

He had been hoping they could both get just a few hours more sleep.

As he drove along, he replayed the conversation with the old bartender in his mind. *Ten rounds of tequila and a drywall patch.* Cam nearly laughed out loud as he shook his head at his younger brother. To others, it may have sounded like a country music song gone wrong, but for Corb, it was just another night. Though he had reached some measure of predictability by the time he hit his thirties, Corb had always been a spitfire, a trait that contrasted starkly against their uncle's even keel. It also contrasted against Cam's quiet repose, which most believed was a natural gift.

They were partially correct, Cam acknowledged to himself. A gift and a curse from his mother, Cam's unflappable coolness made him the obvious choice for peacekeeper. In many of the few memories he possessed of his parents, he could picture his cherished mother's voice, like a tranquilizer, assuaging his father's mercurial moods as he threatened to blast off on yet another drunken tirade. When it was over, she was too drained to cry, having mitigated the crisis at the cost of her own serenity. It was an endless cycle — instead of Dad finding his own peace, he would consume hers with an insatiable ferocity, like a wildfire gobbling its way through the forest. Many of Cam's remaining memories of his father were similarly unpleasant. The sound of a truck squealing out of the driveway, or glass shattering against the wall. Yearning for a hug and a kiss, but knowing he was better scurrying out of Dad's way. He would lie awake at night and watch for his police cruiser, his little mind toiling between concern he might never come home, and curiosity about what their life would be like if he didn't.

Now, Cam was the forest, and Corb was the fire. Rolling down the road, Cam passed Nan's house and the barn where Corb would usually lay his head.

No. Tonight, his little brother was staying with him. He'd drag him into the camper, make up a bed for him in the dinette, pump him full of water, then dutifully watch over him until it was time to head back to the station. Putting out Corb's fire was a tiresome obligation, one that had begun long ago, when the boys were both still teens. But, unlike their father, Corb had actually achieved peace once, and Cam was determined to be there to help him find it again.

Cam parked, then looked over at his brother. Corb was now sleeping soundly, which was typical after he punched something. He was like some unbalanced scale, always seeking the physical turmoil to counteract the mental and emotional commotion thundering in his skull. As a result, as he reached adolescence, his hair-trigger temper and scrappy spirit became his most notorious qualities.

Cam recalled watching their poor Aunt Sandy's copper hair become streaked with silver during their teenage years as she lectured Corb through fight, after fight, after fight:

It was twenty years earlier, and Aunt Sandy pursed her pink lips, then squeezed her hands together, resting them on the dark, floral tablecloth that covered their oak pedestal table. Her nails were shaped and ladylike but short and unpolished, a testament to the various duties she performed in her life. Pancake-maker, chicken-feeder, lawn-mower, dish-doer, check-writer, bath-runner, weed-puller. While Uncle Jack was patrolling the growing town of Cattail, it was up to Sandy to hold down the fort and farm, which included the managing of their three children.

At that moment, she was the discipline-disher. Under the garish, brass dining light, she cinched her auburn brows and squinted her powder blue eyes, practicing her best expression of disappointment.

"Corbin Neil," she began.

From across the table, the teenage boy let out an exasperated sigh and rolled his eyes, looking away. As he turned his head, sandy blonde waves fought with his ribbed crewneck collar, which had been stretched so that it hung down and out like a sad lower lip, exposing his hairless chest. The tee and his holey jeans both bore spots of blood, and his bony knuckles were swollen and purple.

"Fighting will not be tolerated in this household," she continued. "You are not an animal, young man. How many times must I tell you to hold that temper of yours?"

"He called me a fucking orphan," Corb shot back, turning his face towards her. His trembling lower lip now matched his shirt, and his green irises glowed against the red backdrop of dilated blood vessels in his eyes. They were wet with rage.

Sandy's expression softened as she sighed. "And between you and I, nobody really blames you for hitting that little brat. But," she started.

"Big brat. He's in the grade above me," Corb corrected.

"*But,*" she resumed. "You didn't just bloody his nose. You broke his jaw, Corbin."

"Pretty sure his ribs, too," Corb smirked. "Serves him right."

Sandy suddenly pushed away from the table, jumping to her feet and raising her voice. "Do you think this is funny? That this is just going to be how you deal with things from now on?"

Corb shrugged. "I-dunno," he squeaked. His voice had grown deeper in the last year, but it still cracked sometimes, returning to a child's tone.

"*What causes fights and quarrels among you? Don't they come from your desires that battle within you?*"

she quoted the Scripture to him, prodding him with her eyes.

"Easy. James 4:1," he replied smartly.

"So?" she asked.

"So? I don't desire nothin'," he snorted, resuming a man's voice again.

"Something brews in you, I can see it," she answered. "I pray about it. You may not be my blood, but you are like my son. I can see that storm under the surface."

"But I'm not your son, am I?" he began to shout. "I *am* a fucking orphan, just like Billy said. I'm a fucking orphan with worthless, dead parents. Dad killed her, did you know that?"

Sandy sat again, pulling her mouth tight and gently reaching for his hands. He flinched, pulling them away.

"I think that is oversimplifying it a bit," she pointed out quietly. "Your father. . .well, I honestly didn't know your father. But I know a great deal about him. I believe he had some demons inside him, and it drove him to wildness. To drinking," she explained.

Corb closed his eyes, staring down at the puddle that had begun to sink through the woven squares in the tablecloth. "And what if I have those demons? Sometimes it just feels like. . .like I swallowed a ball of fire. Like today. I was so mad."

"You're not him, sweetheart. Is that what you're afraid of?" she reached out again.

This time, he reluctantly let her take his hands, wincing as he bent his mangled fingers, returning her embrace. "I hate him," he whispered.

"Oh, honey," Sandy tilted her head, blinking away the tears in her own eyes. She walked to the boy and leaned over him, wrapping her arms around his shoulders.

Uncle Jack suddenly pushed open the front door, hat in hand. "I just got off the phone with the damn school, and—"

"Jack," Sandy interrupted him sternly. She shook her head.

"I hate him!" Corb repeated, shaking in Sandy's arms as he sobbed. "And I'm gonna be just like him. I know it."

Oh, Jack mouthed. He closed his eyes and took a deep breath. After a moment, he walked across the floor to the dining room, then carefully cupped his hand around the back of Corb's head and lovingly thumbed over his hair.

"Corb, you are not your father," he began.

"Just leave me alone!" Corb sputtered.

Jack looked at Sandy helplessly. She nodded.

"Alright, I'll give you some space," he agreed. He put his hat back on, walking down the hall to the stairs. He climbed them, finding Cam in his room. The teenage boy sat on the bed, staring blankly at the bare wall across from him. A spattering of dark red stains starkly contrasted against his plain, white tee.

"So, you were sent home from school too?" Uncle Jack remarked.

Cam nodded in agreement. "But I wasn't fighting," he stated calmly.

"Principal said you were in the middle of it," Jack pointed out. He gestured to the boy's shirt.

"I was the one who pulled Corb off," Cam insisted. "Not before he got Billy good, though. I thought he was gonna kill him," he realized, finally blinking and breaking his stare.

"I'll bet he was," Jack groaned.

"You heard what he called us. Fucking. . .er, effing. . .orphans. Can you believe that?" Cam shook his head, attempting to process his own distress.

"Sounds like Billy earned that ass-whoopin'," Jack spit angrily. "But you did the right thing, helping your brother by breaking it up like that."

Jack motioned to Cam to scoot over, then sat by him on the bed. "Your dad used to get so mad, Camden. I remember some guy said something about your mom, once. . ."

"What did he say?" Cam perked up, his attention piqued at the mention of his mother.

"Well, she was an attractive woman, your mother. All I'll say is it was inappropriate, and within earshot of your dad. So, your old man, he takes his nightstick, and he just whales on this guy. And he keeps going, and going, and going. Put him in the hospital. . .luckily, not the morgue. I had to fight tooth and nail just so he could keep his job. And that's even with your grandpa as the boss."

"He sounds mean," Cam responded.

"But he wasn't mean," Jack released a dry chuckle. "And Corb ain't mean, neither. That's the thing, Cam, your dad was a teddy bear until suddenly. . .he wasn't. It was like something would just snap, and he'd see red."

"Is that why he hated us?" Cam asked plainly.

"Hated you? Are you kidding?" Jack patted Cam's knee. "Your dad loved you boys so much. Your mother, too."

"He never came around," Cam responded. "Or he didn't stay long. Sure seemed like he hated us."

"I think he hated himself," Jack countered, looking down at the worn, wooden floor. "And he just poured whiskey on that hate until it was numb and gone. You know, back in those days, you didn't hear a lot about things like mental health or depression. I think back on the time I had with your dad, and I can't believe that I missed the signs."

They sat in silence for a moment.

"You never talk about him," Cam observed.

"I don't really like to," Jack admitted.

"Why?"

Jack looked out the window, watching the blowing fields for a moment.

"I guess I just feel bad," he answered finally.

"What for?" Cam quickly followed up.

Jack shook his head. "I should have been there," he said quietly. "I was his big brother. Maybe I could have stopped him. Helped him."

"Like I helped Corbin today," Cam muttered.

"Yeah. Something like that," Jack exhaled, getting to his feet.

"Sandy always says Dad hit rain on the road," Cam pointed out, looking up at his uncle. "That it was just too slick. Is that what you think?"

Jack paused.

"No, Camden, that's not what I think," he finally answered.

Cam returned to staring at the wall, mulling over his thoughts as Jack exited the room.

"Hey, Uncle Jack?" he suddenly called.

Jack popped his head back inside the doorframe. "What's up, buddy?"

"I don't think anyone could have stopped him. It's not your fault," Cam said sincerely.

"Oh. Thanks, son. That means a lot," Jack managed. He ducked out again, nearly choking on the sudden lump in his throat. He walked back down the hall and bit down hard on his tongue, barely stopping the guttural sob from escaping as he quickened his pace down the stairs.

Outside, Jack released his clenched jaw, and the taste of blood filled his mouth.

SIX.

Though he was on the older side, wearing lightweight shorts, a white tee, and faded tennis shoes with their laces tied in neat loops, Jack blended in with the handful of parents at the high school assisting their kids' coaches with summer practice. At the football field, teenage boys would soon be starting their first shift during "double days", a long training session split into two segments: one in the early morning, and one in the late afternoon. The policy had been deemed antiquated in more progressive states, but Jack didn't think so. He remembered he and his brother, Connor, working through their own double days when they made the varsity team. The first week, the test of his physical endurance in the hot, summer sun caused him to nearly lose consciousness more than once. Soon, though, the drills became more manageable, and he appreciated avoiding the sweaty sessions during the worst heat of the day. Plus, the break in between practices gave him a few hours of summer freedom while still keeping him accountable for coming back later, and not with a belly full of booze. Indeed, he'd made that mistake just once, and he'd spent practice curled up on the bleachers, puking up the sickly-sweet Annie Green Springs so violently that he thought it might come out his eyes. The smell of peaches still made his stomach churn.

For now, he was alone on the track itself, save for his four-legged friend, Fritz, the station's K9. Fritz was a black Belgian Malinois with a bright temperament that matched his watchful, russet eyes, and today, he wanted to run. Jack began with an easy gait, making his way around the field. Tall and agile, he was a natural athlete, though these days, his knees gave him more trouble than he liked to admit. In high school, he had spent endless hours at this field, practicing during the day and starting as the Cattail Cougars' quarterback on Friday nights. His brother, with his stockier build and Irish temper, covered Jack's blind side as left tackle, slamming his body into anyone who dared even come close to the ball. Sometimes, Jack recalled, he'd plow through them even when they didn't.

Connor had earned an impressive amount of attention during his time in the position, and though they both felt that college was for rich kids, Connor jumped on the opportunity for a full-ride scholarship when the University of Idaho offered it to him. Jack stayed behind, going right from his high school graduation to the police academy. He was on the beat shortly thereafter, hoping he'd follow in Pop's footsteps to become Chief of Police himself one day. After a few years, Connor squeaked by with a degree in general studies and crawled back to join the family business, too, but with three additions: his college girlfriend, Lucy; his new baby boy, Camden; and a crippling drinking problem. Sure, they'd both always drank to unwind, but Connor's alcoholism now ran deeper: when he wasn't on-duty, he was rarely without a beer or a whiskey in his hand, and even when he was working and supposedly sober, Jack often wondered how close he was to the legal limit. Of course, it was all fun and games until suddenly, the reality of addiction reared its ugly head.

Though it was almost thirty years ago, he still recollected that night's call clearly:

The insistent rapping at the front door echoed in Jack's subconscious as he realized he'd passed out on the scratchy, tweed couch in front of a flickering television. As he sat up and blinked his eyes, he could feel the burn of whiskey sloshing beneath his bony ribcage. It threatened to shoot out his dry, cracked lips, and he swallowed hard to keep it down. Still, fumes escaped, swirling up his esophagus and into his mouth and sinuses, where they tingled his nostrils with their sharp and rancid stench.

"What do you want?" he managed to croak from the dry cavern of his throat.

The rapping became a pounding.

"Chief, open up," he heard the familiar voice of Master Corporal Charles Ritter with the state police. "Chief!"

As the man spoke, Jack realized his colleague had been calling out to him for some time. He must have been sleeping hard. He got to his feet and began to push his legs into his pants, but jelly knees collapsed under his weight.

Maybe he was still drunk.

He remained seated as he resumed dressing.

"Just a minute, just a minute," he hollered. He blinked harder, trying to decipher the dining room clock's face in the dim light of black and white reruns. The numbers and hands blurred together.

Jack stood again, dragging his feet to the front door while he buttoned his jeans. He turned the deadbolt, then pulled the door open. The cool autumn breeze whistling inside the entry brought goosebumps to the bare skin on his chest, but its brisk embrace was a welcome wake-up.

"Alright, Chucky," Jack began. "What's all the fuss. . ."

Reading the man's facial expression, his voice trailed off, and the liquid in his stomach turned to concrete.

"Who?" Jack asked.

Chuck removed his black campaign hat, and its gold cords glimmered in the light of his patrol car's headlamps. He said nothing.

"Where's Connor?" Jack's voice quivered.

"He's gone, Chief." Chuck whispered the painful statement, forcing his stare to rise from the splintered porch planks and focus directly on Jack.

Jack slammed his eyelids shut. "FUCK!" he shouted. The jelly in his knees returned, and he dropped to them.

"I'm so sorry. . ." Chuck began, then ceased, aware that the words were a hollow and pitiful offering in this moment.

"Fuck. Motherfucker. Fuck. Fuck." Repeating the mantra to himself, Jack squeezed the mud-streaked entry rug tightly in his grip, as if he'd fall off the Earth if he let go.

"How?" he finally managed.

"There was an accident," Chuck explained. "They, uh. . .they failed to navigate the corner where the highway meets Buckboard Road."

"*They*." Jack said the word softly. "Lucinda?" he suddenly asked, opening his bloodshot eyes and looking up at his friend.

Chuck shook his head sadly. He reached out, resting his hand on Jack's trembling shoulder.

"Who else knows?" Jack swallowed.

"Just me an' Pete," Chuck responded, referring to his partner.

"You didn't call anything in?" Jack asked, surprised.

"Waiting on you. Wasn't sure how. . .how you wanted to handle it," Chuck explained. He spoke the words cautiously.

"Oh," Jack suddenly realized. "Yeah, I'm sure he was drunker'n a skunk," he admitted. His tone sharpened. "Let's go, then. Daylight's coming."

He released the rug, and the blood returned to his white knuckles. Using the brass doorknob to pull himself to his feet, he clung to the frame for a moment, weaving as he stood.

"Guess I'd better get a lift, too."

Outside, the rain hung suspended in the air, forming a heavy mist that clung to Jack as he stumbled to the cruiser. After they'd descended the stairs, Chuck ran ahead and opened the passenger door, then offered his arm to help Jack inside. Jack waved him off, declining assistance. He slid onto the black leather seat and removed his hat, then opened the window, lifting his face out into the fresh air again. Though it was damp now, earlier, the weather was sunny and crisp, a perfect day to drop the tailgate and barbecue some burgers and dogs with a beer in hand. No doubt, Connor and Lucy had each cracked a few cold ones waiting in the University stadium's gravel parking lot for the homecoming game to start. Afterwards, they'd have drifted downtown for a nightcap. If he knew his brother, more than a few nightcaps.

Jack had been invited.

He pushed the thought from his mind, pulling his head back into the car and rolling up the window. Buckboard was just inside the county lines, but thankfully, past city limits and the prying eyes of the townsfolk. Chuck coasted along, taking back roads from the McNulty property to the crash. At this hour, the sky was still black, and the absence of anything but wheat fields made for little light pollution from homes or businesses. For a few miles, they sat in the quiet darkness, illuminated only by the dull glow of the instrument panel.

Soon, the patrol car dropped to a crawl, carefully approaching the scene. To the untrained eye, maybe nothing would appear amiss. But to Jack, the scene told a story. In the cruiser's headlights, yaw marks came into view. The curved scrubbings were normally a sign that the driver had approached the corner too fast, then turned the steering wheel while braking to try and avoid going off the road. Typically, the rear of the vehicle swiveled towards the outside, and the tires would slide sideways even as they were still rolling. The driver would lose all control.

Here, those tell-tale marks disappeared into the grass at the road's edge.

Chuck stopped before the crest of the hill. He cleared his throat.

"You really don't have to come see this, Chief."

"I really do," Jack insisted.

"Alright," Chuck acknowledged. "Let me prepare you, then. Neither of them had a seatbelt."

"Okay," Jack slowly processed.

Chuck continued. "Lucy was thrown from the vehicle. She appears to have died upon impact. Her neck is broken. TBI apparent as well."

Jack pictured the vibrant, beautiful woman as a lifeless corpse, her head and limbs twisted into an unnatural state.

As if reading his thoughts, Chuck turned to him. "Pete's got a blanket over her for now."

Jack sighed gratefully.

"And Connor?" he asked.

Chuck took a deep breath. "He's still inside. The vehicle rolled multiple times. First on its side, then end-over-end towards the bottom of the hill," he explained. "The steering column crushed his chest, causing him to bleed out."

Jack closed his eyes.

"Quickly, I believe," Chuck hastily added, attempting some measure of comfort.

Without a word, Jack opened his door and stepped out of the cruiser. The wet grass at the shoulder of the road was soft underfoot, and the soles of his boots sunk with each step as he staggered forward. Chuck caught up to him just as he reached the edge. The bright beam of Chuck's flashlight bounced as he scanned the field for a minute; then, the totaled silver and blue pickup was illuminated. Pete stood stoically alongside the vehicle as if guarding a tomb. Noticing the men's arrival, he tipped his hat in recognition. Jack nodded in return, then carefully began to navigate down the hill, following the muddy gouges in the earth towards his brother's truck.

Near the bottom of the long descent, Pete approached him. A Native man, Pete was young and normally cheerful, with a round face and round eyes that smiled when he talked. Tonight, his black eyes were wet and swollen, and his mouth sank at the corners.

"I haven't left his side, Chief," he offered.

"I appreciate that," Jack responded. "Connor would have appreciated that."

"Before you get in there," Chuck began. "Once we saw the truck and realized who was inside, we didn't touch anything. His eyes are still open, some of his organs are . . .well, fuck. He's just in really bad shape, Chief. I guess that's all I'm trying to say." The man removed his hat again and rubbed his bald head, frustrated by the crossroads of cold, clinical professionalism and his warm, enduring friendship with the McNulty family.

"Thanks," Jack mumbled.

"I'm sorry. Just trying to help you get ready for what you're about to see."

"My friend, I'm not sure you ever could," Jack shook his head.

Jack left the men on the knoll and strode the last few paces to the bottom of the hill, where the truck had come to its final resting place. His steps were straight and deliberate now, and vibrations ran up his body each time his foot contacted the ground. The dulling cloak of whiskey had dissipated, leaving every sentiment and nerve exposed to the violent scene before him and the frigid rain that had begun to pummel through his denim coat. He reached the truck, then wrenched the creaking door open.

Aside from pediatric victims, death didn't much bother Jack; from a young age, Nan had instilled in him a reverence for his Savior and the promise of eternal life. Thus, even as his heart ached, when his eyes fell upon his younger brother's mangled body, he tried to find comfort thinking of it as an empty shell, instead focusing on Connor's soul. It was gone, having left this vessel as if it were water springing through the cracks in a broken vase.

His soul wasn't all that spilled out. Jack surveyed the vehicle's interior, which had been soaked by the blood leaking from Connor's caved-in chest and the deep lacerations to his forehead and nose. It carried a metallic scent through the cab, which mixed with the pervasive odor of alcohol. Jack supposed it could be from the crushed, empty cans that dusted the seat and floorboards like silver discs of confetti. Pieces of a whiskey bottle had been strewn about, too, distinguishable from the windshield's glass only by the torn bits of black label still affixed to them. Still, Jack knew it was his brother's own body that likely held the highest alcohol content of all, and he feared what a test of his remaining fluids would reveal.

Jack headed back towards his colleagues, leaving the truck's door ajar. Through the streaming downpour, he addressed them, raising his voice over the rain.

"You find them right away?"

"I can't be sure, but I thought I heard the crash," Pete responded. "Lucy was still warm when I checked her. Couldn't have been on scene long after it happened."

"How long before you came to get me, Chucky?" Jack asked.

"Minutes," he answered.

"Roads weren't this wet then," Jack reasoned. "And no ice yet this year."

Chuck followed his train of thought. "Yeah, no reason to believe conditions were slippery at all."

"So, his fucking drinking cost him his life. . .both of their lives. Gonna cost the boys, too." For the first time since they arrived, Jack's tone was not just sharp or matter of fact, but angry.

"I can't imagine losing both parents," Pete commiserated.

"Connor was a good father, a good cop—" Chuck began.

"Maybe," Jack interrupted. "But the insurance company won't leave a cent for them if they think he was DUI."

"No, they won't. And with all due respect," Chuck addressed him, "I'm worried that's exactly what our guys are going to determine. Don't even need the toxicology report. . .I could smell him before I saw him."

"I know it," Jack acknowledged. "Damnit. Think of the publicity. Embarrassment, once the boys are older. Guilt, even. I can't stand the thought."

Chuck sighed, then crossed his arms over his chest. "So, what do we do?"

"I'm gonna torch it," Jack answered abruptly, glancing at the wreckage.

Pete suddenly piped up. "I could say the vehicle must have hydroplaned in all this water. It was already a ball of fire when we got here."

"Think you can keep this field from going up, too?" Chuck asked Jack pointedly.

"Fall's been wet enough so far," Jack shrugged. "And with this rain now? Probably."

"Good enough for me, then," Chuck affirmed. "We've got your back."

Jack nodded, then motioned to the car above. "You got a gas can?"

While Chuck climbed the hill to retrieve it, Jack and Pete walked the few meters to the brightly patterned wool blanket that shielded Lucy from the rain and the officers' macabre conversation.

Jack kneeled, laying a hand on the woman's body. He fought the urge to remove the covering and see her injuries for himself; he feared it would not only mar her lovely visage that would otherwise remain ageless in his mind, but also brew more disdain for his brother's selfish act.

Chuck returned, and Jack took the red, plastic jug from his hands. The liquid within sloshed as he walked to the crumpled truck.

Connor's body came into view once more, and Jack studied him more closely this time. His brother's typically twinkling, blue-green irises were choked by hemorrhaging blood vessels, and each orb bulged from its socket like a water balloon sagging from a gushing garden spigot.

Chucky had warned him not to look.

Jack averted his gaze, focusing instead on the subtle silhouettes of a distant doe and her offspring tiptoeing through the grain. "I'm taking your boys. I'll raise 'em up right," he started.

"This will never—" Jack's words caught in his throat. His heartbeat drummed through his chest, shaking his entire body.

My baby brother.

"This will NEVER happen to them," he finished.

With that, Jack quickly but thoroughly spread the can's contents until the last drop had been shaken out. Standing back, he cupped his hand and lit the match.

"I won't fail you again," he promised through tears.

* * *

The Cattail Police Department was a simple, flat building with a faded, brick exterior and a line of black-and-white cruisers down the east side. A flimsy white awning offered a few square feet of shade outside the front door, which was adorned with a crisp, vinyl crest.

At 5:03 A.M., Cam and Corb tip-toed through the front, each carrying tall, gas station coffee cups that were already halfway empty. Scanning their access passes, they reached the command center. This early, the only employee at her station was Luella, the dispatcher. Luella was a plump Filipina woman with a lovely smile and silver hair at her temples. She greeted them warmly.

"Good morning, Lieutenant. Detective. Chief will be back in just a few," she stated. "He took Fritz for a quick jog."

"Sounds good, Lu. We'll be in his office," Cam responded.

Down the hall, the Chief's office was furnished with a fine, walnut bookcase filled with pictures and plaques. Alongside it, an American flag was perched in a gold stand. On the leather pad protecting his desk, the Chief had scattered various papers relating to the Robbins investigation. At the top of the pile, Cam eyed what appeared to be a résumé.

PAGET JAMES, PH.D.

He picked it up, then sat on the edge of his chair as he quietly skimmed the document. He sipped his coffee.

"POG-ette? PAW-jet?" he finally tried.

"That for the new guy?" Corb asked. Cam nodded.

"Lemme see," Corb replied. He set his coffee on the Chief's desk, then snatched the document from Cam. He plopped down in the Chief's stately, leather office chair and began to spin around.

After two 360's, he stopped.

"Here we go. This cat's originally from Louisiana. N'awlins. So, you just French it up. *PAW-zhay.* Monsieur PAW-zhay, I drink Chardonnay. . ."

Cam chuckled.

A woman suddenly entered the room and cleared her throat, startling the brothers.

"It's PAD-jit," she announced in a rich, silky voice. Over dark eyes, she furrowed her brow. She was tall and thin, with flawless mocha skin and ebony hair that ran nearly to her waist in smooth waves.

Corb jumped to his feet. "My apologies, Mademoiselle," he offered, flirtatiously extending his hand.

"*Docteur*," she sharply corrected him.

Corb glanced down at the C.V. again. "Right. Dr. James," he mumbled, tossing the document at his smirking brother.

"But you can call me PJ," she offered in a kinder tone, taking Corb's hand and giving it a firm shake. The brothers introduced themselves.

"I'm a Supervisory Special Agent with the FBI's Cyber Crime division," she elaborated. "I specialize in profiling celebrity stalkers."

"So, you think somebody's got a crush on Mrs. Robbins," Corb concluded.

"Somebody is completely and dangerously obsessed with her," PJ clarified, setting her slim, black briefcase on the vacant club chair by Cam.

She looked at Cam, and her eyes fell to his coffee.

"Where can I get me some of that?" she pleaded.

Cam shot a glance at his younger brother.

"I'll round some up," Corb confirmed. "Least I can do."

As he strolled from the room and down the hall, PJ pulled a streamlined laptop from her briefcase.

"How was your flight?" Cam began politely.

PJ set the laptop before them on the desk, then opened it.

"Busy," she responded. "Britlyn Robbins has only been active for about two years, and she's already attracted millions of followers."

In the web browser, PJ navigated to the woman's blog, then opened several other tabs, one for each social media site.

"I've skimmed it. Makeup, clothes, home decor. . ." Cam stated. "I did learn my Tupperware is vintage."

"Riveting, isn't it?" PJ remarked sarcastically.

"Just hard to believe it pulls in so much dough," he responded.

"Believe it. She's got almost three million followers on her apps, not to mention the traffic that flows through the blog itself. Plus, commission on sales for any of these products she's wearing or furnishings in her house. The figures would make your head spin," PJ explained.

"It does already," he agreed. "And it sounds like a mountain of data."

"Yes, tons to comb through," she replied. "We can web-crawl some of it, but it's not a substitute for human assessment. We still have to view the material."

"Where do you even start?" Cam lamented.

"Our team is tracking her last movements and interactions via social media and her blog. Hopefully, we can get some definitive answers to our most pressing questions before trolls start mass-creating dupes."

"Which means what exactly, in English?" Cam smiled.

"Sorry," she shook her head, slowing her speech. "Individuals often create spam websites and social media accounts to capitalize on breaking and popular news. Sometimes they're searching for clicks; other times, they're phishing for personal information."

"Ah," he nodded, finishing his coffee and tossing the paper cup into the black plastic liner of a nearby wastebasket. "Well, we're certainly glad you're here, Agent James. I have to say my experience with fishing trolls is limited to writing tickets to folks using barbed hooks on the river."

"The sweet nostalgia of real-life crime," PJ responded with a smirk. "I did that for a while. Now. . .my job starts and ends with this box." She patted her laptop, then moved her fingers to the trackpad. She clicked one of Britlyn's posts. Cam recognized the sweeping views of the Palouse through the home's windows. The photos showed before and after shots of the Robbins' updated farmhouse.

Corb shuffled in, handing PJ a sleeved paper cup and glancing over her shoulder.

"Probably doesn't help that any damn person with the internet has a complete blueprint of her house," he chimed in.

"Thank you. No, it doesn't," PJ agreed, taking the coffee.

She reached the bottom of the post, then began to go through the comments section.

"We've been reviewing the individuals who are engaging in dialogue here," she began.

"Whoa, hold up," Cam suddenly directed, inching his face closer to the laptop's screen. Corb leaned in to look, resting his hand on the back of his brother's chair.

"What is it?" PJ asked.

With a gentle laugh, Cam shook his head. "Uh, it's nothing."

"You were gonna say that looks like Amos Sinclair, weren't you?" Corb quizzed him.

Cam turned his head, locking eyes with his brother. "Isn't that crazy? Yeah, I was."

"You two know think you might know this guy?" PJ perked up, rejuvenated by both caffeine and the excitement of a lead.

Corb walked around the desk to the Chief's chair, sipping his own coffee as he mulled it over. "No," he decided.

"He looks like someone we went to school with, but it's impossible," Cam explained.

"Why impossible?" PJ asked with a puzzled look.

"First off, because that dude's missing about a decade's worth of beard," Corb began, nodding in reference to the photo on the screen. Cam chuckled.

"And second," Corb continued, "Why would Amos be on some women's fashion site?"

"Amos wouldn't be on the internet at all," Cam added. "Doesn't believe in it."

"What do you mean 'believe' in it? Is he Amish or something?" PJ inquired.

"Or something," Corb muttered.

"It's more than that," Cam expounded. "The folks at Anthem Hold don't believe in anything modern. Not technology, not vehicles, not medical treatment. . ." he trailed off.

A somber air filled the room. "That has to end poorly for some folks," PJ said quietly.

"It does — Amos's twin brother included," Cam replied. "Back before Anthem Hold had its own schoolhouse, they went to school in town. With us. He got leukemia in 7th grade, and the family refused to treat him."

"Well, that's not entirely true, Cam. They prayed about it," Corb added bitterly.

"Shit," PJ said sadly.

"Yep. Obviously, he didn't make it," Corb concluded.

"Anything happen to his parents?" she asked.

"Not in this state. Idaho's faith healing exception has been a sore spot for law enforcement for years," Cam disclosed.

"His parents died in a house fire, though," Corb added. "Funny thing is, it probably could have been prevented with smoke detectors." He took another swig of coffee. "That karma. . .*she is a bitch.*"

"That's right," Cam remembered.

"So, what happened with your friend, then?" PJ wondered.

"No idea. They keep the whole compound pretty well shrouded in secrecy. He's still alive now, if that's what you mean," Cam answered. "As for his past, I don't know."

"Is there any way to find out more?" PJ asked.

"About Anthem Hold? No idea. Maybe someone with a better grasp on their history?" Cam wondered aloud.

"Actually. . .maybe I do have an idea," he realized. His eyes trailed to his brother.

"No. Nope. I know what you're gonna say, Cam, and the answer is no," Corb exclaimed.

"She was close to all of it, Corb. Lizzie will be able to point us in the right direction on this," Cam reasoned.

"Absolutely fucking not," Corb stated firmly.

"Who's Lizzie?" PJ interjected.

"Elizabeth Shetler. A defector, of sorts. Oh, and Corb's ex-girlfriend," Cam answered, amused. He turned back to his brother. "You owe me."

"No," Corb refused again.

"Mornin'," Chief Jack McNulty greeted them, suddenly appearing in the doorway in athletic apparel and sneakers. Sweat beaded on his brow, and his breathing was still slowing to its normal rate. He released Fritz from his leash, then hung it on a rack beside his door. A consummate morning person, in addition to exercising the dog, he'd have already done 50 push-ups, read the paper, started the coffee pot for Aunt Sandy, showered, and reviewed yesterday's field notes. Cam's routine was similar. Corb felt tired just looking at either of them.

"Good morning, Chief," the trio returned.

"Accommodations work out alright for you, Agent James?" Jack asked.

"Yes, thank you," she acknowledged.

"Where'd he put you up?" Corb asked.

"The Cattail Inn," she confirmed.

The brothers grimaced.

"We'll get you moved today," Cam promised. "There's a few vacation rentals in town you'd probably find a little more. . .suitable."

"It was late," Jack offered, shrugging.

"It was fine," PJ insisted. "I may be from the city, but I don't expect five-star lodging in the middle of Idaho. No offense."

"You probably don't expect to witness a drug deal, either," Cam responded. "Trust me on this one."

"The Cattail Inn? Seriously?" Corb asked the Chief. "Did you at least arrest anyone while you were there?"

"No, I did not arrest anyone while I was there," Jack answered, mimicking his tone.

"But *could you have* arrested someone while you were there?" Corb pressed, grinning.

"Oh, cut the shit, Corbin," Jack growled. "Fine. We'll move her today."

PJ stifled a smile. Especially without the shadow of Jack's cowboy hat, she could see the family resemblance.

"ANYHOW," Jack began. "State lab ran the blood at the scene. It does not belong to Mrs. Robbins."

"None of it?" Corb asked, picturing the blood-smeared walls.

Jack shook his head. "Not so far."

The three younger officers sighed with relief.

"So, we've got ourselves an injured kidnapper," Cam derived. "That could be helpful for narrowing things down."

"Should be. No matches so far, but you know the limitations of our databases. Remind me to ask Santa

Claus for a catalog of the world's hair follicles," he remarked sarcastically. "You got any leads yet?"

"Not really," PJ admitted.

"You'll get there, just keep digging," Jack encouraged them. He reached over to a wooden valet stand tucked behind the door, picking up his jeans and suit jacket. "I'm off to handle the damn press."

"The press, already?" PJ clenched her teeth. "Who spilled the beans?"

"Not any one of ours. Husband told some of her blogger friends, and now the whole world knows."

"Just that she's missing?" Corb asked.

"And left a bloody crime scene behind," Jack confirmed.

"Isn't he law enforcement?" PJ asked in a baffled tone. "He should know that blabbering about the details is going to compromise the investigation."

"Yep. I'm learning there's a pretty large discrepancy between what that man oughta know and what he actually does. Anyhow, me and ISP agree he's taking a leave of absence. Didn't give him much choice but to stay in his lane."

"That seems unusual," PJ remarked. "For them to push him out of the office entirely. I mean, when he could be working on other cases."

"Not really, considering I asked to have him kindly yanked for the time being," Jack responded.

"Good riddance," Corb piped up.

"Those reporters are going to dig at you like a dog for a bone," Cam changed the subject.

"Let 'em. We're not showing our hand with our victim unaccounted for and our suspect at large."

As Jack turned to leave, he suddenly stopped and squinted at the laptop screen behind them.

"Well, I'll be!" he said aloud, walking out the door. "If I didn't know better, I would swear that's Amos Sinclair."

* * *

The morning jog had been good for both the man and dog, Jack noted as he studied Fritz's satisfied expression. Following Connor's death, there was nothing more he wanted than to wash himself in whiskey, drowning in the liquid respite of blacking out and forgetting, if just for a moment, the tragedy that had befallen his family.

With two little boys, that was no longer an option. Instead, he needed sustainable and healthy relief. One night, after dinner at Nan's, he'd gone for a walk while his nephews joined her to watch TV. His walk broke into a run, and soon, he was sprinting over the rolling hills of the Palouse, rushing head-on into the black night, praying the answer to his grief might find him. His lungs burned, and in cowboy boots with thick socks, his feet were slipping in sweat.

But then, something else happened. A familiar wave of relief, much like the one that followed the first few sips of an ice-cold beer, swept over him. He unclenched his jaw, and the tension in his neck subsided. As the years passed, he ditched all the bad habits and most of the guilt, but he leaned on exercise frequently as a way to power through the more stressful eras of his life. Today, under the intense pressure that came with the well-known woman going missing in his hometown, he had needed the break.

Upon entering the station, he'd encountered both nephews ready for the day's busy schedule, although Corb smelled more like he would rather crawl back into bed. His younger nephew didn't smoke, but the odor of cigarettes and an unmistakable sweet scent on his breath clued Jack in: he'd been at the bar, and probably late. He had been ready to chew his ass, but then, he caught Cam's eye. With a look, he determined that Cam had already handled it. He was innately responsible and poised, and during their childhoods, Jack had frequently found himself letting Cam take charge of his younger brother.

They'd talk about last night later.

In addition to the brothers, his FBI agent had arrived from Salt Lake. The higher-ups had extolled her intellect and expertise in the area of social media stalking specifically, but they had neglected to mention her beauty. The African American woman was stunning, with upturned, almond eyes that shone brightly from under thick black lashes and sculpted brows. Her starched, white shirt and delicate gold jewelry cut clean lines against her smooth, dark skin, which she mostly covered in a form-fitting but professional black suit. In his shorts and sneakers, he suddenly felt silly. He eyed

Camden, clad in the navy, summer uniform of a police lieutenant, complete with various patches and pins denoting his rank and service accomplishments. Even compared to Agent James's sophisticated polish, he didn't look so bad.

Jack's eyes shifted to Corbin again. Aside from a badge that dangled in the center of his chest, it was hard to believe he was a detective. His wrinkled shirt was already soaked in sweat, and his sandy scruff was looking especially scraggly that morning. Adding in his cowboy hat and worn, leather boots, he looked like he belonged at a bar as much as he smelled like one.

They were in over their heads, Jack worried.

However, after a few icebreakers, he found that the female agent was not nearly as formal as her appearance suggested, and the trio quickly adjusted to working together. When Jack left them in his office, the brothers and Agent James were already delving deep into the investigation. He'd laughed at what appeared to be a familiar face on her laptop, but as he walked down the hall, he again found himself recollecting the past.

How had time treated Amos Sinclair?

After another quick shower, Jack donned his regular uniform and headed outside, where he was accosted by a swarm of cameras and news anchors with colorful blazers and voluminous, sweeping hair.

"Chief, have you located Britlyn Robbins?"

"Does your team even have the experience—"

"Are the residents of Cattail safe?"

"How are you handling this situation?"

"Is the Department overwhelmed?"

"Isn't it true you don't know where she is?"

"You don't know if she's even alive, do you?"

"With all the blood at the scene, aren't you afraid you're too late?"

The reporters lobbed their questions like grenades.

Chief McNulty cleared his throat and tendered a confident expression. "I am extremely proud of the diligent efforts of the Cattail Police Department and our partner agencies. Our primary goal is to bring Mrs. Robbins home unharmed. It is important that the general public does not panic in this situation. . .we have no reason to believe this was not an isolated incident. The best thing Cattail citizens can do is to remain calm and let us focus our resources on the investigation." After years of experience, Jack didn't flinch under fire, and his response came across as cool and collected.

"But Chief—" the rebuttals began.

Jack tipped his hat, abruptly ending his statement. He pushed through the reporters and the small crowd that had gathered, continuing until he had reached the bottom of the stairs. He picked up the pace, carefully navigating the uneven concrete so as to not catch a toe on the sidewalk, which humped in places over the hundred-year-old tree roots that swelled beneath. Between the buildings, Jack caught glimpses of the babbling water where the Palouse River slowed to a crawl behind the town's Main Street. Walking the block, he passed the Creekside Cafe and the corner gas station, inhaling the tangled aromas of fried foods and fuel. Near the end, on the left, he ducked inside the used book store, retreating into that maze until he was entirely obscured by stacks of dog-eared novels. He sucked in a breath. He'd first met the Sinclairs decades ago, but he remembered it like it was only yesterday:

"Adam Sinclair," he recalled announcing over the boy's bare body.

The man and woman nodded. They were older than he'd expected the child's parents to be, and they both appeared to be in poor health, with sallow skin and long, yellow teeth.

"You say he passed this morning?" he asked.

"We'd been praying for a miracle," the mother offered. "But at least he is home now. With our Father."

"Right," Jack replied, deeply rubbing his brow as if he could massage his anger back into his skin. "Well, Dr. Black and I will be removing his body—"

Out of the corner of his eye, Jack saw a figure skitter across the hall.

Instinctively, he moved his right hand to his pistol.

"Who's there?" he commanded.

"Just our other boy," the father explained.

"Didn't we talk about him being at school when we came?" Jack sharply reminded the parents.

"Didn't want to go. He won't leave his brother's side," the mother chimed in emotionlessly.

Jack suddenly felt queasy. *Of course, he won't.*

"Come here, boy," he instructed, gentler this time.

After a moment, the young man showed himself, then tiptoed down the hall towards Jack. His pale blue eyes were red and swollen.

"This is your brother?" Jack asked.

The boy nodded.

"Your twin brother," Jack suddenly realized, examining their identical features.

He nodded again.

"You know, we have to take him with us now," Jack explained carefully. "I'm so sorry."

"I know," the boy responded. "I just. . .don't. . . want. . . him to go," he managed to sob.

"He's already gone," Jack explained in a delicate tone. "But so is his pain. His suffering."

The boy drew closer, laying his hands softly over his brother's dusky, lifeless forearm.

"The kids at school say he should have gone to the doctor," he suddenly stated. "Is that true?"

Jack took a deep breath and looked down. "I don't think that's my place to say," he commented politely. His outrage continued to simmer just below the surface.

"Would you have taken him? If he was your son?" the boy pressed.

"Amos! Hold thy tongue," his mother cautioned.

"Enough questions! Go outside!" his father followed suit, rapping his knuckles on the table and pointing a finger towards the door.

"It's perfectly alright—" Jack began.

"Soon, we'll have our own school. One without all this newfangled nonsense," the man interrupted angrily.

"Without you people trying to tell us how to live, how to treat our own ailments. Trying to change our ways. . ."

"Your ways?" Jack scoffed.

"God's will is for sickness to be healed," the father continued. "If He didn't heal Adam, it's because we've been defective in our faith."

Jack's rage boiled over.

"Yeah, kid. Damn right I would have taken him." He raised his gaze as he answered, meeting young Amos Sinclair's wide eyes for a moment.

Nearly twenty years later, leaning against creaking shelves of books, Jack couldn't shake a sense of déjà vu: when he glanced at the laptop screen, he felt like he had met those same eyes again.

SEVEN.

"Hit the lights," Agent James commanded.

The bright, overhead bulbs were extinguished, and the squad room grew dark, save for a single light projected at a dry erase board at the front. The enlarged silhouette of Agent James's slender fingers came into view as she adjusted her materials against the light source.

"Good morning, officers. As your Chief has surely informed you, I'm Agent James from Cyber Crimes in Salt Lake. I've been assigned to assist with the Robbins matter based on my expertise in the area," she explained. "Specifically, I have training and experience in the area of psychology, and this knowledge has been instrumental in the apprehension of dozens of stalkers in the northwestern United States. Now, can anyone tell me, what is a stalker?"

The room remained silent.

"Wake up, fellas," The Chief prodded firmly. He stood beside her, sipping coffee and squinting at his officers from under his cowboy hat.

A young deputy cleared his throat. "Uh, I can't remember the specific language in the statute, but it's basically when you're harassing an ex or something." His smooth cheeks grew red.

"That's right," Agent James praised him. "And what kind of behavior might constitute harassment?"

"Showing up at their work. Or their house," another deputy piped up.

"Could be. Your average stalker might be a scorned lover, intent on keeping that connection. They might go to the victim's workplace or residence. Maybe send gifts. Typically, these are people who had a relationship with the victim, like an ex-boyfriend or girlfriend. Or sometimes that was a different relationship, like a customer or client. Now, thanks to the internet, we can't always narrow down our suspects to the immediate proximity."

Agent James loudly shuffled her papers on the overhead projector. Looking towards the doorway in the rear, where Cam and Corb lurked behind the rows of chairs, she shot the brothers a raised eyebrow; she had already chided them once for the ancient technology, which thwarted the presentation of the slick PowerPoint she'd prepared.

"Thanks to the internet," she resumed. "We have people from different towns, states — even different countries — zooming in on your backyard. They can see the car in your driveway. They can find your professional profile and see where you work. They can discover your family and friends. And thanks to our oversharing society, they can do all of this from afar. . .just sitting back while the victim publicizes the most intimate details of her life. I'm talking birthdates, children's names, anniversaries, number of piercings, favorite foods — pretty soon, you've got a secret admirer who feels like they know you very, very well. Some may be content to obsess from afar. But, when we factor in some mental health issues, problems can start to emerge. Afar isn't good enough. . .the stalker wants to meet in person."

"In our case, Mrs. Britlyn Robbins was kidnapped from her home by someone we believe was a cyberstalker and follower of her blog. Someone we believe was an erotomaniac."

As she uttered the last word, a dozen more flushed cheeks fell towards the floor.

"Which is not quite as kinky as it sounds, boys," she chuckled softly. "Erotic brings to mind sexual desire, nudity, and the like. But erotomania is something else: in short, these individuals believe the victim is actually in love with them. This is true even if they do not know the victim or if the victim rejects them—*they will not take no for an answer*. This type of celebrity stalker believes the victim is sending them secret messages in their lines on TV, their song lyrics, or in the case of Mrs. Robbins, their blog posts."

"You got a suspect in mind?" one of the officers asked.

Agent James's eyes met Cam's, then Corb's. Both brothers shook their heads.

"Not quite," she responded. "There are some areas we are prioritizing based on Mrs. Robbins's online activity, but we still want to rule out the possibility that this was simply a local yokel attracted to a pretty face. Or some other motive in play. She was mostly a homebody, but she did leave the house for necessities. We'll want to check the grocery stores, coffee shops, anywhere she could have given someone the wrong impression or made some enemies. Detective McNulty has already put together some places to comb through."

Corb approached the front. "Sanders, Sabato — I'd like you to look into the wine shop on Spokane Street and that hippie foods store. Bauer — check out Creekside Cafe. Ellwood, Sitar — you'll stick to your regular patrol, but keep your eyes peeled. Based on the limited video we were able to analyze, we're looking for an individual roughly six foot three, 180 pounds. So, almost certainly male. May have visible injuries."

"Remember," Agent James added. "This person does not feel that he has done anything wrong; he will believe Mrs. Robbins wanted this attention. As a result, he may not appear suspicious at all. He may not be wary of you, or run from you, or even try to avoid contact. In fact, he may seem strangely pleasant and happy — in his world, he has successfully connected with the love of his life."

* * *

The tender spot where her hair had been yanked was the first to wake her, followed by achy, sore muscles and a splitting headache that resonated behind her eyes. Whatever sedative she'd been administered was slowly leaving her system and was being replaced by pain and nausea. She recollected the incident: *a man came in my house. He tackled me to the floor. He stuck me with a needle.*

She suddenly noticed the sound of a beeping monitor. Before she opened her eyes, Britlyn listened for a moment to its tone, slowing her breathing as she focused. Then, she recognized the feeling of a device clipped to one of her fingertips.

I'm in the hospital, she realized excitedly. *I'm safe now.* Ramón must have heard her cries for help. Or maybe, Shawn came home and saved her.

As she opened her eyes, her joy was replaced with confusion. Around her, the walls were comprised of various metal pieces: street signs, trailer siding, diamond-plated panels, and other items formed a random patchwork around the room.

Then, she smelled it.

Not the bitter, chemical, antiseptic scent of the hospital. No, instead, the faint smell of manure nestled in her nostrils.

Britlyn gasped, then started to scramble out of bed. She was startled by the sound of chains clanking against the frame's metal rails. She looked down, realizing that they were wrapped around her wrists.

"Hey, Brit," a voice greeted her.

From behind her, a man emerged. He was clothed in black pants and a white shirt, and he donned a felt, black hat with a wide brim. Blood seeped through the right side of his shirt, evidencing the impact of one of her letter opener jabs. She looked up, recognizing his light eyes as belonging to the man in the balaclava.

"Who are you?" she stammered with fear.

The man smiled. At one corner of his mouth, two teeth behind his canine tooth were missing. His thin lips quivered beneath a hawkish nose that stuck out sharply above a frizzy, blonde beard that hung to mid-chest.

"I think you know the answer to that," he insisted.

"I don't."

"Come on," he pressed.

"I don't fucking know!" she shouted, her voice echoing off the metal panels surrounding them. She resumed pulling her arms against the chains to no avail. As she started to shout, the beep of the monitor quickened.

"Shhhh. . ." he cautioned. "You wouldn't want to hurt the babies."

Britlyn caught her breath and closed her eyes, burying her face in her shoulder. The beeping slowed.

"I understand this is all a rough transition, so I'll forgive your memory lapse," he offered. "Look at me."

She opened her eyes, and he removed his hat, holding it over his abdomen. With the other hand, he pulled his beard off and over his head, stretching the elastic strap he used to fashion the hair to his face. Underneath, his chin was bare and cleft.

Britlyn's eyes widened.

"Now, this is probably how you're used to seeing me. I talked you through building that shelf out of pallets, remember? And your recipes. . .I always compliment your recipes," he attempted to refresh her memory.

"The pallet shelf," she muttered, thinking.

"The pallet shelf in the kitchen. With the cup hooks for your coffee mugs," he added. "We did a wood burn on it, then we clear-coated it?"

She gasped. "You're that. . .DIYGuy?"

He nodded. "DIYGuy85. I knew you'd remember," he beamed. "But that's just a handle, of course. You can call me Amos."

"You followed me?" her mouth gaped in disbelief. "Like, in real life?"

"I mean, really, *you* followed me," he explained. "That's how I knew it was truly meant to be."

Britlyn's face grew pale. "What do you mean, I followed you?" she stammered.

"To Cattail, silly," he exhaled. "Out of all the places in the world, you relocated to my backyard? I knew it was a sign."

She swallowed. "No. You've got it all wrong. I liked the farmland. And the prairie. I didn't come here for you," she said quietly.

"You may not realize it, but you were led here by a divine force. The same force that blessed us with twins.

You didn't know I was a twin, did you? It's an amazing bond."

"These are not your babies," she hissed. "Don't talk about them."

"They are *our* babies," he corrected her. "I've been watching them grow, you know. Watching your womb swell. It's so beautiful. I can't wait to share this life with you. To hold them."

"You'll never touch them!" she shouted. The beeping increased again.

"Ah-ah-ah," he cautioned. "Let's keep things cool. You're going to feel a lot better when we get home."

"What do you mean, home?" she inquired worriedly.

His eyes twinkled. "You'll see. Just rest now. I have a prior engagement to attend. Can't have people worried about me—they might come sniffing around here."

At the mention of other people, Britlyn began to scream for help. As her voice grew louder, tinny reverberations shot back towards her from the metal enclosure and welled in her ears.

"No one can hear you," Amos informed her. "And if you can't calm down for the girls, I might have to make you calm down," he threatened.

Britlyn remembered the warm darkness that had enveloped her in her office and closed her mouth. Her teeth chattered as she shook, both from the memory and from the room's uncomfortably cool temperature. "Can't you just loosen my arms?" she asked after a moment, pulling again against the chains binding her to the bed. "I want to feel the girls. To feel my belly."

Amos shook his head firmly, then pointed to the bloody stain on his shirt. "This was a close one," he stated. He lowered his finger to his upper thigh on the same side. "And you got me here, too. I can't risk that again. Not right now."

She scowled at him, then nodded towards the larger wound. "I hope you fucking die from that," she announced.

Amos pulled his beard back on and adjusted his hat. "Oh, I don't think you do, Brit. See, I'm the only one that knows where you are. Without my say-so, there are no signals in here, and no signals out. If I die, you and the girls won't be long after me. So, chin up! I think it's time for you to start accepting that the moment has finally come for us to be together. It's a great day."

Britlyn began to cry.

* * *

Amos exited the apartment, sliding the entry hatch back into place. As he pushed, a searing pain shot up his side. He groaned through clenched teeth.

Britlyn had gotten him good.

For a moment, as he'd twisted the gleaming, chocolate strands of her hair around his fingers, he considered abandoning the plan altogether. He could simply disappear, departing immediately. The money he'd set aside was more than enough to establish a new life, a new name. A new face. He thought about just killing her there.

But, he'd reasoned, he'd be alone. Sure, he'd find another pretty face, but it wouldn't belong to Britlyn Robbins.

And she belonged to him, promised to Amos by God himself. The twins, too — he was sure of it.

Soothed by this spiritual connection, he'd sedated her instead, then managed to slip her by the groundskeeper and into his carriage. She slept the entire journey home, even as he carried her past the farm and to her makeshift bedroom inside his office. He was eager for her company, but he'd elected to prolong her sedation, administering enough anesthesia to keep her under for the entire evening. Then, he planned to take Friday to rest and muster the strength for their trip. This measure was not anticipated, but it had become necessary as a result of the deep jabs she'd inflicted.

Once he had gotten her chained up in the office, he had begun to treat those wounds. He'd foregone the futile honey ointment and burdock leaves his parents would have used and went straight for his medical kit, beginning the process by swallowing a hearty dosage of opiate painkillers with a mouthful of moonshine he'd made in his own still. He cleaned the wounds, applied antibiotic cream, then bandaged them. If she'd missed his organs, it would be enough. Anyhow, it was all he could do for now. He wasn't worried: though he couldn't determine yet if he was in the clear, soon, his doctors would review the damage and make the necessary repairs.

It would be part of a long list of fixes Amos envisioned. He stuck his tongue through the gaping hole at his gums as he pictured the sparkling, white implants and veneers that would encase his worn, neglected teeth. His brows and hair would be groomed and colored, and he'd laser away the wrinkles and spots where the sun had damaged his alabaster skin. After he found Britlyn, he had started to exercise and become more toned, but he was still toying with the idea of also augmenting his hard work with plastic surgery, beefing up his scrawny frame so that it was a suitable match for his fit, future bride.

Mostly though, he longed to correct the crooked hump that gave his nose a sinister and bird-like appearance. The hump, a lump of cracked bones and scar tissue that jutted from the bridge of his nose towards his left eye, was a gift from his father, received via the handle of a shovel when Amos had supposedly not been working fast enough. He was just thirteen and still reeling from the loss of his twin brother not even a year prior. Grief had him in its grip, and his relentless routine afforded him no opportunity for healing the hole in his heart that Adam's passing had left behind. His parents, on the other hand, bounced back immediately, demanding and graceless as always. Amos was still expected to be awake by 4:00 A.M. daily, tend the property, feed the goats, and assist with the soapmaking. Prayer and religious study consumed what little free time that remained before he crawled into bed, too tired to fight off the cornhusks that poked at his skin through his threadbare mattress.

Amos still had bruising under both of his eyes when he came to the realization that he was better off alone. He despised his mother, a bossy, spiteful woman whose large, unwieldy breasts had hunched her shoulders down over the years and curled her spine into a question mark. He imagined they were once an asset, as he could think of no other valuable feature she could have possessed worthy of luring any man to her bedside. Somehow, his father had found her, and the pair began their dutiful quest to churn out children as they'd been instructed.

Still, as much as his mother repulsed him, it was his father that drew most of his ire. His arrogance was rivaled only by his stupidity, and he foolishly followed the faith-healing regimen dictated by the elders even as Adam grew drawn and frail, and the life drained out of his cheeks. Amos had suspected that a more effective treatment existed, and though his father had tried to beat the conversation from his memory, the lawman had confirmed it.

And so, the seed of hate was planted. The loveless atmosphere of bare tolerance for the boy fertilized it, and his daily whippings quenched its thirst.

But it was their forgetting that truly made it grow. They'd forgotten Adam, pausing their busy lives only for a span of hours to clean out his side of the bedroom and stow his sparse belongings. This forgetting was a ray of sun for Amos's hate, pulling it towards reality until it was no longer buried in the depths of his resentment, but sprouting up into the light.

By that time, Amos wanted to end them for what they'd done.

And so, he did.

EIGHT.

Along with PJ, the Cyber Crimes department had sent two additional agents to assist with processing and analyzing the technological aspects of Britlyn's kidnapping. In a larger, more progressive city, that might mean poring over footage from neighbors' smart doorbells, nearby business surveillance, and traffic cameras. Ideally, they would then pinpoint the suspect's ingress and egress of the Robbins' property, then simply trace the matching vehicle and its route.

However, while Britlyn herself — and her upgraded home — kept the agents busy mucking through the bog of her blog and other social channels, the town of Cattail was otherwise primitive in its ways: smart security systems were swapped for shotguns and big dogs, nosy neighbors helped watch over each other's homes, and the minimal traffic was controlled by a small handful of rudimentary lights and stop signs. Rather than emailing prospective witnesses and digitally inspecting pertinent files from behind a desk, many aspects of the investigation would require actual boots on the ground, face-to-face interviews, and combing through paper records.

To begin, the two other FBI agents, along with various Cattail deputies, arranged the conference room into a temporary headquarters while the brothers and Agent James headed down to the archives. The stairwell to the police department's basement storage area was dimly lit and poorly maintained, each wooden step slightly concave from decades of boots hurrying between floors.

PJ shot the brothers another patronizing glance. "Can I at least hope to see file cabinets or are there hieroglyphics painted on the walls?" she joked.

"Some of this handwriting will have you hoping for hieroglyphics," Corb snorted.

"It's well-organized," Cam reassured her. "Just old."

"2002 is hardly old," she countered. "No one was using computers here then?"

"Cam still doesn't," Corb pointed out.

"True," Cam shrugged. "Notepad works fine. Besides, Luella likes to type them in for me."

"Anyhow, all our current reports are in the system," Corb explained. "We've got modules in the cruisers, even. We just never digitized the old records, not unless they were necessary."

"And Amos Sinclair wasn't important enough to fall under that umbrella," PJ guessed.

"Amos Sinclair isn't important enough even now. Shit, I don't think anyone's said his name out loud since the fire, and probably never would again if it weren't for this wild fucking goose chase." With that, Corb clopped down the stairs, ignoring the cold, steel handrail bolted to the adjacent cement wall.

Cam smiled apologetically. "Don't let it bother you. He's just all fired up that I'm making him go see Lizzie. Doesn't help that he can't stand these folks."

"At Anthem Hold?"

Cam nodded. "As our detective, he's the one out there with the coroner investigating when these kiddos turn up dead. Usually once every year or so. Almost always preventable. Seems every time I finally get him simmered back down, he's heading back to the Hold again."

"Hm. How do they like him?"

"Do you? Does anybody?" Cam chuckled. "If there's one thing he's mastered, it's rubbing people the wrong way."

Cam gestured for PJ to follow his brother. She gripped the railing tightly, then thoughtfully planted a stiletto-clad foot in the center of the slippery top step. Cam slowly brought up the rear.

Downstairs, under a canopy of spiderwebs, rows of almond-enameled file cabinets were arranged as if in military formation. Corb stood before one, its top drawer ajar, and thumbed through a crisp manila folder. "This unit here covers the structure fires around that time," he announced. He pointed to a cabinet several feet away. "And anything on the Robbins property should be in that area."

PJ walked closer and glanced over his shoulder, catching a glimpse of glossy photos depicting the charred remains of a modest dwelling and its occupants.

"Bad one," she noted.

Corbin furrowed his brow. "Yeah, worse than I remember. Guess we were kids; I didn't think much of it then. Cam, do you remember Uncle Jack talking about this at all?"

"Not much. He made sure we knew Amos wasn't hurt, since we were old classmates. He did say it ripped through the house pretty bad, though," Cam answered.

"Leveled the house, more like," Corb corrected. "Looks like a damn bomb went off."

"I know the fire investigator determined it was accidental, but did he find the source?" Cam asked.

"I'm still looking. There's some conjecture in the field notes about their soap-making materials possibly serving as a sort of accelerant, but not much else so far." Corb continued to shuffle through the pages.

"Was Amos not home?" PJ inquired.

"Teenagers take a break away from the group when they reach a certain age. Gives 'em time to decide if they want to come back and join up, I guess," Cam answered.

"They call it 'Reflection'", Corb added.

Cam continued. "That's right. Amos was right in the middle of his Reflection when this happened. He'd have been living with older friends, or maybe in a hostel."

"I'll keep digging, find out exactly where he went," Corb chimed in.

"Thanks," PJ responded. She eyed the rows of files, then turned back towards the brothers.

"Honestly, the Robbins property history doesn't interest me much. According to my intel, they paid a pretty penny for that place, and almost all the upgrades were after the fact. So, this doesn't smell like any sort of real estate dispute."

Corb nodded. "No, it doesn't. And I ran through some of the usual motives. Nothing seems to add up."

"Like what?" she asked.

Corb closed the drawer, keeping the Sinclair property fire's folder in his hand. "First off, revenge or retaliation," he began. "Someone Shawn might have pissed off."

"I've heard he is arrogant. Off-putting." PJ cocked her head. She was silently beginning to think the same of Corb.

"Oh, he is," Corb snorted. "But he doesn't work in the field. And he's not been in his current position long enough to offer damning testimony at any trial or anything. So, it seems unlikely."

"What other things did you consider?" she asked.

"Drugs. My witness says Shawn's a pill-popper, but nothing heavy. Britlyn, on the other hand, is a clean-living type — lots of yoga and shit like that. My next thought would be money. These two have got money, but they're not stupid rich. Not enough to try to get a ransom. Then lastly, there's the suspect who randomly commits a crime like this just for the thrill. Or due to mental illness or something. But they're remote enough that it's not likely to be random, especially with the skills necessary to learn and override the home's security protocols," Corb mentally ran down his list.

"An affair is probably out, too — can't imagine she ran off willingly, especially in her condition," Cam noted.

"And with all that blood," Corb added. "But I do think that's the root of it, kind of."

"What is?" PJ asked.

"Sex. Attraction. Lust. Love. Maybe unrequited love? There was something off about the way the guy was carrying her that just gave me the creeps. Anyhow, that's what the Chief was hoping you could help with," Corb explained. "Like you said, someone is obsessed with her. Maybe it's someone following her online."

"Well, I'd love to know more about the status of the house. Regular guests, any household employees, what sort of technology they're using in and out of the home. . . that's going to paint a better picture of who has access and how," PJ noted.

"Shawn's got a satellite office right off the conference room," Cam noted.

PJ's demeanor brightened. "Yes, that's a good idea. I know he's your colleague, and you felt he wasn't a suspect, but I'd really like to get a better feel for how things unfolded that day. Maybe go through his work computer, his desk, any current files he's working on. . ."

"By all means," Corb grinned broadly. "Tear it up."

"Appreciate it," she responded, returning the smile.

For the first time, PJ noticed that the dimples in Corbin's cheeks were slightly asymmetrical.

They weren't dimples. They were scars.

"I'll show the way," Cam responded, ushering PJ back up the stairs.

* * *

By the time PJ and Cam wrapped up the review of Shawn's office, they were ten minutes late for their 6:00 P.M. rendezvous at Creekside Cafe, a Main Street staple and a short walk from the police department. Upon arrival, they quickly spotted the Chief sitting across from Corb, who was trying to convince him to share a pile of crispy, golden fries. Cam excused himself to the restroom, and a teenage hostess showed PJ to the table, where she slid into the maroon, vinyl booth next to the Chief.

"I told you, I'm not supposed to eat that garbage," he insisted to his nephew, patting his trim abdomen. "Your aunt would know about it the minute I walked in the door."

"What, like she's going to smell it on your breath or something?" Corb teased. "Breathalyze you for fried foods?"

"She's watching my cholesterol," Jack explained.

"If Aunt Sandy won't let you eat a single fry. . .well, that's the most un-American shit I've ever heard," Corb declared.

Their waitress, who also appeared to be another teenage girl at her summer job, arrived to take PJ's drink order.

"Iced tea for me, please," PJ requested. The girl smiled energetically, then bounced off.

"Oh, I wouldn't call it un-American. You know they're 'French' fries, right?" PJ informed Corb with a smirk. "Not American fries."

Corb shrugged. "Belgian, if we're getting technical."

PJ furrowed her brows.

"Soldiers during World War I thought they were in France, so they called 'em 'French fries.' Turns out, they were actually in Belgium," he explained.

"Oh. I didn't know that," PJ humbly remarked.

"Nobody knows that," Jack grumbled. "Because nobody needs to know that."

"Suit yourself," Corb continued. "Agent James, you know what I told myself when I was eating through a straw for eight weeks? When my jaw was wired shut?"

"I don't," she replied curtly.

"Well," Corb began, pausing to munch another greasy slice of potato, "I guess I didn't tell myself anything, because I couldn't say anything. But I thought to myself: Self, you are going to get out of these wires, and you are gonna chew yourself a big, ol' burger and a pile of fries. And then I was just thinking about fries. . .where they come from. . .who even thought 'em up. The history of fries, if you will."

Cam rolled his eyes as he arrived at the table and sat by Corb. "He's not talking about the fries, is he?"

PJ cracked a smile.

"Jesus. We need to get you out more, brother," Cam razzed him, nudging him with his elbow. He reached into the pile, downed a few fries of his own, then shared their findings with the group.

"So, Shawn Robbins is clean. Sloppy as hell, but clean," Cam informed them.

"We went through the devices in his office, and it's like Corb first said," PJ confirmed. "Agent Robbins had lax security. . .even more so than his wife's personal laptop at home. His firewall was disabled, and he gave out all sorts of permissions for third-party applications. His systems were surprisingly open to attack, especially considering his knowledge of the precautions he should be taking."

"Why'd he drop all the security?" Jack wondered aloud.

"Porn," Corb hypothesized flatly, licking salt from his fingers.

"How do you figure?" Jack frowned.

"Shawn — and people like Shawn — are shallow. Materialistic. He married brunette Barbie, and now she's got cankles. So, he's beating off to other hot chicks because that's how he strokes his own ego," Corb surmised.

Their young waitress blushed as she delivered PJ's iced tea and filled their coffees, pretending to ignore Corb's crude assessment of the situation.

"He's not wrong, actually," PJ chimed in. "Pornography *is* what we found on the agent's devices."

"What kind of porn?" Jack asked warily. "Anything we need to worry about?"

"No kids, thank goodness, if that's what you mean," PJ clarified. "It ranged from merely degrading scenarios to acts of aggression. Violence towards women. Rape. Cheating. Most of it featured women crying."

"Unsurprising," Corb muttered. "It fits. I'm guessing he's insecure about his power in their relationship. She holds the purse strings."

Cam nodded in agreement.

"In any event, that's why we think the devices were so easy to compromise," PJ shared.

"At this point, PJ and her team can see that the home's security system was infiltrated, but they don't know who's behind it yet," Cam finished.

"And what about our guys?" Jack asked. "Did they go over her routine?"

"Nothing weird. She stopped going into the wine shop once she announced she was pregnant, and the natural grocery store says she's been doing online orders, so they bring them right to her car," Cam responded. "She still gets coffee sometimes, but the baristas say they've never seen anyone lurking around her or anything."

"You check this place?" Jack pressed, gesturing to the surrounding cafe.

"She's only ever been here with Shawn," Cam replied. "And just the once. Guess they weren't impressed with the vegan and gluten-free offerings — or lack thereof. They put it all in an online review. Ruth was pissed, apparently."

Corb cracked a smile picturing red-faced Ruth, Creekside's plump co-owner and primary cook, huffily responding to the Robbins' special dietary requests for tofu scrambles and quinoa waffles.

"You know, fries are gluten-free," he joked.

PJ smirked.

"Well, shit." Jack nodded towards Corb. "How about you? You dig up anything on that Sinclair kid?"

"Just the one thing. Not sure how it relates to our victim, though," Corb answered, chewing.

He swallowed, then resumed. "I'm pretty sure he blew his fucking house up. With his parents inside."

Jack's blood ran cold. "What makes you say that?"

"These people have been making soap for like a hundred years. They didn't just carelessly splash their ingredients around the house. Besides, soap's not really flammable. Not on its own."

"The accelerant wasn't soap?"

"Fire investigator didn't bother to test the samples. He found the residue, then I guess he just figured that was the cause."

"So, he took the samples, but didn't bother to test them." Jack shook his head. "Lazy bastard."

"Yep. Maybe lazy. Maybe didn't give a shit. Can't say I blame him, with how those folks treat their kids. This was only like two years after they let Adam die," Corb reminded him.

Jack didn't need his memory refreshed; as Corb spoke, a scene played clearly in Jack's mind: the boy's eyes, red and swollen from mourning his brother, implored him. . .*would you have taken him to the doctor?*

He swished coffee around his mouth, as if it might wash the recollection away.

"But you have the samples," he prodded Corb, getting him back on track.

"Lab ran 'em today," Corb announced. "Glycerin, like in soap, is not flammable. Nitroglycerin, on the other hand. . ."

NITROGLYCERIN, Jack mouthed the word. "Wait. Like dynamite?" he asked incredulously.

"I thought those pictures looked worse than a house fire. More like someone dropped a bomb on it. Turns out, the bomb was already inside," Corb explained. "The majority of the samples came from inside the woodstove. Well, what was left of it."

"Where did he get his hands on this stuff?" Jack drained his coffee, then waved their server over for another refill.

"I was curious about that myself," Corb answered. "So, the fire investigator was partially right: the glycerin does come from the soapmaking. As for the remaining ingredients, that is where things started to come together."

"Some sort of acid. . .?" Cam racked his brain.

"Sulfuric and nitric," Corb clarified.

"Who's gonna have that? The hardware store?" Jack asked.

"It crossed my mind. I figured Amos would have known that was suspicious, though. Imagine, you get a tip from the local hardware store that says this kid with no indoor plumbing is loading up on drain cleaner the day before his house burns to the ground." Corb threw a crumpled napkin atop the remaining limp fries.

"Right," Cam agreed. PJ nodded.

"But he didn't have to buy it. He got it from work," Corb revealed.

"Work? Ah, that's right. That was during his Reflection. He was away in Moscow, working at. . .some factory, I think. Working at. . ." Jack tried to recall.

"A fertilizer plant," Corb finished. "Which utilized both of those chemicals."

"Holy shit," PJ exhaled.

"Speaking of shit," Cam wondered aloud, "he's been mucking around in manure his whole life. Why pick some fertilizer place in Moscow for his Reflection? Why not go somewhere more exciting? More fun?"

"Most kids go to Coeur d'Alene," Jack informed PJ. "Plug right into hospitality jobs at the Resort there. Waiting tables, slinging drinks—"

"And spending their downtime partying their tips away on the Lake," Cam interrupted.

"I wouldn't stick around, either," Corb answered. "So far, I only found one real advantage. Well, two, actually."

The group listened intently.

"First, proximity to the college. And second, tuition assistance," Corb disclosed.

"College classes?" Cam questioned doubtfully. "Which ones?"

"It's just a guess, so far. I don't know yet," Corb admitted. "But it's the only perk I can see. The plant pays for six credits of college courses as a sign-on bonus."

"I thought these kids didn't get past eighth grade," PJ chimed in. "How does he pick right up on college curriculum? I mean, would the school even let him?"

"They'll waive certain requirements if he can test in," Jack added quietly. "And he would have. Boy was a whiz."

Corb frowned. "How do you know?"

"Remember that gifted kids program you were in, back in middle school?" Jack asked him.

"Yeah. 'Gifted and Talented.' You paired me up with a bunch of damn nerds," Corb recalled.

"Nerds just like you," Jack teased playfully. "You were eating books for breakfast."

Jack turned to PJ. "It was great. They took him on so many field trips: museums, cultural centers, archeological sites. . ."

Under Corb's scruff and scars, PJ thought she detected a hint of flushed cheeks. The fry comments suddenly made more sense.

"Anyhow, Amos tested into the same thing. 'Cept his parents wouldn't let him do it. They were furious with the school for even letting him try," Jack explained.

"So, theoretically, he's away taking college classes when the house goes up," PJ pieced together. "He comes back after the fire. . .then what? Did he stay? How long was his Reflection?"

"That's what I'm going to find out," Corb responded.

"At Lizzie's?" Cam inquired.

"Lizzie?!" Jack exclaimed. "That's right, she was right in the thick of it. God, it's been years. . ." he trailed off.

Corb abruptly scooted out of the booth. "Got some more researching tonight. Maybe tomorrow," he shrugged, obviously eager to drop the subject.

With that, he brushed the crumbs from his jeans and made his way to the door, jingling its bells on the way out.

NINE.

Before Anthem Hold had its own educational facilities, its children attended the public institutions in town. They'd met in grade school, when Lizzie was eight and he was ten. Despite their age difference, they were tablemates: Lizzie was sharp, and she was completing work two grades above her own. Though he was also bright, Corb was too stubborn and surly to sit with any of the boys in his class. Mrs. Sutherland, their teacher, had sniffed out his soft heart and paired him with the little girl, a slight, skittish child who frequently exhibited bruises on what minute amount of skin she was permitted to have outside the confines of her scratchy, cotton dresses. Lizzie kept him on task, and he protected her from being teased. What began as a special friendship blossomed with adolescence, and Corb longed for the time when she'd be sent on her Reflection and he could ask her out. To a movie, maybe, or for a cheeseburger.

Soon, however, it became clear that escape would happen sooner than either of them had planned.

One sunny, July day, they'd followed the creek down to Lake Himeen, where Corb had stashed an old, aluminum jon boat underneath a blanket of pine boughs just beyond the east shoreline. Together, they'd pulled the small craft down the muddy banks to the blue-green water's edge. Then, like always, Lizzie had carefully removed and folded her simple dress and apron, laying her bonnet on top. She placed the dreary uniform on the smooth trunk of a large, fallen tree that leaned over the beach. Underneath, she wore shorts and a tank top she'd covertly sewn herself from her mother's fabric scraps. Corb usually smiled at the sight of her suntanned arms and legs, evidence of not only her rebellion against the sect, but also their growing time together that summer. As promised, once school was out, he'd taken her fishing every Friday, an excursion she secretly bracketed in between legitimate errands in town. This time, however, her bare legs brought him concern: from just under the hem of her shorts, on the right side, Corb spotted the tail of a long, dark bruise that appeared to extend up towards her buttocks.

"What happened?" he'd worriedly asked. Lizzie had turned suddenly to face him, quickly concealing the mark.

"It's nothing," she insisted.

"You fall off your horse?" he pressed. She shook her head.

"Then you better come up with something, 'cause that's black and blue," he noted.

"It doesn't have anything to do with fishin'," she explained. "Or you. So don't worry about it."

"Did somebody hurt you?" he dug deeper.

"I said, it's none of your business." She bit her bottom lip like she was bottling a jug, pushing any words she might have wanted to say back down into her throat.

Corb stopped rolling the rope in his hands, then bundled it and tossed it into the boat.

"Alright, Lizzie," he quietly agreed. He took her hand in his, helping her onto the bench seat, then pushed off the shore with a gentle shove. They'd launched into a large patch of yellow cowlillies, then rowed out past the inlet till they were hidden from view. Once they reached their regular fishing spot, he reached for her hand again.

"Show me," he pleaded.

"You just want to see me undress," she scoffed playfully as she pulled her hand away, hiding behind her humor.

Corb raised his eyebrows. "Maybe I do," he answered honestly. "But that's not why I'm askin'."

Lizzie sat silently as he patiently loaded a fat worm onto her hook. After a moment, she sighed. "You can't tell anyone."

He nodded, setting the pole aside and focusing his gaze on her.

She rotated onto her left hip, then pulled her waistband down to expose the right side of her bottom. It was tiger-striped with black and violet strokes, some apparently so deep that they had bled and scabbed over.

"He likes to play games," she began. She paused, looking out over the peaceful water as she fumbled to finish her sentence. "That I don't want to play anymore."

He'd known since damn near the day they met that her family was rough on her — Lizzie always had bumps and bruises, or a red cheek, or swollen knuckles — and she'd told him before about Anthem Hold's views on corporal punishment. But her father had also been sexually abusing her for years, she shared. This time, when she tried to speak up and defend herself, he'd dragged her to the elders, who held a private disciplinary session for her in the back room of the church. They'd lifted her dress to her waist and yanked her underthings down, bending her over a communion table. Then, they'd taken turns flogging her with everything from clammy palms, to wooden paddles, to leather belts.

"Fuck that," Corb had shakily replied. "That ain't about God. God doesn't want a bunch of old perverts with their hands all over your ass. Look what they did to you!"

The tears welled in her eyes as she pulled up her shorts. "I don't know what to do."

"Come home with me," he insisted.

"I can't leave," she dissented.

"What are you going to do when we all go back to school in September, and you're alone with them folks all day long?" Corb asked. Now fourteen and having finished eighth grade, Lizzie would not be allowed to return to school in the fall; instead, she was set to spend her remaining teenage years learning to keep a house and husband.

"So, what if I do go with you? They'll just come find me. And then it will be worse," she answered.

"Then we'll hide," he countered. He reached across the boat, taking her shoulders in his calloused hands.

"I'll keep you safe, Lizzie," he'd promised.

Eventually, she'd taken him up on the proposition, and he'd stashed her in Nan's hay loft like a squirrel secreting away his winter rations, hoping he could keep her hidden until the time was just right. *Nan heard voices anyhow,* he'd thought to himself, *so no one would believe her if she heard them chatting in the night.* He brought Lizzie books and water, and he snuck her portions of his meals throughout the day. They managed to keep the arrangement under wraps for almost three weeks, when Aunt Sandy finally noticed that Corb was eating nearly twice as much food yet hadn't gained an ounce. In fact, he'd lost weight, and his eyes were ringed with dark circles. Her concern had him in the front seat of the car and nearly en route to Dr. Rosen's office for a check-up. Then, as he gazed out at the fields through the windshield, trying to concoct a plan, Corb caught the brim of Uncle Jack's hat in his peripheral. In Jack's right hand, he clutched the arm of Corb's red-faced, sweet little acorn. The jig was up.

But then, Uncle Jack realized that no one at Anthem Hold had reported Lizzie missing. When Corb was confronted with the situation, he spilled to Aunt Sandy about the spankings, and Lizzie reluctantly let her see for herself. After that, Corb knew Lizzie wasn't going anywhere. Still, Uncle Jack had a duty to advise her parents that he'd located their juvenile runaway, though he had plans for Child Protective Services to get involved due to Lizzie's condition.

In response, they told him to keep her — they considered her a deviant now that she'd run off with some boy, and she was already excommunicated from the church as a result. After dinner that night, Uncle Jack had gently broken the news to Lizzie: she was never going back. Corb remembered mashed potatoes going dry in his mouth as they all watched Lizzie's face, waiting in agonizing silence for her to mentally process Jack's words and the current state of her life.

It was the first time Corb saw anyone cry happy tears.

* * *

Huckleberry trotted the dry road, his hooves clopping in the dust that bore his same honey coloring. The handsome Appaloosa had been a gift from Lizzie many years ago, back when Corb first came on the force. He'd let his little sister Cayla name him. As Lizzie and time slipped away, Cayla came to be the one to care for the horse, then ride him, then basically adopt him. These days, Huck spent most of his time lazing away in the shade, eating apples and playing in the field at Nan's. As Corb gently rocked in the leather saddle, he guiltily realized it had been far too long since he himself had sat atop the beautiful animal. He'd just gotten busy, he guessed.

Or did Huck just remind him too much of her? Corb wondered.

Then, just after the fork that led to her cabin, he got his answer.

The subtle trickle of the creek filled the dry air with cool, water music, and the plush cattails at its banks danced along. Just beyond, a grouping of birch trees joined tall grasses to obscure a small cabin. For a while, this hidden valley had been his paradise. Then, his third day in the field with the Cattail Police Department, everything changed.

The suspect had already killed the other two occupants of the condemned, old house — a known drug den — by the time police surrounded the residence. The gunman was flushed out, and Corbin had the guy in his sights as he emerged onto the sagging stoop. Just as Corb squeezed his trigger, the shooter began yelling and firing out across the yard. Corb's bullet pierced the other man's chest, but it was too late: Corb had stepped directly into the line of fire. He turned his head instinctively, and what would have been a killshot instead threaded itself through one cheek and out the other. The incident left deep, ugly pits on each side of his face, chipped several teeth, and fractured his jaw, but miraculously, he was otherwise uninjured.

Lizzie cared for him tenderly: she blended all his foods while his jaw was wired shut, she administered medication, she fluffed pillows, she kept the gawkers away. Mostly, she remained steadfast by his side. Imagine her surprise when, shortly after he could speak again, he expressed his desire to end things between them.

What would you do if I got killed next time? he'd asked her. *What would our kids do?*

She'd tried to reason with him, pointing out how he and Cam had turned out fine even after losing both parents. Still, he stood firm: he wouldn't leave her and his children on this Earth wondering why he'd choose to risk death when he knew they were counting on him to come home.

No. He knew how that felt.

As he continued to trot along towards the cabin, Corb stuck his tongue against the subtle raised area inside his right cheek. Of course, Lizzie had pleaded with him to just take a less dangerous position, pointing out that he needn't risk death at all. But, he'd realized, he enjoyed the danger. The stomach-churning, breathless sensation of his life in peril was like the tip of the sharpest knife just grazing his skin, refining and purifying all his scrambled thoughts into a singular, simple equation:

Did he want to die?

Or did he not?

That day in front of the drug house, his brain had autonomously turned his head away from the impending bullet. Still, for a second, he was ready for it.

Grateful, even. He'd thought of his late father, tumbling down the hillside in his truck like a rag doll in an aluminum garbage can. Corb wondered if he had felt the same relief as he let everything go.

Once the idea took hold, it spread like a virus in his mind, eliminating Lizzie and her dreams of their family with it.

Paradise was lost.

The sudden echo of a shotgun racking commanded his attention.

"You're not welcome here," Lizzie shouted. Her straw-colored ringlets grazed her shoulders, which were bare under a spaghetti-strap, cotton sundress that hung loosely to just above her knobby knees. Predictably, it and her hands bore smudges of paint.

"You know it's a felony these days to assault a peace officer?" Corb asked, ignoring her as he and Huck drew closer.

"Is that what you do, Corbin Neil? You bring peace?" she asked sarcastically. He cringed at the sound of his middle name. He'd always hated it.

"Not here to fight, Lizzie," he assured her.

"I don't give two shits why you're here. Not another step," she threatened.

"I think you might," he insisted, now mere yards away. "We've got a missing lady. I'm here officially. Just wanna ask some questions."

"Don't care," she retorted.

"Missing *pregnant* lady," he emphasized. "Twin girls."

Lizzie bit her lip.

"You're really gonna play the baby card with me?" she looked at him with disgust. After a moment, she huffed, lowering the shotgun and laying it on the railing that surrounded the front porch. In its place, she picked up an amber bottle that caught the sun and scattered refracted rays at her feet.

"Jesus, is that a beer?" he asked, referencing the glass bottle in her hand.

"It's Saturday," she shrugged.

"It's eight o'clock in the damn morning—" he began.

Corb suddenly straightened. *"Saturday!"* he exclaimed.

Lizzie gave him a quizzical look.

He thought of yanking his phone from his pocket, but as he reached down, he remembered his present location. Cell service was fine in town and even at the McNulty property, then spotty on the main roads until Anthem Hold, where it was nonexistent. However, though Lizzie's property wasn't far from his own, the valley obscured it from nearby cell towers. Though they'd considered foregoing the convenience of any communications, when Corb dug the trench for their other utilities, he'd run a landline. After all, he didn't want her — or their future children — stranded during an emergency.

"Can I use the house phone?" he pleaded.

"Now you want to come inside?" she asked incredulously.

"It's related to the investigation," he promised.

She gulped her beer. "Oh, hell. Why not?" Lizzie retreated into the cabin, slamming the antique-style screen door behind her.

Corb dismounted and followed her in, softly wiping his boots on a wool entry rug braided in shades of hunter green and burgundy.

Lizzie had paused a few feet in to assess the space. Though they had once shared the small cabin, it was now her private sanctuary. The walls were packed with canvases in various states of completion, and nearly every flat surface held easels, tubes of paint, and containers of brushes of all shapes and sizes.

"Don't mind the mess," she said quietly, failing to hide a vulnerable note in her voice.

"What mess?" Corb responded graciously.

Lizzie sighed with apparent relief. "Well. . .just don't ask me to fix you a damn sandwich or anything," she said, resuming her normal sarcastic tone.

The phone, a cream-colored set affixed to the wall in the hallway, was exactly as he remembered. The spiraled cord was stretched to what he figured was three times its factory length, a result of Lizzie pulling it every which way around the house.

Get a cordless, he'd say.

I'll lose it! she'd respond.

You'd lose your head if it wasn't attached, he'd tease her.

The sound of his bootheels clicking across the hardwood kitchen floor interrupted the sudden, vivid memory. He plucked the handset from its cradle, then dialed his brother's number.

On the second ring, Cam picked up.

"Lieutenant McNulty," he announced.

"It's me," Corb answered.

"Whose phone?" he asked.

"Lizzie's," Corb responded.

"Thought I recognized this number. She let you in the house, huh?" Cam whistled.

"Barely." Corb took a deep breath. "Listen. She reminded me: it's Saturday."

"Saturday. . ." Cam chewed on the word a moment. "Oh, shit. Farmer's Market Saturday."

"My thoughts exactly," Corb confirmed.

"Think we can get close?" Cam pondered aloud.

"Don't see why not. You could chat Cayla up a bit. She's a good cover," he reasoned.

"Yeah. PJ isn't," Cam noted.

"No. Not really," Corb admitted. "Fed through and through."

"I could put her in some clothes, make it like we're there as a social thing. Probably find her something in the closet at Nan's. . ." Cam trailed off.

Corb pictured PJ's tall, slender figure and realized Cam was asking, not telling.

"Yeah, put her in Mom's old stuff. Something country. She'll blend right in," he approved.

"That's what I was thinking," Cam sighed. "You getting anywhere?" he asked.

Corb stretched the cord around the corner into the kitchen and peeked into the living room. Lizzie was perched on one elbow, staring out the window at the horses and swirling a dripping, new beer bottle in her left hand.

"Well, she put the gun down," he pointed out.

Cam chuckled. "Sounds like a step in the right direction," he offered. "Listen, I'm sorry I had to ask, especially after the other night—"

"No," Corb interrupted, raising his stare to meet Lizzie's. She had seen him at the corner of her countertop and had left the horses, turning instead to face him. She raised an eyebrow as she took another sip.

"It's time," he finished.

* * *

Nestled inside handcrafted wooden frames, horses and prairie landscapes claimed the wall space around the living room, their textures brought to life by the sheen of oil paint in the natural light.

"Still painting, I see," Corb commented as he sat.

"Still painting," Lizzie confirmed, handing him a cup of coffee.

"They're nice," he noted. "You've always been a good artist." He gulped the hot liquid.

"Thank you," she replied. "Finally got into a few galleries. Mostly here, but some in Texas and Montana, too."

"I thought I saw some stuff up at Rocky's that looked like your work," he casually mentioned. About an hour north, in Coeur d'Alene, Rocky's Gallery was the premier showcase for local artists. Featuring fine Western art, the gallery catered to the elite clientele that summered along Lake Coeur d'Alene's ever-bustling shores, eager to shed their Californian roots and authenticate their turnkey, waterfront homes with something more unique than a tired, vintage Pendleton blanket or another antler chandelier. Rocky's shared its brick storefront with a wine bar downtown, a stylish but small joint offering artisan cheese, specialty cured meats, and live acoustic guitar to pair with its local vineyard selections.

Years ago, Corb and Lizzie had cruised by Rocky's once after a day on the lake, feeling instantly out of place in tank tops and flip flops. After tossing back a $10, four-ounce pour of Rosé like he was swilling Boone's Farm from a plastic cup, Corb had promised her they'd be back for a proper date.

Only weeks later, he responded to the scene of the call that would alter their lives forever.

Since that aftermath, Lizzie had used her unexpected alone time to evolve from an awestruck observer to an admired local artist, working diligently to improve her skills and market her work. It seemed like she'd finally reached a point of comfort, where she had a growing camp of collectors and exposure in several galleries. Most notably, she had recently earned a dedicated corner at Rocky's.

Lizzie looked him up and down. Dust caked his jeans, and his button-up shirt was faded by the sun and soaked under the arms. It was unfastened at the top, revealing a patchwork of short scruff that stretched from his equally sweaty chest up to his jaw, where it joined his beard. His lower lip was neatly tucked under his upper, forming a fat pocket for the same chewing tobacco he'd preferred since he was fifteen.

She rolled her eyes. "Yeah, you look like you get your fancy ass to Rocky's all the time, Corb."

Corb shrugged, oblivious to the insult. He smoothed his hand over the arm of the loveseat, an elegant, clawfoot piece that Lizzie had reupholstered in a rust-hued velvet that echoed the warm tones of the paintings that surrounded it. Before him, a vintage steamer trunk on a large, cowhide rug served as a coffee table. He set his empty stoneware mug, which he realized was another of Lizzie's creations, on the corner, leaning in and resting his elbows just above his knees. Across the small living room, Lizzie sat in a wooden rocker and pulled her own knees to her chest, wrapping herself in an afghan blanket. From beneath feathered, black lashes, her aquamarine eyes peered out at him over the edge of the knit, ivory cocoon.

She was always cold, he remembered. Many a morning he had caught her clutching that same blanket, poking at the dying embers in the woodstove until they'd eked out their last bursts of heat. With her long, blonde coils framing her pert nose and rosy cheeks, and her plain, poplin nightgown sticking out around her ankles, she'd resembled some frontier child's misplaced doll, lost in a modern world where folks traded freedom and fields for high-rise apartments and high-tech devices.

Time had been kind to Lizzie: save for a slightly shorter haircut and soft crinkles in her brow, she was nearly unchanged, with bright eyes and dewy skin that made him question if it had really been nearly a decade since he'd seen her. While he pondered the lapse of time, the sound of the whinnying horses she boarded on the property outside softened the harsh silence between them.

"So," she finally began. "You're not here to talk about horse paintings."

Corb cleared his throat. "No, I'm not. Actually, I'd like to know more about Amos Sinclair."

Lizzie raised her eyebrows. "Haven't heard that name in a long time."

"Doesn't need to be recent history."

"Well, I don't know what to say. His twin brother died when we were kids. You remember," she said softly.

Corb nodded.

"Then his parents died a few years later in that house fire. Poor kid. During his Reflection, actually. But he came back while I was still there. Now he's grown and sells soap, like his family did," she finished. "But you knew all that."

"I did," he agreed. "So, tell me what I don't know."

"I left when we were still kids, Corb. And not even for a proper Reflection — just up and gone. You know what happens when you make that choice? You're shut out; cut off. I don't exist to them anymore," Lizzie explained.

"You still talk to your sister, though," he pointed out.

"Only every few years," she countered. "And it's not something she wants to flaunt. Frowned upon, for sure."

"She ever share anything memorable with you?" he asked.

"About Amos? Oh, I don't know. I don't think they have any reason to cross paths. He's got his goats; Rachel's husband makes furniture. . ." she contemplated.

"Anything?" Corb pressed her, rubbing his brow with his fingers.

Lizzie frowned. "I really can't put my finger on anything important. Um. . .I think she mentioned it was Amos who helped them with credit cards. A website or something. Sales took off after that, so they're doing pretty well now. That was a few years ago."

Corb snapped upright, meeting her eyes.

"What website?" he demanded.

"I don't know. All Rachel said was that Amos had this idea that if they could list things on the internet and accept credit cards, they'd sell more. An online store. Got the church leaders to agree. Not sure who runs it."

"Anthem Hold. Online." He shook his head.

"Ain't that some shit? I have to imagine he was pretty pissed those fuckers broke their own rules to turn a profit but not to save his brother." Lizzie freed an arm from her swaddle to pluck her beer bottle from the floor beside her. She bundled back up, then sipped it pensively.

"That's some shit," Corb agreed, fighting a smirk. Watching Lizzie's perfect, rosebud lips spew profanity with a sailor's forte was a pastime he admittedly missed.

"You're sure it was Amos's idea?" he pressed.

"That's what she said," Lizzie confirmed. "Been awhile since I've sent her a letter, though. I just don't see how any of this—"

"I need you to get me in," Corb said suddenly.

Lizzie laughed out loud. "What? Have you lost your mind?"

"Please," he insisted.

"It's not like they'll just open the doors and welcome me in. I've only gone back twice since I left the Hold behind. . .both times just to see my niece and nephew after they were born," Lizzie explained. "Not just dropping by to say hello. And even that barely got me past the elders."

"So, tell them you're really sick or something. Or you're going on a long trip. Or that you're getting marr. . ." He stopped himself from finishing.

Lizzie shot him an icy stare. "You're cold, you know that?"

"Damnit," he muttered. "Hang on —"

She raised a hand, silencing him. "I think we're done here."

"I'm sorry," he countered. "I didn't mean that, Lizzie, and I'm sorry."

"For what? Bringing up that I'm still alone after all these years? Or that you abandoned me after I fed you through a damn straw for two months? After I left everything for you?" Her words were sharp.

He sighed. "All of it. I'm not good at these things. I didn't mean. . ."

"Or that you were supposed to be my home? And now I can't even go back to the home I had?" she continued, her voice growing louder. She stood, letting the throw slip from her bare shoulders. "Get out."

"I never meant to hurt you," he sheepishly offered. Corb crumpled a fist and rested it in the center of his frown lines.

She looked down as her voice finally cracked. "You know, some people touch death, and they hold their loved ones closer. But you — you pushed me away."

"You're right," he quietly acknowledged. "I didn't mean to be cruel. But I see how it could have come across. . .maybe. . .as cruel."

"Only 'maybe', huh? Is that seriously your apology?" she snapped.

"Liz —"

Lizzie shook her head. "Just shut up."

"Fine!" Corb threw up his hands, shouting. "You wanna talk about it, let's talk about it. You think I even had a choice!? What was I supposed to do?"

"Of course, you had a choice!" she shot back. "You could have chosen us. But you chose to crawl back inside your fucking head and shut everything out."

"You don't know anything about what's in my head," he hissed.

"Because you wouldn't ever tell me!" she quickly countered. "You can't just hold it all in, Corb! All that anger and self-loathing. It will eat you alive."

"It's been workin' out just fine," he grumbled. He turned his body away, closing his eyes and resting his face against his fist once again.

Lizzie cleared her throat and dried her wet cheeks with her hands. "Whatever. I'm not doing this right now," she laughed to herself, recharging her composure. "Why are you even here? Why don't you just get a warrant?"

Corb opened his eyes, saying nothing.

Lizzie's jaw dropped. "You can't, can you?"

"I could get one. Probably. It would just take some time, and maybe tip him off. . ." Corb explained.

"Unbelievable. What would Cam say? Or Jack?" She shook her head.

His chest swelled. "I don't care. This lady could disappear, maybe get seriously hurt or even killed. I don't have time for a warrant," he stated loudly.

"Go, then. You don't need me," she responded. "Never have."

"Just march on in, right?" Corb asked sarcastically. "When I come knockin' at Anthem Hold, I'm usually with the coroner. Not like I'm some friendly guest."

She scowled but continued to listen.

"Last year, two kids died of strep throat," he continued. "Fucking strep throat, Lizzie. I may not be able to charge these people under the law, but I sure as hell don't have to like it. And believe me, I let 'em know, every time. They'll fight letting me in."

Lizzie lifted her beer bottle to her lips again. It was empty.

"Strep throat?" she finally exhaled in disbelief.

"Four and five years old. They were cousins. The boy went into cardiac arrest. The girl was septic, and her organs failed," he explained. "When we found her, her lips were blue. And their dumbass parents had done nothing," he spit angrily.

She shook her head sadly. "I'm sure I know their families, too. You ain't supposed to be telling me all this stuff, Corb," she reminded him.

"Yeah, well, that's never stopped me before, has it? I'm sorry I'm fucked up. I'm sorry I couldn't be your home. But I'll never regret taking you away from that God-forsaken place. At least now I know you're safe."

His voice softened, and she was flooded by the memory of the same gentle tone from a teenage Corb, holding her tightly in his arms as they hid in his grandmother's hay loft. *You're safe here with me, Lizzie.*

Her posture relaxed. With a sigh, she walked over and sank into the seat cushion beside him.

"Is she hurt?" she asked.

"Don't know. Found blood all over the crime scene, but it's not hers. Not so far," Corb revealed.

"That's DNA, right? Can't you just run it?"

"DNA ain't magic," Corb sighed.

Lizzie frowned. "Seems like you could just run it and find out, like they do on TV."

"Since when do you watch TV?"

Lizzie nodded towards a small display atop an old, oak ice box in the corner of the room.

"Got a computer, too. Cell phone, even. How about that?" she winked.

He looked around, noticing for the first time that the cabin's rustic charm had been balanced with an assortment of modern features: from the butcher block island, a sleek humidifier sprayed a fine mist into the air; behind it, Uncle Jack's old hand-me-down fridge had been replaced with a stainless model that seamlessly operated without the omnipresent buzz of its predecessor; and in the entry, a glowing wax warmer dispersed botanical scents. The outlets throughout the cabin, once nearly vacant, were plugged full, powering everything from mobile device chargers to countertop appliances.

Perhaps she'd changed after all.

"Look, DNA is like a library," Corb explained. "If I'm searching for a book, and that book is in the library, then I've got a match. But if it doesn't happen to be in the library, nobody knows where to find it. We don't just keep everyone's DNA. Not every person is part of the library. Mostly just criminals we've caught before."

"And you've got no one. Nothing," she surmised.

"Oh, *now* you want the confidential details," Corb chuckled. "No. We've got fuck all."

"But Amos? How can you be so sure?" she asked.

"It's a hunch, I guess. All these little things just seem off. They don't like photos, right? But I saw his face, right there on this lady's website. So, I started thinking. He lost his twin; she's pregnant with twins. Anthem Hold's not big on technology, but you're telling me the whole compound is wired for internet now. That it was his idea. Then, somehow between milking goats and tying little twine bows on his soap, he just learns to build websites? Bullshit."

"A hunch isn't good police work," she answered flatly. "And that's not from TV. I've heard that right outta your uncle's mouth."

"Pff," Corb scoffed. "He's just a stickler for procedure. Every investigation starts out with a hunch, doesn't it?"

"Smooth," she conceded.

He smirked.

"Here I thought I was done with you getting me into trouble," Lizzie sighed.

"Listen," he pleaded. "Cam's looking into him now. Gonna go check things out at the Farmer's Market. If he thinks I'm wrong, we'll turn back."

"What if you're not wrong?" Lizzie asked. "What if you get hurt? I'm not playing nurse this time. You should just follow the rules."

"I won't get hurt," he assured her. "And I might save somebody else from getting hurt, too. Three somebodies."

Lizzie crossed her arms in defeat. *He'd always known just how to persuade her.*

"Fine. What do you need me to do?"

155

T E N .

Sleep paralysis: the warmth of a dream suddenly ripped away by a pressing lucidity, an awareness that the events taking place are only happening in waves of the brain, as the body lies frozen and inaccessible to its owner.

Britlyn had felt the sensation in the past, mostly when shifting between various herbal supplements or drinking coffee at night. It was a frightening and unpleasant experience: she had been unable to move her arms or legs or even speak for several minutes before finally managing to shout for help. Her husband would soothe her, and she would settle into her down pillow, drifting back to sleep. She would then awaken naturally; her consciousness and muscle control would resume in sync once again, and the episode would be forgotten.

Tonight, in her hospital bed, she was mentally screaming at her paralyzed body to move. Alas, she was trapped in a persistent nightmare, all too aware that she couldn't escape.

Was it a nightmare, or was it a memory?

She was in the kitchen of the new house, and she had just finished making Shawn his protein shake. He quickly thanked her, then he returned to his work. At the end of their marble counter, he pecked away on his laptop, finishing the last piece of some investigation he'd been assigned to since just after they'd moved to Cattail. She considered blending her own protein shake but decided on a yogurt instead. She withdrew a small, glass container from their massive, stainless fridge. As she popped the top, Shawn raised an eyebrow, as if the noise had disturbed him. Britlyn sighed.

"We still haven't talked about names yet, you know," she pointed out, digging a slender spoon into the tangy, white curd.

"I told you, I'm fine with whatever," he responded nonchalantly, continuing to focus his eyes on his computer screen.

"But I want you to participate," Britlyn insisted. "I want you to like what I pick."

"Mm-hm," he acknowledged. "Yeah, okay. Fine. What are you thinking?"

"Well," Britlyn gushed, "I've always had this thing for princesses, right? But like, I can't just name both girls after different princesses, 'cause one princess might be prettier than the other, or else younger, or richer, you know?"

"Yep," Shawn feigned listening to his wife.

"Besides, those names are old-fashioned. Boring. Who wants to be named Diana or Grace? Just grannies. Definitely not cutting-edge," she added.

"Totally," he remarked.

"So, I was thinking like 'Reina' and 'Regent'. Royalty names," she revealed.

"Regent? Like a Board of Regents?" he asked. "Like overseeing a college?"

"Huh?" she replied, puzzled.

"My vote is no. It doesn't mean what you think it means," he rolled his eyes.

"Oh," she said softly. "Okay. Well, what about cities? I had a few really amazing cities in mind, like 'Raleigh' or 'Rio', or maybe 'Rome'. I mean, you could even add the letter 'A' to make it more girly, like 'Roma' or something -"

"Roma?" Shawn interrupted, chuckling. "You want to name our kid after a fucking tomato?"

Dejected, Britlyn huffed, then burst into tears. She could hear him calling after her as she ran upstairs, but he didn't follow.

Inside the nursery, Britlyn's pulse slowed as she admired her hard work. Soon, the girls would be nestled in their cribs, swaddled in tiny muslin blankets and pink caps. She walked to a stylish reed basket next to the gliding chair. Bending down, she withdrew a fuzzy, soft rabbit.

Wiping her tears, she held the plush toy close, breathing in its subtle scent. The toy, with its compacted, white fur and aqua, eyelet jumper, had been hers as a child, one of few meager belongings she'd salvaged during her family's many moves around the country. It didn't smell much like anything pleasant; mostly, it carried the scent of the inside of a cardboard box combined with the passage of time. In her new, lavish surroundings, the odor of a worn, old item was strikingly unique, and it comforted her as she seethed at her husband's sometimes selfish and careless manner.

She walked with the rabbit to the edge of one of the cribs, resting her elbows on its side.

"Little Bunny Foo Foo, hopping through the forest—"

Her voice cracked mid-song. She had wanted a child for so long, and through the amazing technology of in vitro fertilization, she was finally going to be a mother.

"—scooping up the field mice, and bopping 'em on the head."

As she whispered the last line, movement in her peripheral vision caught her attention. She cocked her head, staring at the nursery's camera.

After a moment, she continued.

"Down came the Good Fairy. . ."

The camera moved again. This time, the lens barrel slid forward, zooming towards her.

She looked into it, speaking tenderly. "I know you're feeling pretty bad, now, aren't you?" she asked. "It's okay, honey. Roma is silly, you're right."

The camera panned down, focusing on the rabbit.

"I loved this one when I was a little girl," she shared. "My mother would sit at the foot of my bed and hop

Bunny Foo Foo all over the covers." Britlyn smiled, and the camera shifted up again, focusing on her face.

She resumed singing.

"Little Bunny Foo Foo, I don't want to see you, scooping up the field mice, and bopping them—"

Suddenly, Shawn snuck up behind her.

"Hey, I'm sorry," he began.

Startled, Britlyn dropped the rabbit into the crib below, turning just in time to see the camera return to its normal position.

"But you—" she started, looking at her husband. "The baby camera. Baby monitor. You were watching me!"

Shawn frowned. "Watching you?"

"On the camera. I was singing, and. . ." she trailed off.

Shawn took a deep breath. "Are you sure stopping your meds was a good idea?" he asked worriedly.

"Yes. It's what's best for the babies," she insisted.

"Is it what's best for you?" he pressed.

"I swear. The baby monitor, it was moving, it was watching. . ."

She swallowed, but her throat was dry.

Both Britlyn and Shawn looked towards the motionless device.

Shawn took her hands. "Listen. I was a dick, sure. That's why I'm up here. To say sorry. But don't let it wind you up like this."

Britlyn sighed. She took a deep breath, held it, then exhaled. After a few moments of this grounding exercise, she nodded at him.

"You're right," she conceded. "I'm on edge. It just felt like—"

"Shhhh," he soothed her. "This tech shit is my job, baby. No one is watching you. I'd never let that happen."

* * *

While the woman slept fitfully, Amos tapped away, sinking into the office chair behind his sleek desk. Next to him, a hefty pour of rosy, bronze liquor glittered under the flickering lights of his monitors. This time, he had foregone his homemade hooch for something from his special collection, selecting a soothing single-malt aged in sherry casks. He paused to take a sip and allowed his backside to melt into the chair's memory foam, silently cursing the rigid seat of his carriage.

In the beginning, he had just stuck his toe into the pool of the internet, scouring the many profiles he'd come across on social media. He found musicians and athletes, judges and barbers and writers. Bringing his focus closer, he was surprised to see many, if not most, of Cattail's residents had a presence. Everybody who was anybody was online, which he quickly realized was full of a lot of nobodies, too.

Though he was captivated by the vast size of these social media networks, he was more engrossed by their implicit promise: *you can be anyone, or anything, at any place, at any time.* He had known for years that he desperately needed to leave Anthem Hold, but he had always thought it would drag behind him like a ball and chain, something he'd be forced to acknowledge to every future employer. Friend. Lover. He figured the stink of the religious cult would be on him forever.

But then, he'd realized as he tunneled deeper into the dark web, nobody portrayed themselves how they actually were in real life. The friendly barista had an active warrant under a different name. The football coach snapped stealthy photos of young men changing from inside the locker room. The happy housewife and PTA president was a closet alcoholic. He latched onto the more insidious circumstances, steadily siphoning a princely sum from ransomed secrets. He was amazed at the riches a person would part with just to maintain this manifestation, this shell they had created of themselves.

Then, a door opened. A potential victim, impressed by Amos's skills, offered Amos the opportunity to push his abilities to a greater level. He brokered a deal with the leader of that organization, a syndicate with their fingers in every pot from drug trafficking to biological warfare. The gig was simple: seek and destroy. Amos would locate damning digital evidence, then delete it from existence. With each completed contract, he rose from anonymity. Soon, his reputation preceded him, and he was the go-to clean-up guy for nearly every major crime ring.

"Amnesia," they'd called him.

Amos logged out and stood, removing his headphones and finishing his scotch in a single swig. He scanned the security feed, then shuffled to the bathroom in fine leather and Australian shearling moccasins. With a water flosser, he sprayed his gumline, then polished his teeth with an electric brush. After soaking his face with a warm, Turkish cotton cloth, he pressed cream into the creases and spots that riddled his skin and made him appear several years older. In the mirror, he inspected himself closely.

Tomorrow, he would play Amos, the local Bible-thumping, horse driving soaper, destined to die alone amongst his dairy goats.

But he had become someone else now: the dark web wizard, the scene sweeper, the money maker, the security savant. He was accustomed to a certain level of respect, and he commanded a sizeable salary. He was not weak. He did not spawn pity. He had a plan in place and the manpower to achieve it.

It was the last time he would be Amos. He'd treated the wounds as best he could, but his plan to skip town before the market had been thwarted by his weakened state. Skipping the weekly event would surely draw attention, and attention was the last thing he needed while he had Mrs. Robbins under lock and key. He could picture his neighbors and their wives starting a meal train, then helping themselves to a tour of his home under the guise of serving up casseroles. They weren't really a helpful, selfless clan; no, they were a nosy, intrusive people, and the thought of them scoping out his place turned his stomach even more.

After the Farmer's Market, while fellow vendors were busy inventorying their wares and accounting for their sales, he would grab the girl and go. It was a short ride to his plane, at which point, they were only a quick flight from the larger, more luxurious jet that awaited them. He could change clothes, nestle into the luxurious leather seats, and say goodbye for good to American airspace.

He was ready to say goodbye to Amos, too.

* * *

It was a bumpy ride into town, and each rut in the road jolted his injuries, sending ripples of nausea through his body. Amos watched the horse before him lift its thick, black tail, and the smell of manure hit his nostrils almost as fast as it tumbled out the animal's anus and onto the road below. He wrinkled his nose, looking out over the monotonous, rolling prairie. It was a view he'd experienced every day of his life; with the seasons, the gradual hills shifted color from emerald green, to gold, then icy white, but their shape remained the same. As a young man, he had begun to wonder if there was really anything else out there. Sure, the bit of education permitted by his parents afforded him the opportunity to see the world as a globe, or through pictures in books. Still, it never felt real: even staring at the deepest blue ocean, he could never escape the Palouse under his feet or the smell of farm animals mixed with his own rank body odor.

Even during his Reflection, he'd lived and worked in Moscow, in nearly the same expanse of fields. But he'd picked the fertilizer plant for a reason, one unknown to all but Amos. His mother and father were pleased he was close to home, boasting of their son's dedication to the Word of God and his abstinence from the other youths' sometimes wild excursions, which often took them to Coeur d'Alene, Spokane, and even Seattle. In truth, Amos didn't give a shit what they thought. No, the local job was part of a plan he had only just hatched, a plan that was slowly putting out buds on its bare, green branches. With the fertilizer plant's generous tuition assistance, he'd enrolled himself at the university, intent to find a way to get out of Anthem Hold.

On the first day of school, they'd watched a video on the internet: a live stream from a web camera half a world away. Amos had never even watched television before, let alone tapped into the deep well of information and entertainment available online. He remembered being mesmerized by the aquamarine waters of the Indian Ocean lapping at a sugar-white beach that glimmered below swaying palms. After that first computer course, he'd delved into operating systems and programming languages, tirelessly absorbing the material until he was adept enough to continue through self-study. After a short pause to effect his parents' demise, he moved into the next stage of his scheme, which involved building the capital to finance his dream.

Now, he was a mere flight and a ferry ride from his Maldivian villa, an overwater bungalow with peekaboo windows set into the floors and an infinity pool on its expansive deck. He'd owned the property for a few years now, but he'd never had someone to share it with. Then, while mindlessly skimming through featured feeds on his home page one day, he'd been intrigued by the dark, chocolate eyes and mischievous grin of a certain fashion blogger. He'd scavenged the web for every bit of information about her, longing for the opportunity to catch her attention. Though he'd been discouraged by her halfhearted responses to his carefully crafted profile and engaging comments, he was pleasantly surprised to learn that she'd taken an interest in him after all, relocating to his very hometown. After that, it was only a matter of planning and time before he could reveal himself in person. She'd been more shocked than he expected, but he was prepared to whittle that lingering confusion away, until all that remained was the desire and love for Amos he knew existed deep inside her. He could see her yearning for him in her every move: the way her eyes squinted when she laughed, or when she wriggled into a new outfit, or the unveiling of a new project for her social media audience. She was a caged bird, and she needed him to set her free.

As he'd gained access to her home — an easy feat through her dimwit husband's inept security measures — he'd enjoyed even more opportunities to get to know Britlyn. He knew the way she applied her lotion, brushed her teeth, and fluffed her pillows. He'd watched her favorite movies with her, and he'd sung along with her to everything from romantic ballads to upbeat pop. He had learned both what made her mind tick and what made her grip the bed sheets. Lately, he'd even been privy to her whispered, sweet words to her unborn daughters-to-be.

Watching her pour her heart into the nursery, then stand and admire her work from the doorway, he realized their moment had arrived. His parents and elders had buried him for years under a mountain of guilt and humility they'd insisted was "God's will", but the more he'd studied and analyzed their source of that so-called knowledge, the more Amos convinced himself that they'd gotten it wrong.

In fact, it was God's own words that finally set Amos free:

"Be fruitful and increase in number; fill the earth and subdue it. Rule over the fish in the sea and the birds in the sky and over every living creature that moves on the ground."

God didn't want him to toil away at this endless prairie, watching his loved ones die preventable deaths from common illnesses, shitting in holes in the ground and taking cold baths with water lugged into the house in buckets. No, God wanted him to use his acquired talents to take the world in his hands like a wet washcloth and wring every last drop out of it, until he'd gotten everything his heart could ever desire. Now, it was time to squeeze: he'd leave this place with his new family and finally begin to enjoy the fruits of his labor in a hidden paradise half a world away, where they could never be found.

By the time Amos pulled his carriage into the vendors' lot of the Farmer's Market, his pain had subsided, having been replaced by excitement and joy for the next 24 hours. Beneath his thick, faux facial hair, he was beaming.

ELEVEN.

Since Cam was a boy, Cattail had grown tremendously: downtown, a coffee stand popped up every couple blocks, and the riverbanks now boasted two restaurants with more than just deep-fried offerings. In addition to the standard grocery market, a natural foods store had opened, and a wine and olive oil spot after that. Cattail even had a few thrift shops. Still, it lacked any real clothing or department store, and with time slipping away, Cam knew they couldn't afford to take their chances hoping to find something secondhand.

Bless their hearts, Aunt Sandy and Cayla would have been glad to help him out by opening their closets at a moment's notice, but neither had the figure for sharing clothes with Agent James. Sandy had looked matronly as long as Cam had known her: she couldn't be more than five-foot-three, and her heavy bosom matched her wide hips. Though Cayla cut a more athletic figure, she was slight in stature like her mother, with legs as thick and muscular as a draft horse.

Luckily, he did know of one woman with a tall, willowy silhouette. Shortly after Corb called, they hopped in Cam's cruiser and made a quick run to the family farm.

Nan's house, like his uncle's, was a Victorian-style, two-story design, though hers was much larger and yellow in color, rather than light blue. Though it was worn in places, its ornately carved, white bargeboard exquisitely contrasted against the lemon exterior. Save for a few spots blistered by sun, Nan's thickly painted, taupe porch looked mostly as it did when Cam was a child, though the steps were clear of chalk drawings and action figures these days. *One, two, three, four, five, six, seven,* he silently counted, climbing the stairs as he had a million times before. At the top, a heavy, wooden swing still hung on creaky chains to the right of the front door.

From the swing's padded bench seat, a person had the perfect view of Nan's flower beds. Even as she struggled to piece together her thoughts and her balance, she was a meticulous gardener, cultivating deep-purple irises, balls of hydrangea, tumbling petunias, and roses that climbed along the picket fence and over the dainty, white arbor above the front gate. Beyond, yellow fields churned in the wind, encircling the farm's small pond like a golden frame. The shimmering crown jewel of the magnificent property, reflections of cotton-candy clouds drifted around its lily pads and the happy ducks paddling across the surface.

Just as the swing pulled others towards it with its picturesque promise, Cam was repelled by its sight.

He hated the fucking swing.

At night, the beauty was gone: the flowers closed, the fields grew dark, and the pond was a mucky, black pit. As he would sit awake and hope for headlights, the chains would taunt him, creaking loudly with his every move. A few special mornings, he found himself returned to his own bed, warm under a nubby quilt someone had lovingly pulled over his bony, bare shoulders. Other times, he woke next to his mother, sleeping in his father's empty place. Mostly, he opened his eyes to find that he was still on the porch, shivering under an unsympathetic blanket of cold morning dew.

The last time he'd woken on the porch swing, his uncle was lifting him from its weathered cushion and curling him up into his strong grip. Uncle Jack had never held him that tightly before.

"Shhhh, it's alright," he'd soothed Cam. "You're comin' with me for a while."

The gravelly promise had brought Cam comfort, and he closed his eyes once again. Nuzzling under the crisp lapel of his uncle's jean jacket, he was greeted by the sweet and intoxicating aroma of gasoline.

"So, this is your Grandma's house?" PJ piped up.

Cam cleared his throat and the decades-old memories from his mind, then met PJ's question with a smile and nod. "Our Nana, yes. She goes by Nan. Doesn't sit out here too often in this weather, but as you can see, she still loves her gardening." Cam gestured to the colorful blooms around the yard. "My little sister, Cayla, lives here with her now. Helps her out around the house and such."

"It's lovely," PJ responded.

Cam nodded politely, then opened the front door and gestured for PJ to enter.

Inside, the smell of old, wooden things greeted them. PJ discerned the prints of a cat's paws across the dust on the kitchen table. In the adjacent sitting room, she could see the orange creature napping on a faded, striped sofa. Cam strode to the cupboard and began to rummage. He sighed.

"I'd make you some coffee, but it looks like Nan's out," he apologized.

"No worries," PJ assured him in her rich, warm tone. "Cayla doesn't drink coffee?" she asked.

"Always profiling, huh?" he teased her.

"Oh, I didn't mean. . ." PJ began.

"I'm pulling your leg. Cayla drinks some God-awful stand-in for coffee, last time I checked. Ground mushrooms or something. Nothing fit for human consumption," he assured her.

"This is your sister we're going to see at the Farmer's Market?" PJ asked.

"Yup," Cam confirmed. "She's got a little of everything. . .fresh eggs, cut flowers, herbal tea, even some baked goods from Nan's wheat."

"I wouldn't say no to a muffin," PJ admitted, rubbing her stomach.

"Well," Cam answered, motioning towards her to join him down the hall, "lucky for you, her muffins are a hell of a lot better than her coffee."

PJ followed behind him, her heels clicking on the antique, wooden floors. From down the hall, the promising, cheerful sounds of a game show boomed from a television.

"Your Nan?" PJ whispered.

Cam put his finger to his lips. "We'll chat with her later," he replied quietly. "Or we'll be here all day."

He opened the second door on the right and ducked in. PJ followed.

She masked a gasp.

Inside, the four-poster bed was neatly made, dotted with lacy throw pillows and anchored by a soft, crocheted blanket at the foot of the bed. The nightstands showcased matching ceramic lamps, each featuring a painted rose at its center. The lampshades were yellowed. On the closer table, a woman's antique brush lay next to a framed photo of two towheads in Christmas outfits. The boy in the picture held a baby on his lap.

The boy was Cam, of course, and the room was a relic to their deceased parents. Cam opened the wardrobe, which held even more belongings: flannels and jackets on his father's side, and sweaters and dresses on his mother's. On a shelf above the hanging clothing, various pairs of embroidered, leather cowboy boots leaned into each other for support as if they, too, were still grieving.

"Your uncle told me about the accident," PJ finally managed.

Cam closed his eyes as he cringed at the word. *Accident* suggested something unexpected. Something unavoidable.

"Thank you," he acknowledged courteously.

"He seems like a nice man. Your uncle," she offered.

Cam pawed softly through the clothes, pushing his father's aside.

The silence stretched for a moment.

"He is," he finally said. "When I was a kid, I always thought maybe God felt so bad about the crash, he finally gave us a father worth having."

"Oh. Were you not close with your dad?" she asked. Instantly, she blushed and cupped her palm over her mouth. "I'm sorry for the interrogation — it's just my nature. I didn't mean to pry."

Cam turned, meeting her dark eyes with his stoic, slate gaze. "It's alright," he assured her. "I don't mind. To answer your question, no, not close to my dad. Just my mom."

PJ scanned the room until she spotted her picture. The young woman wore voluminous, feathered hair that cascaded over the puffy sleeves of her blouse, which was tucked into high-waisted jeans. The boys both shared her wide, inviting smile.

"She was beautiful," PJ remarked.

"Yes," he agreed, turning his back to PJ again.

She looked once more at the picture of the boys. "But you are close with your brother, I take it?"

Cam snorted. "Ha! Of course. Someone has to keep him from killing himself."

PJ smiled. "He does seem a little bit. . .spirited. Irish temper, maybe?"

"I'd say that's an accurate assessment," Cam chuckled. "It's just how he deals with things. Always has been."

"And you," she continued. "You're quieter. More cautious. Reserved."

Cam stopped digging through the closet and ran his fingers down a line of soft, blue fabric. He pulled a cedar hanger from the closet rod, then laid the garment across the bed.

"Well, I guess that's just how I deal with things," he responded, tilting his head as he admired his selection.

The dress, a denim and floral number, featured a sharp collar and engraved, metal buttons down the front.

"Very 90's," PJ commented.

"I hear the 90's are coming back," he shrugged, grinning. "So, it's in style, right?"

"Our fashionable captive would approve, at least," PJ cracked a smile.

"What, are you worried you'll stand out?" Cam asked.

PJ raised her eyebrows. "Lieutenant, I'm a Black woman in Cattail, Idaho. I already stand out."

"At least now you won't look like a Fed," Cam answered with a wink. "If you're alright with that one, I'll let you get changed. I'm going to run down the road to Uncle Jack's real quick."

She gingerly raised the dress and draped it over her arm. "Thank you."

Cam nodded, then stood and walked towards the door. "As for you standing out," he added as he pulled it closed. "You know, that's not a bad thing."

* * *

As he descended the creaky, brownish-gray steps, Cam's phone began to vibrate from within his denim pocket. He read the name on the screen, then quickly answered.

"Back in service, I see. So, you made it outta the hole?" Cam asked. He jumped in his cruiser and turned the key.

"Alive and intact. Just barely," Corb joked. "I'm heading up the hill now, so I'll probably lose you in a second. We're going out to Anthem Hold."

Cam raised his eyebrows. "To the Sinclair place? How do you figure you're going to swing that?"

"I was invited," Corb answered.

"*Invited*," Cam repeated skeptically.

For a moment he was quiet, then he changed the subject. "Well, how's Lizzie?"

"Found her drinking beers in the morning sun," Corb responded plainly.

"Damn. And you still think you're not meant for each other?" Cam teased.

"Funny," Corb snorted. "No, she's okay. Painting a lot these days. Still stables some horses, too."

"Are *you* okay? It's been a while," Cam pointed out.

"Oh, I'm fine. I'm good, she's good. . .it's all good," Corb reassured him, albeit in a wistful tone.

BBBBBRRRRRRRR. As Cam pulled into Uncle Jack's driveway, the loud, fluttering sound of a horse's snort echoed in his ear.

Cam exited the car with a frown. "Corb, is that Huckleberry?"

"Relax. . .we're just taking him to see her nieces and nephews," Corb advised.

"Uh-huh. And are you sitting on his lap?" Cam pressed. "He sounds awful close."

Corb paused. "Well, we figured we'd just avoid the church elders seeing me at all. . ."

"So, you're hiding with Huck in the horse trailer?" Cam interrupted.

"I'm just going up there to poke around!" Corb countered.

"A literal Trojan horse. That does *not* sound like you were invited," Cam scolded. He opened the barn doors, then peeled back the heavy, tan cover from the red car. He gently opened the door and slid inside. "What do I tell Uncle Jack? You ran off to play cowboy cop?" he guilted his brother.

"I'm not going inside anywhere. Not unless I'm certain," Corb defended his position.

"You'd better not. If we have him dead to rights and you've tainted anything—" Cam began.

"Fruit of the poisonous tree, blah, blah, blah. Yeah, I know. The court will throw the evidence out."

"Rob. . .both Robs. . .will have your head," Cam added. "This is a big case."

177

"Cam, you know I don't give a shit. I just want to find this lady alive," Corb argued.

Cam sighed. "Me, too."

"Anyhow, you guys heading into town soon?" Corb changed the subject.

"Yup. Just grabbed the Pontiac. Figure we'll stand out anyhow, but it's better if folks think we're an item instead of on duty," Cam explained.

"Think of all those poor, brokenhearted girls when they think you're off the market," Corb jested.

"Riiiight," Cam chuckled.

"Seriously though, did you guys find something decent for her to wear?" Corb asked. "I honestly don't remember any of Mom's clothes."

As Cam pulled back into Nan's driveway, he caught a glimpse of PJ gently rocking on the porch swing. He felt his chest squeeze, and for a moment his breath caught in his throat.

"Uh, yeah. We sure did," Cam confirmed. "Hey, I gotta go. Just be careful," he insisted.

"You know me," his brother quipped.

* * *

As Cam rolled to a stop, the friendly tweets of morning songbirds were muffled by the vintage car's throaty growl. Its cherry-red paint, which appeared to have been freshly waxed, gleamed in the sun. Descending the steps, PJ let out a low whistle.

Cam got out, his feet crunching across the gravel as he headed around to the passenger side to open her door. He pulled his shades down. "I could say the same for you," he remarked. Each button joined perfectly, pulling the dress just so around her slim figure. The bottom was split above the knees, showing off her shapely legs and chocolate brown cowboy boots, which nearly matched her skin. Fitted but not tight, alluring but still demure — the dress made a statement on PJ.

"Oh, please," PJ rolled her eyes, lowering herself into the passenger seat. "I look like I'm going to a Shania Twain concert. I mean, no offense to your mom or anything."

"Are you kidding?" he laughed back, closing his door. "My mom would be pumped you just said that. I'm just surprised you even know who Shania Twain is."

"Can't say I'm proud of it," she shook her head.

Cam revved the engine, jolting forwards towards town.

"Anyhow, who does this beauty belong to?" she asked, slinking a slim arm out her window and patting the door.

"You don't think it's mine?" Cam feigned hurt feelings.

PJ raised her eyebrows.

"Alright," he conceded. "Uncle Jack's had this hot rod for years, since back in his heyday."

"And he lets you guys take it out?"

"Correction, he lets *me* take it out. Corb lost his chance when he crashed it. . .into that tree, actually," Cam remarked as they passed his uncle's property.

"So, it's a family compound," PJ remarked, gazing out the window. The golden fields rolled by.

"I suppose. My parents lived with Nan, so we were there until Uncle Jack took us in. Then Aunt Sandy came, then Cayla was born. Cayla moved to Nan's when Nan started needing more help. And Corb and Lizzie lived on their own for a few years, but now he's staying in the barn," Cam explained.

"He actually lives in the barn?" PJ shot him a quizzical look.

"Made himself an apartment in the loft," he clarified.

"I see. And you?" she inquired.

"Me. . .I have my trailer pulled all the way to the other side of the property," Cam advised. "Little quieter that way."

"Like a camper trailer?" she asked.

"Don't need more space than that," he responded.

As they curved around the bends that wound into town, PJ chewed her lower lip.

"This Lizzie, she was more than your brother's girlfriend, then," she speculated.

"Lizzie was like family. . .she even lived here a while until they built the cabin together."

"At Jack's?"

Cam laughed. "Corb would have liked that, but no. At Nan's. She was still just a girl when she left Anthem Hold. Couldn't have been fifteen."

"They were high school sweethearts," PJ mused.

"And thick as thieves. They'd be married if he hadn't gotten shot," Cam confirmed. "I think things became dark after that. It changed their dynamic. Changed his mind."

She eyed the bare ring finger of his left hand as he gripped the smooth, walnut steering wheel.

"You ever been married?" she pressed.

Cam slowed as they neared the only stop sign on the way to town. He looked over at her as he rolled to a halt.

"Only to my job," he answered, raising a half-smile that caused a dimple to suddenly appear. "You?"

Under the intensity of his gaze, her cheeks suddenly felt hot. "Same," she nodded, looking out the window again.

They continued the ride into downtown Cattail. Spring through fall, a bare parcel downtown transformed into the Farmer's Market, and visitors stuffed into the nearby library's lot for parking. Cam and PJ inched closer to it, drowning out the sound of light traffic with the Pontiac's deep rumble.

As he parked, PJ noted several carriages in the lot. The horses that pulled them flicked their tails, brushing flies away from their backsides.

"Think one of those is Amos?" she asked.

"Possibly. Amos makes soap, but Anthem Hold churns out furniture, quilts, wooden toys, you name it. This is the place they all come to peddle their wares," he answered.

"But," he continued. "They're exempt from license plates, so I can't run any registration information — those carriages could be anybody."

"It doesn't make any sense," PJ said, shaking her head. "They don't use the internet; they don't drive cars. Even with the stuff about his parents, I'm finding it harder and harder to believe that this could be our guy," she admitted.

"I know it," he agreed. "It's a wild theory. But his face. . .wait until you see his face. He's a dead ringer, PJ, in the same little town. It was enough to cause Corb some suspicion, and I have to say I feel the same."

"I guess if it's our only lead," she accepted. She scanned the other vehicles, noting that they were mostly old pickup trucks and dated sedans. "Isn't the GTO a little ostentatious?" PJ wondered aloud.

"Well, like you said — we'll stand out anyway," Cam reasoned. "I figured we might as well embrace it. I'm showing off the car, taking you on a little Saturday outing. It won't look like we're here investigating; it'll look like we're on a date. People won't even think twice."

Cam exited, then rounded the car to open her door.

"In that case, I suppose we should hold hands," PJ suggested with a wink, standing and stepping towards Cam. "Really sell it."

Cam looked downwards, meeting her eyes and struggling to hide a boyish grin. "I like the way you think," he replied. With that, he slipped his thick fingers between hers, gently pulling her across the parking lot.

The entry to the market was designated by a large, wooden arch that had been painted dark red. Wooden fencing in the same shade encircled the market, which was set up on an empty dirt lot. Every year, it was poured over with fresh cedar chips. Inside, the vendors were arranged in a horseshoe shape surrounding a small stage, which currently featured a bluegrass band strumming away for the churning crowd.

Cam pointed to a table covered in baked goods and vases of cut flowers. "That's Cayla," he shared, turning in her direction. As they approached, Cayla met his eyes, then instantly smiled with recognition.

"Cam-Bam. What's up, bruh?" she greeted him. Above her slightly gap-toothed grin, Cayla's ornate, tribal-inspired septum ring hung nearly over her upper lip.

"Oh, we just figured we'd swing by the most happening spot in Cattail," he said sarcastically. "Thought we'd at least get to see the girl with the million-dollar muffins," he added, warmly hugging her shoulder.

"Nothing is ever happening in Cattail," Cayla complained woefully, returning his hug. "But it's true, I do make the best muffins in the whole wide world. Does your girlfriend want one?" Cayla smiled, tossing a long, auburn braid over her tattooed right shoulder.

"Actually, this is my colleague, Paget James," Cam gestured to PJ, correcting Cayla. "We're sort of working a case right now. Undercover."

"That's too bad. I never see him here with a girl. Anywhere with a girl, really," she shared matter-of-factly.

"Oh, come on," Cam groaned.

"I've been starting to think you don't like girls," she continued loudly, looking to Cam. "Which would be fine, of course. You can come out to me. Wouldn't be the first time someone has. . .I have a trustworthy face, I guess."

She wasn't wrong, PJ noted, analyzing the girl. Cayla looked friendly: her eyebrows were natural and full but not unkempt, and with each jest at her brother, her freckled, fleshy pink cheeks nudged large, tortoiseshell glasses. Most importantly, she exhibited a *Duchenne* smile: with it, her bright blue eyes crinkled at the corners, a marker of true enjoyment.

"I like girls just fine," Cam quickly reassured her. "I'm just busy."

"I get it," Cayla continued. "It can be scary putting yourself out there—"

"Thank you, Cayla," Cam interrupted sternly.

PJ struggled to hide her own true smile.

Having inflicted a satisfactory amount of embarrassment, Cayla turned to her muffins. "Well, I've got oatmeal raisin, blueberry poppyseed, brownie bran — also known as my B.M. muffins. Lots of fiber, remember Cam?" she ribbed him again. "They'll get you regular!"

"You know," he responded, "Speaking of brownies, I heard a nasty rumor that you churned out a mega batch — of the special kind — for some college students this past spring. April 20th, to be exact."

Her freckled face flushed.

"It would be a shame if someone were to float that information by Uncle Jack." Cam continued.

"Oh, *you would*," the exuberant girl rolled her eyes. "Alright, for-real, lemon streusel is the favorite for summertime. It's on the house," she noted, gently dropping the muffin into a white paper pastry bag for PJ.

"Thank you," PJ replied, clearly amused by the siblings' exchange.

"We're on to bigger and better things, sis. But don't forget — I'm watching you," Cam teased, drawing an imaginary line with his fingers between his eyes and hers. With that, he took up PJ's hand again, leading her down the row of booths.

"Whatever," Cayla cackled at him. "Nice to meet you!" she added, purring enthusiastically after PJ. "Love the outfit, by the way. Vintage vibes."

PJ waved back at her.

"Your sister seems fun," PJ offered.

"Tons," he chortled. "Like it's her life's mission to flip me shit. Took the pages right out of Corb's playbook."

"I'm the oldest, too," she commiserated.

"How many?" Cam asked.

"I have three sisters and one brother. He's the youngest," she answered.

"Your dad wanted to keep trying for a boy," Cam guessed.

"Oh, yeah. I think he wanted to even the odds a bit," she smiled. "It was sort of a madhouse growing up."

"I can't even imagine," Cam replied. "Was that in Louisiana, too?"

"Lake Charles," she confirmed. "You heard of it?"

He shook his head. "Can't say I've traveled far from here. Spokane. Missoula. That's pretty much it."

"What's that, like a four-hour radius?" she gasped.

"Sounds about right," he chuckled.

"Well, Lake Charles is only a few hours away from New Orleans. A lot smaller, though. My parents chose it for that reason," she explained. "That and it's a beautiful city."

"Did you like it?" he asked.

"Not back then," she said thoughtfully. "Not as a teenager, anyhow. I thought I was missing out on something more exciting somewhere else. But now I see why they settled there. I have a lot of good memories."

"Lake Charles, huh? That's quite a ways from Salt Lake," he observed. "I thought there was an FBI office in New Orleans."

"There is," PJ confirmed. "But I wanted to get away. A little adventure."

"So, you picked Utah?" he teased. "Walk me through that decision."

She shoved him playfully. "I don't mind it. Besides, I didn't choose it for the field office. I was going to go to law school."

"Law school?" Cam raised his eyebrows.

"My dad's a lawyer," PJ expounded. "Personal injury. I wanted to be just like him. I'd always escape into his study and read his old books, or just curl up on one of his big, leather chairs. It made feel so important. So capable. Utah State had a generous scholarship package, so when I finished my undergrad at New Orleans, I jumped at the chance."

"But you don't have a law degree," Cam noted.

"No," she confirmed. "I got my Ph.D. in forensic psychology."

"What changed?" he asked.

"I thought there would be too much paperwork with law. Too many late nights," she shrugged.

"And how does that compare to your job now?" he grinned.

"Ha!" she laughed out loud. "Yeah, tons of paperwork and late nights. But it's a lot more riveting than your average 'slip-and-fall.'"

"I bet."

"Besides, I think I like to put things together behind the scenes, rather than act it all out in court," she added. "I worked in mental health services at the prison for a while, but then I realized I could be more effective in the field. I like the proactive approach. So here I am."

She smiled.

Suddenly, she released her hand from Cam's grip, pulling the yellow-glazed treat from its packaging.

"I'm starving," she apologized.

"Please, eat," Cam insisted.

After a few bites, she chatted him up again.

"So, you know my story. What's yours?" PJ prodded.

"What do you want to know?" Cam asked.

"Well, you've got your sister and brother. Your Uncle. Any other family around?"

"Just my aunt and my Nan," Cam answered. "Another distant aunt, maybe, if she's even alive. No one's heard from her in years."

"And you grew up here," she continued.

"Yup," he confirmed.

"And you've never left," she deduced.

"There's nowhere else I care to be," he explained. "I can work here; I live on a big piece of property. I can hunt, fish, float the river, whatever. I don't need to leave."

"You don't want to visit the ocean?" she pressed.

"Not my style," he answered.

"Or a big city?"

Cam raised an eyebrow. "I'm good."

The less he spoke, the more she dug for answers.

"Alright, Mr. McNulty," she grinned. "What about Cattail is so damn great that you won't even bother with anywhere else? Sell me on it."

"First, why don't you tell me about your average morning," he directed.

"Mine?"

"Please."

"Okay. Um, my alarm goes off around five. Sometimes I run on the treadmill. Or else a virtual cycling class on the Peloton. Shower, pour myself a cup of coffee, get ready. Watch the news. Check my email. Then grab another cup of coffee on the way out the door."

"Your own house?"

"Apartment," she clarified.

"How's traffic?" he continued.

"In Salt Lake City? A little congested in the mornings and afternoons. Not terrible, but yeah, it's busy."

"Hm. You ready to hear about mine?" he asked.

"Go for it," she confirmed.

"I'm up around dawn. No alarm, just Nan's rooster. I run outside, all four seasons. I can go a mile in any direction before I even see another house, and I've known every one of my neighbors my entire life. I don't have a TV. But even if I did, I don't need to watch the news, because there's nothing that can't wait until I skim a newspaper at work later that morning. I also don't need to check my email, because if anything affects me directly, someone will come knock on my door and tell me in person. I grab eggs from our chickens, then eat my breakfast overlooking our fields. It's so quiet outside, I can hear the bugs walking up the grass. When I leave, there's no traffic. Shit, sometimes I'm the only vehicle on the road until I get right downtown."

"Hmph. Sounds lonely," PJ teased.

He smirked. "Peaceful," he corrected.

As they slowed their pace, Cam surveyed the booths, looking for their soaper. He quickly identified a table scattered with waxy, multi-colored discs wrapped in yarn. Next to that pile, Amos Sinclair manned a cash register. His familiar features only solidified Cam's feeling about the photograph on Britlyn's blog. A shiver shot down his spine.

He turned his back to the man, facing PJ instead. "My six," he said in a low voice.

She peered past him, scanning the market for their suspect. Suddenly, she spotted him.

"Oh my God," she remarked. "You weren't kidding. Either this Amos character is our guy, or he is seriously a doppelgänger. Wait. He's looking at me," she noted, quickening her speech.

"Close your eyes," Cam commanded. With that, he reached his arms under hers and pulled her close to him. As they embraced, he spun her away from Amos's line of sight.

They parted, and PJ exhaled. "I must have been staring," she acknowledged.

"All he saw was a little PDA," Cam reassured her. "He has no reason to think we're onto him."

"I haven't been in the field for a while," she apologized. "Not face-to-face."

"Relax. Everyone is looking at us, right? That's the point: to throw his ass off the scent of why we're really here. Some annoyingly smitten couple, not two LEOs digging up dirt," he reiterated.

"I know. I just can't believe how much he looks like him," she snorted. "Unless it really *is* him."

"Let's go find out," Cam urged.

PJ nodded, tucking the rest of her muffin back into its bag and into a small, leather purse she wore across her torso. They turned, gliding towards Amos's booth to the tune of bluegrass music.

TWELVE.

As they approached the soap-covered table, the perfume of various essential oils filled Cam's nose. Peppermint was prominent, but he caught a whiff of lavender and orange with each advancing step. On the right side of the L-shaped display, a small platform held a cash register, a business card holder, and a cradled tablet. Behind the register, Amos watched his potential customers draw closer.

"Soaps are buy 3, get 1 free," he announced in a friendly tone. "Goat's milk is a natural exfoliant — full of lactic acid, vitamins, and minerals for younger looking skin."

"Wow, goat's milk?" PJ pretended to be intrigued. "Are they your goats?"

"Yes, indeed," Amos answered. He pushed round, wire-rimmed glasses up the sharp bridge of his nose, then reached for a small album alongside his register. "This here's my whole operation. The farm, all the

191

goats." He flipped to the first page. "Daisy there is my oldest. She's about ten."

"She's cute," PJ offered.

"They are truly special animals," he responded with a smile. "And it is a truly special soap. Are you looking for any scent in particular?"

"Hmm. . ." she wondered. "Something warm, maybe? Like a vanilla?"

Amos stiffened his legs and rose from his wooden stool. "I think my Oatmeal Almond will be just the ticket."

With that, he made his way to the corner of his display. Cam couldn't help but observe his movements were strained, and by the second step. . .*yes*. . .an observable limp. Cam studied his face from the side. *Was that a wince?*

Finally, Amos procured an oat-encrusted disc and held it out to PJ. "Let me know what you think of this one."

Taking the soap, she held it to her face and inhaled deeply. As she inspected the item, Amos suddenly turned his eyes to Cam.

"Long time, no see, Camden," he greeted him.

Cam chuckled. "Yes, it has been a while. How are you doing, Amos?"

"Well, I thought I'd at least improved my appearance after years of growing this," he stroked his beard. "But you were able to recognize me, no trouble!"

"Hardly. It's the business cards," Cam winked.

Amos looked over at the glossy cards neatly displayed on a handmade, wooden stand. "Ah, that's right. Guess nothing gets past you. I hear you're a cop now!"

"Not today," Cam assured him. He put his arm around PJ and pulled her close. "Finally taking a day off. I thought I'd show my girl around. . .she's from out of town."

"I'm Jamie," PJ smiled warmly, extending her hand. "Nice to meet you."

Amos returned her greeting and shook her hand. "Welcome to Cattail, Miss Jamie. Cam's an old friend. You can enjoy that first bar on me."

"That is too generous!" she exclaimed. "Please, let me purchase a few from you. I insist."

Amos nodded, then hobbled between the soap piles, collecting a variety. He wrapped them in tissue and bagged them in a modest but crisp brown paper sack. "These are my bestsellers. That will be eighteen dollars, then."

PJ glanced at his tablet. "You take credit cards, right?"

"Oh, that newfangled thing. Sometimes it can be so tricky, but let me see. . ." The pitch of Amos's voice rose as he answered. He plucked the tablet from its cradle and furrowed his brow. Despite Amos's expressed frustration with the tech, Cam noticed his fingers seemed to glide with a fluid familiarity over the screen.

He was bluffing.

"Okay, I think I'm ready," Amos announced, reaching for PJ's payment. She handed him a special card which bore her undercover moniker.

With a quick swipe, he returned the card.

"These are great," PJ thanked him. "I can't wait to try them all."

"Enjoy your visit to Cattail," Amos responded. "And Cam — please, say hello to Cayla. I see her across the way every weekend, and I always forget to stop by. I'd trade some soap for scones!"

"I'll let her know." The hairs on Cam's arms bristled at Amos's mention of his baby sister.

* * *

Within the safe confines of the classic car once again, PJ let out a giddy breath.

"Did you see that limp?" she anxiously asked Cam.

"It's definitely suspicious," Cam observed. "You pull anything off his tablet?"

PJ shifted in her seat, pulling her purse onto her lap and unzipping it. From within, she withdrew her phone and phony credit card. Using a small attachment, she swiped the card's magnetic strip over the phone, then tapped away at the screen.

"Done," she informed him. "My team will scan this and see if we can tie his merchant accounts to anything we've previously flagged."

Suddenly, the phone in her hand began to chime.

PJ frowned.

"Agent James," she answered. "Oh. Really. Okay." She raised her eyebrows.

"What?" Cam whispered.

She held up a hand, silencing him.

"I believe Detective McNulty is with another potential witness right now, but the Lieutenant and I can be there shortly."

Cam pulled from the parking lot towards the street, then shrugged at PJ, pointing both directions.

She pointed towards her lodgings.

"Yep. Give me. . .twenty minutes," she finished. She ended the call.

"What was that about?" Cam asked.

"Your brother's witness remembered something he wanted to share with us," she revealed.

"The landscaper?" he asked.

"Uh-huh. Any reason why he wouldn't have told Corb everything in the first place?"

Cam shook his head. "Not that I can think of. Could be the tequila shook it loose."

PJ wrinkled her nose. "What tequila?"

Cam sighed. "I probably shouldn't be telling you this. But they were out partying together right after the interview. That's why Corb looked like death warmed over yesterday morning."

"Do they know each other or something?" PJ asked, puzzled.

Cam sighed, shaking his head. "I didn't think so. Guess they do now."

"Where is Corb, anyhow?" she pressed. "He's still with Lizzie, right?"

Cam deliberated quietly. *You don't want to know,* he thought.

Turning onto Third Street, Corb continued towards PJ's vacation rental, a small cottage a few blocks away from downtown. He'd personally recommended the property to her, as he knew the homeowners kept it in meticulous shape, and Big Rob had used it for traveling expert witnesses before.

"Cam?" PJ urged him.

"You don't want to know," he repeated, aloud this time.

"What does that mean?" she worriedly replied.

Cam pulled in front of the bungalow, parking on the street. He looked over at her. He wanted to trust her, to tell her everything. *Was it her dark, kind eyes?* Or perhaps, he was simply blinded by her part in their charade: a beautiful woman, clad in that country dress, on a weekend visit to see her boyfriend. It was all pretend. Still, the feel of her hand in his sure didn't seem that way.

It wouldn't betray his brother to share, just a little.

"Well, he's at Anthem Hold," he informed her.

"WHAT?" she asked, her jaw hanging open.

Shit. He'd overshared.

PJ exited the car, shutting the door in a manner just short of slamming it. She quickened her pace towards the front of the cottage. Cam chased after her.

"Wait," he insisted, running up behind her. "Just, wait."

PJ looked around, noting the close proximity of the other homes in this old, historic neighborhood. "Inside," she instructed.

Once inside the house with the door closed, she threw her purse angrily on the couch.

"What the fuck, Lieutenant?" she began.

They were back to professional titles, he observed. *Not a good sign.*

"He's not going to hurt the investigation," Cam insisted. "He's still with Lizzie. They just left her property a while ago."

"Lizzie is with him?" PJ repeated.

"Yes. Plus, she still has a sister at Anthem Hold. She has every right to visit her," he added.

"You don't think the sight of your brother — who isn't exactly inconspicuous, mind you — is going to catch anyone's attention?" PJ huffed.

Cam swallowed. "I don't think anyone is going to see him," he clarified carefully.

PJ raised her eyebrows and crossed her arms. "So, he's up there sneaking around."

Cam cocked his head, meeting her eyes. "Maybe."

Her chest heaved, causing the buttons that met at her cleavage to pull tight and draw his eyes downwards. Cam quickly averted his stare, but it was too late.

"Seriously?" she chided him.

He closed his eyes and turned away. "Sorry. I'm sorry."

"And here I thought you were the sensible one. That you were responsible. But you're peas in a pod," PJ frowned at him.

Cam took a deep breath, regaining his clarity. He turned to face her again. "I am responsible, Agent James. I told you what I know about my brother, and I didn't have to."

Her expression softened.

"As for your current attire. . .my staring was unprofessional. This all has me a little out of my element," he apologized.

She wanted to scold the man some more, but his demeanor was too sincere.

"I get it," she forgave him. "Sometimes undercover ops can make things confusing. It complicates our roles a bit."

He nodded regretfully.

She glanced at the closed front door and the heavy drapes over the windows, which she'd left drawn upon arrival the night before. With her patronizing tone, she had convinced him she was taking the high road. Yet, in this dark and private space, she was also having trouble keeping things above board.

"It's normal to feel confused about your partner. Attracted to them, even," she reasoned. As she spoke, her voice was shaky, betraying her true emotions. She felt like the explanation was mostly advice for herself.

Cam met her eyes, grinning. "With all due respect, Agent, the fact that you're an extremely attractive woman isn't confusing at all. That part's crystal clear."

She blushed.

"It's how I'm supposed to act in light of that fact that's giving me trouble," he finished.

"Let me help you," she responded, dropping her gaze to the floor. "I'm going to get out of this dress. . ."

"That's not helpful at all," he playfully interrupted.

". . .and back into a suit," she continued, smiling coyly. "Then, we can refocus on our investigation."

She pointed at the door.

"Absolutely," Cam agreed. "Let's get to it." With that, he exited the front room and made his way back to the car.

Her heart was racing.

* * *

"*Hola, Ramón,*" PJ greeted him, standing and pulling the hem of her jacket taut as he entered the room. She'd chosen a navy suit that was well-made and fitted, but slightly less formal than the black version she'd worn yesterday. She smiled, further softening her sharp appearance. The black-haired man cautiously returned the expression, then shifted his eyes to Cam. Cam nodded, closing the door and leaning against the wall near PJ, who had sat on the corner of the Chief's desk.

"*Buenas tardes.* Take a seat, please," she encouraged. While the Department had two interrogation rooms, PJ had insisted on using the Chief's office, a more comfortable and inviting location considering that Ramón was not currently a suspect. Additionally, she had been worried that such fear could prevent him from being entirely forthcoming. As he eased himself into the club chair nearest PJ, she addressed that concern.

"I'm sorry Detective McNulty isn't here to speak with you, but I just wanted to make sure—" she began in Spanish.

Ramón reluctantly held up his hand. "I know your language," he informed her.

"My apologies," she offered. She then continued to explain in English.

"I wanted to make sure you knew that we are not interested in your immigration status," she promised.

"The detective already told me," Ramón replied.

"He did?" PJ asked, surprised.

Ramón nodded.

"He promised you weren't looking to send me back, that you just wanted to find her. He seems straight. Even gave me a ride home from the bar once."

PJ smirked.

"Besides," he elaborated, winking at them both, "if you deport all of us, who will be left to do the work for people who don't know how to get their hands dirty?"

"Fair enough," Cam laughed out loud.

PJ turned back to Ramón. "So, you already shared everything with Detective McNulty, then?" she asked him.

"Like I said, he was cool, so I told him what I knew. I like Señora Robbins; I want her found," Ramón responded.

"Alright," PJ accepted. "So, what is it we can help you with?"

"I forgot to add something that might be important. He said to call."

PJ and Cam exchanged glances. She sunk from her perch on the corner of the desk to the Chief's chair behind it, lowering her gaze to Ramón's level. "Okay, let's have it."

"Well, like I told him — I don't know much," he shrugged. "I didn't see her or hear her at all that day. But then, I usually don't. All the tools are in the garage," Ramón recounted again.

"I get there in the late morning. I start with the flowers in front of the house, then the sides. I mowed the main lawn a few days back, so I just edged it this time. A touch-up. Then, 'cause it was Thursday, I went down to mow and trim the river property. That was after lunch."

"We have surveillance that shows you leaving at about 3:00," Cam confirmed. "You were down in the pasture until then?"

"Yes," Ramón nodded. "It's a big job."

Cam nodded, picturing the large plot of land leading up to the cattail-flocked banks of the Palouse River.

"But I forgot that I did hear something strange. Something made me come up by the house before I was done," Ramón added.

PJ stiffened her posture. "What, what was it?"

His voice lowered. "I am afraid to say. . .I thought it was a scream," he revealed, shaking his head.

"A scream," PJ repeated, her eyes growing big. Cam pushed away from the wall, uncrossing his arms and moving in closer.

"I had my music going, so I ignored it at first. But then I heard it again. I kept working a minute, but I started worrying maybe she fell and hurt herself or the babies. I don't know." His gentle concern describing the pregnant woman contrasted sharply against his rough appearance. "I walked up from the grass and set my trimmer by the back porch. And I went up the steps by the side of the house."

"Could you see where the scream was coming from?" Cam asked.

"It was so quiet by then, I thought maybe I was hearing things, but then I saw it," Ramón confirmed.

"Saw what?"

"The horse," Ramón disclosed.

"On the property?" PJ asked.

"No. Just on the road," he clarified. "In front of the house."

"You decided the scream was just. . .the horse making a noise?" PJ pressed.

"I didn't want to bother her for nothing," Ramón explained, sounding somewhat embarrassed. "I saw her car in the driveway, and the scream was gone. I told myself it was in my head. That it had to be the horse."

"But you don't think that now," Cam concluded.

Ramón shook his head. "No. After the detective told me she was missing, I went through it in my mind again and again. I *know* I heard a scream. A woman's voice.

Almost like. . .like I thought she was screaming for help, you know?"

Cam swallowed the lump in his throat, remembering the blood-soaked office.

Ever the skeptic, PJ narrowed her eyes. "That's a pretty big jump. I haven't spent a lot of time around horses, but I don't think they normally make a sound that would compare to a human scream."

"Maybe not normally, but that's the other thing. Lots of neighbors have farms, and they ride horses. I see horses all the time," Ramón explained. "But it wasn't just a horse. It was a horse and a carriage. Riding away."

Cam's eyes grew big. "Like an old-fashioned carriage?"

Ramón nodded. "And the driver, he was using a whip. *That's* why I thought the scream was the horse: he was whipping the shit out of it."

"Yep. That'll get us a warrant," Cam remarked, quickly pulling his phone from his pocket. As he began to dial, a pounding on the door caught the attention of all three of the room's occupants.

"Agent James?" her colleague demanded from the other side of the wooden slab.

"We're almost finished here," she responded coolly.

"I think you need to see this," the man insisted. "Right away."

* * *

After excusing Ramón, PJ and Cam hurried down the hall to the conference room, which had been converted into a makeshift mega-office to house the investigators the FBI had sent along after PJ, as well as a handful of local officers. While Cyber Crimes continued to review digital evidence relating to online activity, Cattail PD focused on picking through any surveillance footage, conducting interviews, looking into acquaintances, and documenting potential leads. Behind the closed doors, the air had become permeated with the smell of sweat, which was only masked to a point of tolerability by the concurrent aroma of coffee and maple donuts. Now stale, they were scattered alongside the file boxes and laptop chargers littering the long table.

"What is it?" she exhaled, looking over the agent's shoulder at his computer screen.

"That card reader you swiped through earlier," he shared excitedly. "We sent the info you skimmed to the payment processor. They just got back to us with the details on the connected financial institutions, which includes a certain digital wallet."

"Didn't even need a warrant, huh?" Cam shook his head.

"Gotta love that Patriot Act," PJ winked at him. She turned back to the agent. "You said it was one we'd flagged."

"A big fucking flag," he confirmed. "You may want to sit."

"Who?" she asked excitedly.

"Amnesia," he whispered.

PJ's eyes widened, and she braced her arms on the nearest office chair. "No way."

He nodded. "I thought the same thing. Looks like it was a one-time mistake. My guess is he accidentally withdrew the balance as crypto, and his browser auto-filled the fields with his digital information instead of his normal account number for cash. But there it is."

"*Amnesia?*" Cam chuckled. "Sounds like bad guy out of a comic book."

PJ smirked. "That's his handle on the dark web. We've never been close enough to his true identity to call him anything else."

"Until now," Cam pointed out. "But it's a stretch. Sure, Amos looked savvy with that tablet. . .more than he lets on. . .but dark web supervillain? We are still talking about an individual who spends his days milking goats and his nights by candlelight."

"Maybe not," PJ shrugged. "Maybe he's got everyone at Anthem Hold fooled."

Cam squinted. "I suppose he could. You heard Uncle Jack say he was smart enough. . .and an off-grid community is the perfect cover for those activities. Especially if you're secretly on the grid."

"Any way you can reach your brother and see what he's finding?" she asked.

He shook his head. "No cell service up there. I need to find another way to warn him what he might be walking into." He quickly stepped towards the door. "I'm gonna run this by the Chief. Think we can brief everyone in the squad room in say, fifteen minutes?"

"It's tight, but I'll see what I can put together," she assured him.

THIRTEEN.

PJ's heart thumped as she fumbled over an assortment of photographs and documents. For the second time since she'd arrived, she was making use of the Cattail Police Department's outdated overhead projector. However, this presentation was unexpected, and the lack of preparation coupled with the high-profile subject of its focus had her unnerved. As she skimmed the intelligence they'd gathered on Amos, she forced herself to take a long, deep breath.

"Listen up," she heard Cam announce. His voice was firm but pleasant, and it immediately caught and held the attention of his officers. It was clear from their alert and ready submission that they trusted and respected the Lieutenant completely.

So did she, she realized, noticing her pulse slow. During their assignment together, he had been professional yet pleasant, engaging but not overbearing. He appreciated and lauded her expertise while complimenting it with his own. He didn't resent her involvement as an "outsider", and he wasn't threatened or insulted by working the case with a female.

On the contrary, she had found that she was the one becoming more aware of her sex in his presence. First, in the car on the way to the Farmer's Market, when her face flushed in response to his handsome grin. Then, when he'd covertly wrapped her in his arms to obscure her from Amos's view, she'd felt her belly fill with butterflies and a telling, soft tingle where his hips had pressed against hers. In the living room, it was all she could do to turn him out of the house before she undressed. Now, the same voice that inspired trust in his deputies brought her a sense of comfort, and she realized that her hands had finally stopped shaking.

"Go ahead, Agent James," he smiled.

She managed to set aside her wandering thoughts, and her gaze dropped to the stack of papers in her hands.

"Our suspect's name is Amos Sinclair," she began, placing his photograph below the old machine's document camera. A grainy picture appeared on the wall behind her. "Or as the FBI knows him, Amnesia."

"Though we've believed for some time that Amnesia was likely a White, adult male, his physical characteristics were previously unknown. Now, we have been able to link him to this photograph, which is the profile picture for a user on Britlyn Robbins' website."

"Wait — that doesn't look like Amos," one officer piped up. "I mean, kinda. But I saw him just last month with a full beard."

"And that's how he looked when Lieutenant McNulty and I visited his booth at the Farmer's Market this morning. We believe Amos has been living a double life: carrying out his normal, known existence as a member of Anthem Hold and resident of your community, while also becoming very active in the online community as Amnesia. Specifically, he's carved out a presence on the dark web, and he's quite well known for his malicious cyber activities."

"Why Amnesia?" asked another officer.

"When he was first put on our radar, he was still dabbling with basic ransomware. But his techniques quickly became more sophisticated, and around 2015, he changed this predatory strategy and took a more proactive approach: instead of targeting innocent civilians and holding their data hostage, he began contracting with other criminals and charging them to wipe out digital evidence. Police departments began turning to us because they no longer had the evidence to move forward with their investigations. Prosecutions that had already commenced would stall and then end in dismissal. He became the cleaning guy for some major players." PJ shuffled the papers on the overhead so that a news article covering one of the more prominent cases was displayed.

"So, these other departments, are they not backing up their files?" the same officer wondered aloud. "I mean, we're pretty rinky-dink as far as technology goes, but even we know how to make copies. Airplane mode, evidence bags. . ."

"Any copies were also destroyed," she informed him. "We're not entirely sure of his technique, but the theory we're running with is that he's built some kind of software to intercept the low-frequency magnetic radiation emanating from the device, and he uses that channel to funnel the data to a local computer he's remotely hijacked. Once the data is moved to the non-air-gapped computer, erasing that device becomes basic. You're left with empty drives and zero evidence. . .as if the case never existed," PJ explained. "Hence, 'Amnesia'."

Cam approached the overhead, laying down a crude, hand-drawn map.

"Everyone here is familiar with the gates at Anthem Hold. Just past that, through the trees here, is the Sinclair property." Cam tapped the map. "The house burned down a while back, but there should be a new dwelling somewhere at this site. I'm putting the warrant application together now, then we'll get a team assembled for extraction before the Judge's ink is dry. Do not be fooled — he may look like Amos Sinclair, but as Agent James just informed you, he is a dangerous and capable cybercriminal. We think he has the resources to slip away very easily if we can't pin him down today at Anthem Hold."

* * *

Anthem Hold was situated near the top of the mountain, a few miles after the paved road turned to dirt. Its entry was strategically tucked between jagged outcrops of basalt columns and fortified by tall, wooden gates.

Engraved upon them, Corb recognized a line from a Psalm:

HE IS MY REFUGE AND MY FORTRESS.

He heard Lizzie exit the truck, followed by a brief conversation between her and the elder manning the gates.

"I'm getting married," she gushed. "I wanted to share the news with Rachel."

Corb smirked. Despite her outrage, she'd used his suggestion, after all.

"You should have sent a letter," the man snarled. "Her husband isn't expecting you. He will not welcome you at their home."

"*Let marriage be held in honor among all,*" she quoted the Scripture to him. "Surely, her husband will rejoice."

The elder was silent.

"I won't stay long," Lizzie added.

"Why do you bring your horse?" he demanded.

"I thought the children might like to see him," she explained.

"You may be granted a brief visit to apprise the family of your marriage. I will go inform them of your presence," he decided. "But keep your animal in the trailer."

Lizzie thanked him, then hoisted herself back into the truck.

"Asshole," he heard her mutter, echoing Corb's thoughts.

As the heavy gates swung inwards, Lizzie slowly continued on the dirt road constituting the community's main thoroughfare. To the left, a large blanket of loess served as a parking lot of sorts for the modern vehicles occasionally permitted to enter. Corb had parked in the same lot, riding along in the coroner's van, at least a dozen times since he'd started in the field. He and Dr. Klein — a tall woman with spindly limbs and a short, dark bob — would walk the main road like it was a plank over gator-fraught waters, keeping their heads forward and hands in their pockets as Anthem Hold's citizens scrutinized their presence. The community had become emboldened over the years, and the accusations they hurled from the roadside became especially sharp for his female colleague. Sure, they'd disliked Dr. Black before her, but his masculinity saved him from the sect's most loathsome behavior.

With Nadine, they balked at her pantsuits and shamed her for working amongst men. Further, like Dr. Black, she was a medical doctor and board-certified forensic pathologist, rigorous training which earned her the ability to perform autopsies rather than referring them out — a major benefit for the small county. But at Anthem Hold, this prideful and greedy professional title caused them to disrespect her even more. A modest dress and skipping her trademark dark lipstick would have likely made their walk quieter, but Corb preferred her cold indifference: she had mastered a certain aloof poise that silently screamed she could not muster a single fuck for any one of them. The unapologetic duo would carry on toward their destination, usually the home of some dead child, with all the polished finesse of an emery board, roughing everything up along the way.

Of course, the community wouldn't know he was here this time — he'd smoothly slip over to the Sinclair place to survey the property, hopefully pick up a clue on the vic's whereabouts, then sneak back in and snuggle up to Huck. No one would be the wiser.

Lizzie pulled into the parking area, careful to situate the vehicle so that the trailer's man door was out of view.

"Sounds like we don't have much time," Corb whispered as Lizzie opened it, stepping inside.

Lizzie shook her head. "We don't. Her house is about a mile from here. I'll walk slow, but you'll have to hurry."

In all the years he'd known Lizzie, he had never been by Rachel's home. Considering his occupation, for the sake of her family, he prayed he never would. But he had seen her parents' house once, when Lizzie went back to say goodbye to her sister before leaving the compound for good. Corb had tagged along and hidden in the nearby bushes, dutifully observing his new role as her protector. The home was a plain, white structure with a tan chimney, and it sat behind a long clothesline weighed down by a row of neutral linens.

It's how they wanted her to be, he supposed. Simple. Ordinary. Colorless and obedient; silent and sober.

All her young life, she'd diligently followed those orders, and for what? He remembered thinking of the thatching of purple welts across her skin and wondering who else inside the gates had judged Lizzie as disloyal and rebellious for her revelation. Or worse, who didn't believe her. After all, those same sheets that billowed in the gentle breeze, freshly scrubbed clean, bore no trace of the girls' bright, red blood from their father's special brand of attention.

The hypocrisy had filled Corb with a new kind of heat, an anger fueled not by self-hatred or pity, but love for another. He wasn't sure what became of her parents or their house, but he'd never forget watching her turn her back on them, or the heavy feeling of her hand in his as they ran through the woods and away from the Hold.

It was a welcome burden then and now.

"Amos's place is just through these trees?" he asked, peering through the trailer's man door.

"His parents' house was. Amos is past that, up the hill a ways. The same property, but closer to the top of the mountain," Lizzie explained. "How will we communicate?"

"Think this guy will let you stay till one o'clock?"

"Begrudgingly, maybe," she responded.

"I'll meet you back here then," he determined.

"And what if you're not back? Then what do I do?" Lizzie pressed.

"Then you just go," he commanded. "And when you get to cell service, call Cam and tell him I'm still here."

"How will I know if you're hurt?" she worried. "If he is who you say he is, what if he—"

"Elizabeth!" the elder's voice boomed. "Leave the animal and be on your way!"

"I'll see you at one," Corb whispered.

Lizzie nodded, then closed the door, leaving it unlatched.

* * *

Closing the door behind him, Corb easily crossed the lot undetected, though his footsteps had fluffed the light soil into the air so that his jeans and boots were already coated with a thin, tan layer of "moon dust", a term he and Cam concocted as kids. He knew from experience that a longer walk through the stuff would draw the earth up into his nostrils and lungs until it felt like breathing chalk. Luckily, the hill quickly turned to mud and matted clumps of wild grass, and the surrounding pine trees filtered the moon dust lingering in the air behind him while also obscuring him from view as he scrambled towards the Sinclair property. It was only about a half mile away, but then, Corb would need to stay hidden behind the final row of trees, skirting the edge until the last possible minute. He soon reached and passed a large meadow, continuing forward until the Sinclair barn came into view.

Despite its proximity to the original house, firefighters had managed to save the barn, Corb suddenly remembered from the file. The red building was large, with a traditional gambrel roof that shaded the goats playing in the grass below. The spot where the old house had been was now a tidy vegetable garden, its vines budding with cherry tomatoes, squash, and peppers. A muddy driveway that stretched from the barn toward the main road was currently vacant, and Amos and his buggy were nowhere in sight. Corb left the safety of the trees and crossed the field, concealing himself behind old farming implements and water troughs. Beyond the farm, the field stretched up towards another patch of trees, where the woods continued until the mountain's peak.

Corb surveyed the property, attempting to locate Amos's new house. Had he not spotted the sheen of a glass window in the sunlight, he would have missed the cottage altogether: with a stone exterior and a roof that had become overgrown with grass, it blended into the landscape where it had been dug out, directly into the hillside. The only apparent access point was through the front, which was a short walk from the barn.

Corb rested his hand on the pistol at his hip and cautiously surveyed his surroundings. He didn't like being out in the open and funneled right to the front door of whatever bunker this was, but his options were slim. Anyhow, there was still no sign of Amos or anyone else. He glanced at his watch, remembering the curt tone with which the elder had hurried Lizzie along. The last thing he wanted was to jam her up.

Corb followed the barn with his back until he reached its edge, then slowly began his ascent, bending at the knees and ducking low into the tall grass as he climbed. As he reached the front, he tucked himself alongside the far corner of the structure, leaning his shoulders against the stone facade. Like the other homes in the community, the door and windows were as traditional and plain as possible, and the area in front of the home was free of decorations and other embellishments. Corb slid over and gently tried the handle.

It was unlocked.

The ease of access was somewhat welcome, as it saved him the time and commotion of breaking down the door, but it also gave Corb a sense of apprehension. *If Mrs. Robbins was inside, why wouldn't Amos take the precaution to secure the entry?* Then again, the community wasn't big on security. It wasn't just Anthem Hold, either; he'd found that many Idahoans judged the value of a neighborhood based on the ability to leave their doors unlocked.

Corb warily ducked through the door, quietly closing it behind him. Inside, the home's interior was dimly illuminated by the sun that filtered in through the front window. It was furnished with simple, wooden pieces: a rocker sat in the corner, and a coat rack in the entry held a couple of dark jackets and a black hat. Save for a clock and calendar mounted near the rocker, the walls were wood-paneled and bare.

Corb knew better than to look for a light switch; instead, he pulled his flashlight from his belt. He clicked it on as he advanced, washing the space with a bright, white glow and sending tall shadows scurrying up the walls. Beyond the living area, a small kitchen held a table with a single, spindle back chair and a woodfired stove. Corb dragged his finger over the appliance, leaving a trail in the dust. He continued toward the bedroom in the back, which was similarly furnished with strictly necessary items: a bed; a wardrobe; another clock; a large, wooden chest. A narrow dresser held a wash basin, which had yellowed with age. Corb lifted the matching pitcher and attempted to pour from it. It was bone dry.

Corb crouched down, searching under the bed with his flashlight. More dust bunnies.

He turned it off. In the dark, he focused on the sound of his own heartbeat and breathing, then tuned them out. If she was alive, maybe she'd cry for help. *Or if she wasn't, maybe he could smell the decay of her body.* He frowned, shaking off the morbid thought and attending once more to his senses. The only detectable scent was a faint whiff of farm animals and their manure, which Corb supposed was lingering on the garments hanging throughout the home. It was nearly silent inside the cottage's thick walls, save for the ticking of the grandfather clock against the back wall, reminding him of the time that was quickly slipping away.

Tick. Tock. Tick. Tock.

In the dark, it loomed over him, a hulking shadow that boomed as it announced the passing seconds. Without the dull static of everyday background noise — people chattering, the hum of electricity, a radio's tunes, a plastic wrapper rustling, fabric brushing against itself — the clock quickly grew agonizingly loud. Corb thought of trying to sleep in the company of the maddening metronome.

No, Amos didn't live here. Not in these rooms, anyhow.

Corb clicked his flashlight back on.

It was a beautiful clock, with a stately wooden case and a finial on top. Its beveled glass door stretched its full length, allowing the viewer to observe the pendulum and weights inside.

He squinted at the fixture. It was *too* beautiful. Too fancy. Getting to his feet, he walked to the clock, tracing its edges with his eyes. In its polished surface, he could see fingerprints. Corb exhaled as he studied them. The prints were many, and some smudged over the top of others. Still, he was able to discern what appeared to be a thumbprint from a large, right hand on the right side of the clock's door. He noted the location of the hinges, which were also on the right. This wasn't where a person would open the door to service the clock — that would be from the left side. Corb hovered his own thumb over the print, then followed his fingers around the edge of the frame, locating additional prints. *Someone had grabbed the clock around the side.*

Then, Corb felt it — a distinct change in temperature. He switched his light off again and looked down the hall, worried that Amos had somehow opened the front door undetected, letting in the fresh air from outside.

Hearing nothing, Corb swiveled back towards the clock, and he felt the drop in temperature again.

He reached towards the wall, feeling the minute change become more noticeable. He rested his palm against the wall's surface.

It was cold.

Corb clicked on his flashlight. He found the handprint, then traced it again, this time pressing his own palm and fingers against the edge. To his surprise, the heavy clock easily gave way to the wall behind it. He stepped back and pointed his light downward, revealing the brass gleam of ball casters fixed to the bottom of the piece. As he continued to push the clock aside, a recessed handle appeared on the wall. The pull featured a ring inset in a larger, square backplate, and it bore a bronze finish unlike anything else he had seen in the house. Corb finished moving the clock, then looped his finger into the ring. He pulled.

An entire section of wood paneling swung inwards towards him, and Corb was hit by the onslaught of cold air and cool, white light. He replaced his flashlight on his belt, reaching for his gun instead. Corb stepped into the room, its own entryway of sorts, and was greeted by the soft aroma of vanilla and wood. Oddly, it reminded him of Mrs. Robbins' house.

Corb continued past the entry down a narrow corridor to what appeared to be a bedroom. The platform bed was wooden but modern, with sleek lines and a low profile. It was neatly made and spread with a brushed, gray duvet. A similarly contemporary nightstand held a water tumbler and a leather-bound journal, along with a digital clock and a slim lamp. Corb raised his eyebrows as he contemplated their energy source. He shifted his focus to the water.

The glass, with its straight sides and dimpled texture, wasn't terribly unique. However, it had grabbed his attention for another reason: it matched the glass Cam had reimagined from the shards in the robot vacuum, as well as the other four arranged in a single column on Mrs. Robbins' chic bar cart. Five glasses in total, which he was now sure had been sold as a larger set — and he was looking at the sixth.

Had Amos been to her house before, or did he just take it on the way out?

Corb sniffed the air, realizing that the notes weren't merely reminiscent of the Robbins' foyer; he was smelling the exact same scent.

The epiphany and the cool air tickled the goosebumps at his neck, and he raised his firearm, letting it lead him further into the secret apartment. In his closet, Amos hung fake beards amongst modern dress shirts and slacks, and a tray holding partial dentures was tucked on a shelf alongside hoodies and stylish sneakers. In the adjacent bathroom, updated technology prevailed, with a composting toilet and a glass vessel sink hooked to water tanks. Corb entered, and a large mirror came to life with bright, LED lights, illuminating the vanity below.

An electric toothbrush. Half a bottle of cologne. Deodorant. The toiletries were perfectly arranged, yet entirely out of place.

Who was Amos Sinclair?

Corb moved to the kitchen area, where several chrome-accented, digital cooking devices were displayed on a butcher block countertop. Soy protein powder sat alongside an expensive blender, which was stationed by a stainless coffee maker. The last cup still lingered in the glass carafe.

Then, across from the kitchen, another bronze handle caught his eye.

He walked to it, then pulled. This time, the door was heavy, and Corb studied it as he crossed into the room. The inside of the hatch had been paneled in aluminum sheeting that extended onto the walls and ceiling, which were joined in the corners with wire strips. Though some of the metal sheeting appeared to be new, other areas were patched together with street signs, trailer siding, and flattened ducts.

"What the fuck?" Corb muttered aloud.

"Hello?!!?" He heard a woman's shaky voice call out from around the corner.

"Cattail Police!" Corb announced suddenly. "Britlyn Robbins?"

"Yes, yes!" she answered, sobbing. "Help me! Please, help me!"

Corb cautiously stepped further into the room, eyeing the strange materials Amos had affixed to every wall. Then, in an alcove, he laid eyes on the petite woman handcuffed to a hospital bed. Her cheeks were splotchy, and her eyes were red and swollen over her nose, which was caked at the nostrils with dried mucus.

"Jesus Christ," he exhaled, holstering his weapon and rushing to her side. Carefully, he lifted her wrists, which were rubbed raw under the tight, metal bindings. He quickly inserted his own standard, single-tooth key, and the cuffs fell away.

Britlyn mustered up the energy to throw her arms around his neck, then hung against his chest. "Thank you," she whispered. She began to cry.

"It's alright," he assured her. "We're gonna get you out of here." As he noticed her hard, swollen belly pressing against his, he remembered that she was with child.

"How are your girls, Mrs. Robbins?" he asked.

She nodded, still burying her head in his shirt. "They're okay."

"Alright." He sat her up by the shoulders, examining her. He'd noticed an IV inserted inside her elbow when he removed the handcuffs, and he pointed to the tube. "What's in this?"

"I don't know," she shook her head. "To knock me out, I think. How long has it been?"

"Not long," Corb promised. He followed the tube to the IV bag, but it was unmarked. With two fingers, he gently pinched the skin under her collarbone, watching as it sprung back into place.

"He's been keeping you hydrated," he revealed. "Which is a good thing."

"He said he's taking us away," she sputtered. "The babies, too. Like he thought we were going to be a family, or something. He found my website. . .my socials."

Britlyn's voice began to falter. "He followed me online, and then he followed me to my house."

"You ever talk to him, online?" Corb asked.

"He followed me to my house," she repeated, stunned. "And then, then he grabbed me, then—"

"Are you hurt?" he interrupted.

"I don't know. I don't think so. But he is," she remembered. "I had to. . .I had this letter opener in my desk, and I had to. I had to try and get away, and he kept coming, and. . .oh, there was blood everywhere. I don't think it's my blood. I think I stabbed him, two times maybe. He was limping when he was talking to me here. Oh, God. . .he was here, talking to me. He was standing right where you are. . ."

"Shhhh," Corb comforted her with a pat to the shoulder. "That's over. We're leaving, you hear?"

Britlyn's breathing became ragged again.

"We're gonna get the hell out of whatever this place is," Corb continued, "then my brother's gonna take you down the hill and right to Shawn, okay? He's been worried sick about you."

"Shawn?" she said feebly. "You know Shawn?"

"Of course, I do," he replied. "He's helped us with a lot of cases. We really appreciate having skills like that here in Cattail. Tell me, how did you two meet?"

While Britlyn was distracted by her explanation, Corb removed the IV and took stock of the room. For the first time, a cabinet full of computer servers caught his eye. *That explains the cooler temperature,* he thought. Nearby, a large desk held three slim monitors before a black, molded office chair. Above the screens, the glass lens of a small, round camera glimmered in the dim lighting of the room.

Corb wondered if they were being watched, and if so, how long it would take Amos to reach them.

"That's nice, Mrs. Robbins. Are you ready to go home?" he cut in.

"Yes," she confirmed. "Please hurry."

"Let's go." Corb put an arm around her, then helped her swing her legs over the edge of the bed. She winced, and he looked down. Unlike her left ankle, which was bony and slender, her right ankle had ballooned in size, and the skin was bruised purple and black.

"I think it happened at the house," she explained. "I had forgotten about it."

He sat up from the bed, then crouched next to her legs, evaluating the injury. "Doesn't look deformed, really."

"Gee, thanks," she huffed.

"I mean, I don't think it's broken," he assessed. "Could be a fracture. I can't tell here. But more than likely, a sprain. I mean, unless you can tell me you heard it pop?"

"I don't remember hearing anything," she admitted. "It happened so fast."

"We'll figure it out," he stated. "Just hold on tight."

With that, Corb reached under her legs and lifted the woman from the bed. Though pregnant, she was still light and easy to carry. He took one last glance around the room, then headed back towards the exposed, traditional area of the home and out the front door.

FOURTEEN.

Lizzie trekked along the game trail that skirted the main cluster of Anthem Hold's residences, her sweaty soles slipping in her Velcro-strap sandals as she attempted to dodge the thorny branches that gouged her suntanned, bare legs. She'd forgotten that the path to Rachel's included this detour if she wanted to avoid walking past the church and her parents' house.

Then again, she'd forgotten many things about Anthem Hold in the years since she'd called that place home. Some of the lost memories were bittersweet: she could not remember helping Mother plant the garden, or making mud pies with Rachel, or Father reading to the family at night. Others were a burden she was glad to release, and she had smiled when she realized she couldn't recall the church elders' names or the scent of Father's hot breath, or when she fumbled to piece together the layout of the compound.

Though she cursed him for subsequent events, she truly had Corbin to thank for helping her find the path to healing. While that strategy had also included more avoidance and alcohol than she cared to acknowledge, she was finally at a place in her life where she felt like she had found herself. The resulting wave of peace had dampened the noise of these past events, muffling this old life until Lizzie almost felt like she hadn't ever been anyone's child at all, but rose from the Palouse dust as a grown woman on her own.

Her own self. She'd never have to share herself again, unless she wanted to. Corb was careful to respect that, even despite Lizzie's eagerness to spend every night in his arms. For a while, she thought he'd been sent to save her, her own guardian angel in cowboy boots and Wrangler jeans.

Foolish girl. She'd almost lost herself again in the sorrow of being forsaken.

But He would not let her be tested beyond her strength. Lizzie had picked up the pieces and endured, putting one foot in front of the other until the nightmares ceased, and she could finally sleep before dawn. She had found a quiet life after Corb, minding her own affairs and working with her hands.

That is, until this morning, when he had sauntered up on his horse and spoken her name with the gall of a man who had never left. His familiar face and spirit stirred something inside her, and she'd been fighting it into submission since.

Similarly, the sight of her sister roused old memories she struggled to keep at bay. As she approached the back side of Rachel's property, she could see the woman in a bonnet wringing her hands with excitement. The gatekeeper said he would notify her of Lizzie's impending arrival, and Rachel must have known she'd come this way rather than up the main road.

Growing closer, Lizzie could see she was excited, but she was also crying. Unlike Lizzie's light turquoise eyes, Rachel had gotten Mother's warm brown color. Though Lizzie knew the tears in them now were due to joy and not fear, she couldn't help but be reminded of Rachel as a girl, wide-eyed and powerless as Father did his worst to both of them. In the near-pitch blackness of their family bedroom, Lizzie would search the darkness for the light reflecting in Rachel's brown eyes, then escape into them as if she were diving into a deep pool. While he took turns with the girls, the sisters would mentally climb the strands of each other's irises like rungs on a circular ladder until they'd reached a place of near catatonic detachment, immune to the ravages of real life. They had gone to war together, but they'd found refuge in that stare.

"Lizzie!" her sister cried with joy. "Oh, how I've missed you so!"

With that, Rachel threw her arms around her, and Lizzie shifted her thoughts, aching to remember the mud pies instead.

"It's been too long," Lizzie agreed, returning her embrace. As her arms fell, she brushed against a tiny body.

"Look at you!" Lizzie praised the small child hiding in the skirt of her mother's modest, navy cape dress. "You've grown like a weed!"

"Arleta, you might not remember your Aunt Lizzie — you were just a baby the last time she came. Can you say hi?" Rachel coaxed her.

The child grinned and blushed, turning her cheek.

"Micah?" Lizzie inquired as to Rachel's husband's whereabouts.

"He's in the fields. Took David with him. So, it's just us girls today," Rachel smiled. "We're making some strawberry jam, actually. Isn't that right, Leta?"

Lizzie kneeled by the child and spoke softly: "You know, strawberries are my favorite."

"Me, too," Leta whispered through little, square teeth. Suddenly, she raised her arms and looked at Lizzie expectantly.

"Not teaching her about stranger danger, I see," Lizzie joked. "Can I hold her?"

"Please," Rachel insisted. "You'll never be a stranger."

Lizzie sighed gratefully, then scooped the child up under her bottom and rested her on the curve of her hip. They started towards the house.

* * *

After they'd finished pouring the sweet, ruby concoction into jars, the women rocked on the porch in wooden chairs, sipping lemonade and watching Arleta and her young, slender cat chase butterflies through the grass.

"She's beautiful," Lizzie commented.

"She reminds me of you," Rachel noted. "I can hardly keep her in the house. . .she'd live outside if I let her," she chuckled.

"I suppose that sounds like me," Lizzie smirked.

"She likes to paint, too," Rachel shared. "Speaking of which, how's that going for you?"

"Great, actually," Lizzie answered. "I've got pieces on display in other states, even."

She nearly cringed as she said the last part aloud, feeling instantly boastful. "I mean. . ." she began to apologize.

Rachel raised her hand. "You're the best artist I know. It's okay to be proud of your work," she insisted. "I know I'm proud of you."

"Thank you," Lizzie managed. She bit her lip, trying to keep the rest in.

It was futile.

"You know," Lizzie began, "The few times I've been here, we didn't get a chance to talk alone. And I never got around to saying sorry."

Rachel gave her a puzzled look. "Sorry? Whatever for, dear?"

Lizzie swallowed. "For leaving you. Leaving you alone with Father. I never meant to make it worse for you," she apologized.

"I'm the oldest. . .it was me who should have been protecting you," Rachel lamented. "I'm the one who should be saying sorry."

"You were just a kid, too. It wasn't your job to protect me," Lizzie replied.

"Maybe not. But I'm thankful that boy stepped up to take care of you. To get you out," Rachel shared. "Besides, it still did me a favor. After you left, Father was so afraid they'd come for him, he finally stopped."

She suddenly stood and hollered at her young daughter to stay in sight, and a small head of bouncy, blonde curls came back into view.

As Rachel eased back into her rocker, she looked over at Lizzie.

"So, is that same boy your betrothed now?" she asked pointedly.

"What?" Lizzie furrowed her brow. "Oh, right," she mumbled, remembering the fib.

"There is no engagement, is there?" Rachel inquired. Lizzie sighed.

"Why are you really here?" Rachel continued.

Lizzie rolled her eyes. "It involves him, anyhow. My troubles always do."

"Last you wrote, you weren't speaking to one another," Rachel recalled.

"Yep," Lizzie confirmed. "Ten years. Then he shows up and wants my help with some sort of investigation."

"He's still a lawman after his accident?" Rachel asked.

"Apparently," Lizzie answered. "Anyhow, he's got his eye on Amos Sinclair for some wild accusations. He wanted to check things out, but he didn't have a way in. Except for hiding in my horse trailer."

"You brought one of your horses?" Rachel smiled.

"One of his, actually. The gatekeeper wouldn't let me take him out, or I would have ridden him here. The kids would have loved him — he's a gorgeous Appaloosa."

"Yes, they would have liked that," Rachel agreed. "I'm sorry things up here are that way. Some of the others. . . they don't see you like I do."

"Fuck 'em," Lizzie spit.

Rachel chuckled. "They'll never take your spirit from you, at least. Well, should we be worried? I mean, what kind of accusations?"

"I don't know. There's a missing lady in town. . .Corb thinks Amos might know something about her disappearance. He thinks Amos may have had some affections towards her. Following her online and such," Lizzie explained. "The less you know is probably better."

Rachel furrowed her brow. "You know, Micah mentioned how knowledgeable Amos was about that technology when he pitched the web site to the elders. Thought it was odd that he knew so much already. He embraced it so wholeheartedly."

"Corb thought so, too," Lizzie noted.

"There's another thing," Rachel lowered her voice to a whisper. "He has a cellular phone."

"What?" Lizzie's jaw dropped. "How do you know?"

"I went to the farm to buy some of his soap. Amos really does an excellent job with that. Anyhow, I could see him holding this shiny object, up on the hillside. At first, I thought it was some sort of spyglass. But then he held it to his ear. He was talking into it."

"Did he see you?"

"No," Rachel shook her head. "His mannerisms were very guarded. Very secretive. It made me concerned, so I snuck away. We started buying our soap from the Millers instead. I haven't been back since."

"Probably smart," Lizzie added. "You should lay low until we find out more. And don't talk about this. Not with anyone."

With that, Lizzie tilted her head way back, finishing the last of her lemonade. "I have to warn Corb about this business with the cell phone. I sorta brushed it off before, but...what if he's really in danger? What if Amos isn't who we think he is?"

"You still care for him," Rachel observed.

"No matter how hard I try," Lizzie conceded quietly.

Rachel put a hand on her shoulder. "I'm not going to try to talk to you out of it. Frankly, I don't think I could. But I will tell you to be careful," she cautioned.

Lizzie reached up and squeezed her hand. "I will," she promised. As she got to her feet, she waved at the little girl, who had moved on from butterfly-chasing to swinging a faceless, cloth doll.

"Micah is gentle with them?" Lizzie asked.

"Leta is the apple of his eye. And David is his constant companion. He'd never lay a finger on them. Or let anyone else," Rachel assured her.

Lizzie nodded. "Good. Love you, Rachel."

Rachel stood, then leaned in and kissed her forehead. "Love you, little sister."

Lizzie pulled her sunglasses down and returned through the pasture to the game trail, tracing it back the way she came. As her feet pounded against the dirt, she pondered her sister's assurances.

Father stopped, she told her. The relief was immense, and it helped salve the old, nagging guilt Lizzie still carried from leaving her sister behind. Of course, by the time of her own rescue, she had sunken into such a pit of despair and hopelessness that she had been blinded by her survival instincts when presented with an opportunity to escape. Only after she was safe with Corbin did she realize she'd left a wounded soldier on the battlefield to fight their war alone. To his credit, Uncle Jack had flexed law enforcement muscle on the complex in the months that followed Lizzie's escape, sending social workers and police to conduct welfare checks at random. Unfortunately, they couldn't stick Father with charges unless the girls testified. She'd elected to leave that decision to Rachel, who declined. Instead, shortly thereafter, Rachel married Micah, and the family's shameful history had remained buried ever since.

As the vacant lot came into view, Lizzie was interrupted by the sight of her horse trailer, which was now open. It was empty.

"You fucking idiot," she cursed Corb aloud.

* * *

Outside, Corb surveyed the hillside and the Sinclair farm below, noting no signs of movement.

"Alright," he began. "Sit tight. I've gotta check something real quick."

He carefully seated Britlyn against the rock exterior of the home, and she closed her eyes, clearly relishing the sun on her face. He withdrew his cell from his pocket, checking for reception.

Finding none, he pocketed his phone and pulled his pistol instead, ascending higher up the mountain while still keeping an eye on the property. About a hundred yards up, he clambered up a large rock, then stood at its highest point and checked his phone again.

Relieved to find service, he quickly dialed Cam, who answered on the first ring.

"Hey, I've got one bar towards the top of the mountain here," Corb told his brother. "And I've got something else, too."

"Our vic?" Cam asked excitedly.

"Mrs. Robbins, alive and well," Corb confirmed. "As well as she could be, anyhow. Sprained her ankle hashing it out with Amos at the house, but not a scratch on her, besides. Babies are good, too."

"So, the blood was all his," Cam concluded.

"She says he's still limping around from his injuries," Corb revealed.

"I know. We saw him at the Farmer's Market," Cam confirmed.

Corb looked at his watch. "He headed back here yet, you think?"

"Probably. But so are we — Judge Schwartz just signed the warrant," Cam informed him.

"Warrant?" Corb asked, puzzled. "Based on what probable cause?"

"Based on Ramón says he heard a woman screaming right before a horse and carriage drove by the house," Cam began.

"My Ramón? I thought he spilled all the beans to me, I swear—" Corb interrupted.

"He meant to," Cam resumed. "He put it together after he mulled things over a bit. He thought it was the horse making noises at first. . .Amos was whipping on it pretty good."

"Trying to hightail it outta there," Corb figured. "How'd you get a warrant all pieced together already?"

"Baby Rob's been down here helping us out," Cam explained. "Making sure we're not going to have any weak spots for some damn public defender to poke holes in his case."

"Fucking Baby Rob," Corb beamed.

"Yep. But that's not all," Cam added.

"Let me guess, Amos is some sort of cyber freak up to all kinds of no-good shenanigans?" Corb asked.

"Yeah, you could say that. FBI's chomping at the bit to get their hands on him once Mrs. Robbins is in the clear. Apparently, he's been on their wanted list for a long time. Dark web activities. Something about him remotely accessing evidence, then erasing it all from existence. They call him Amnesia."

"*Amnesia?*" Corb repeated skeptically. "And who gets paid to make that shit up?"

"It sounds like that's what he goes by online."

"It sounds like he should be wearing tights and a mask."

"I said the same thing. But it's all they had: this is the first time they've tied him to a real identity," Cam explained. "They were looking in all the wrong places. . . they're pretty surprised to find him out here."

"Can't blame 'em. I can't even believe this is the same person," Corb chewed his bottom lip. "He's got this fucking house dug into the hill like a cave. Back where I found her, there's a whole other setup, like its own apartment. Kinda decorated modern, like hers. Smells like hers. He even took one of her cups. But listen to this: the entire office area is metal. Metal walls, metal ceiling. Even the floor. Got all his tech stuff inside."

"A Faraday cage," Cam observed.

"Yeah. I guess so," Corb agreed. "Some of it looks familiar, like pieces from other crime scenes. He's got prosthetics. And fake beards. It's crazy, brother. Really disturbing shit."

"Guess we'll have to piece that together, too. You two able to get out of there alright?" Cam asked.

"I'll carry her the whole way if I have to," Corb answered.

"Good. Go, then," Cam instructed. "Amos. . . Amnesia. . .could get to you before we do."

"I know it. And I doubt he'll be feeling cheerful about the reunion," Corb concluded. "We're on our way."

Corb slipped his phone into his pocket once more, then plodded back down through the grass towards the house. Britlyn appeared to be napping, and he felt a twinge of guilt for waking her. He firmly but kindly squeezed her hand, and she began to stir.

"Mrs. Robbins? I hate disturbing your rest, but we've got another leg to this trip," he informed her.

She blinked the sleep from her eyes, nodding groggily.

Corb reached under her legs, lifting her body towards his chest.

"Here," he offered. "Just lay right there on my shoulder."

As Corb strode past the farm and crossed into the wooded area, Britlyn closed her eyes again, succumbing to the calm relief of safety.

FIFTEEN.

"Walk up the ramp and towards me. Quickly and quietly. Or I'll blow your pretty little brains out."

For a moment, Lizzie stood speechless and paralyzed at the entry to her horse trailer. She thought the man hiding inside seemed familiar, but her brain glossed over those details, focusing instead on the weapon in his hand.

Amos cocked the gun.

"And your boyfriend's, too," he threatened. "Let's move."

"Amos," she whispered as she put a name to his face. She studied him as she slowly stepped forward with her hands half-raised in surrender. She had seen him a handful of times around town, but he had been mostly seated on his carriage or leaning against the table in his booth at the Farmer's Market. This close, she became aware of his large stature and bone structure, which made him formidable despite his lack of muscle mass. When she reached his outstretched arm, she stopped.

"Sit," he instructed.

Keeping her sights on his gun, Lizzie crouched down, nestling into the pine shavings.

"Where is he?" Amos asked.

"Who?" Lizzie played dumb.

"I don't have time for your stupid games," he hissed. "Corbin McNulty. I know he's here with you."

"I don't know what you're talking about, Amos," she responded. "I was here to see Rachel."

"Bullshit," he snorted.

"Ask the gatekeeper," Lizzie replied.

"Or maybe I ask Rachel, huh? Maybe see if she knows something?" Amos threatened.

Lizzie stewed quietly.

"Maybe her little ones know something?" he continued. "David and. . .Arleta, is it?"

"You wouldn't," Lizzie gasped.

"I would," he insisted menacingly. "I'll ask you again. Where is Corbin?"

"How dare you," she squinted at Amos. "Me and Rachel went through the same shit as you. Worse."

"Old news," Amos shrugged. "You think that makes us comrades? Pals?"

"It makes us something, doesn't it?" Lizzie pleaded. "We were good to you. Good to Adam. We played together as kids, for crying out loud. Now you're telling me you're going to go after her family?"

Amos blinked, struggling to hide the conflicting emotions behind his pale eyes.

"You left, Lizzie. Don't talk to me like you're still part of the Hold."

"Of course, I left! Do you remember what they did to me? Do you even know?" Lizzie asked in an exasperated tone.

"I know," he acknowledged sheepishly. He lowered his gun, but he continued to grip it firmly.

"You didn't have to come back after your Reflection. And you don't have to stay now. Whatever you've got going on with this lady. . ." Lizzie trailed off.

Amos smirked. "So, you are working with Corbin on this."

She sighed. "I know it's only a matter of time before they find her. And you."

"I highly doubt that," Amos sneered. "No one will find us when we get on our way."

"And where's that?" Lizzie asked.

"You got out. I've been finding my way out, too. A little at a time," Amos revealed. "Though, mine will be a far more successful escape than yours. I've got a real paradise. I'll be watching the waves, while you — well, you barely made it down the mountain," he scoffed.

"Yeah. Well, that's my paradise," Lizzie defended.

"Even without your white knight, huh?" Amos taunted.

Lizzie glared at him, seething. "Fuck you."

"I used to think he was tough. Turns out he can't even take a bullet," Amos carried on. "Folks say it messed him up in the head. Or else, you did," he said coldly.

"What's it to you?" she spit. "I don't have anything to do with this. Let me go."

"Oh, I will. Just as soon as I'm sure Corbin isn't leaving here with anything of mine," he assured her.

"I'm not sure why you think I can help you accomplish that. I haven't talked to Corb in years," she maintained.

"That doesn't mean he's over you," Amos countered. "I'll bet he thinks about you more than you realize. Wishes he was back in the good ol' days. . ."

"You don't know what you're talking about," Lizzie frowned.

"You'd be surprised," Amos asserted.

"You're spying on him, then?"

"I have my ways," he said flatly. "Anyhow, he'll gladly trade your safety for dropping this case. Then we'll split, and my lady and I will be airborne in ten. Never to be seen again."

"And if he doesn't?" Lizzie asked.

Amos tapped his gun against the leg of his charcoal, woolen pants. He smiled.

Lizzie suddenly shot up and hurled towards him, releasing fistfuls of pine shavings as she barreled towards his face. She sunk a punch in his gut just before he managed to catch the side of her head with the hard apex of his elbow, sending shocks down her neck and spine and darkening her peripheral vision.

She fell backwards, settling onto the floor once again. Amos staggered forward until he hovered above her. She blinked, attempting to focus as she stared up towards him. In one hand, Amos clutched his ribs. In the other, he held the gun.

Lizzie raised her own hand to her face, noticing a sticky substance clinging to her knuckles. She wondered where she was bleeding from.

No, she realized, watching Amos's shoulders heave as he gasped for breath.

Amos's blood.

Through the small, side windows, sunlight poked in. For a moment, it reflected off the metallic barrel Amos raised towards her.

Then, everything went black.

* * *

As they drew nearer to the last cluster of foliage and trees obscuring the dusty parking area, Corb recognized a tan figure meandering through the brush.

"*Huck!*" he hissed in the animal's direction.

Huckleberry perked his ears, then suddenly stopped, awaiting further directions.

"That yours?" Britlyn inquired.

Corbin paused to gently lower Britlyn down and set her on her feet. "Yeah, he is. But he shouldn't be out."

"Uh-oh. You don't think he jumped out of his cage?" she pondered aloud.

City folks. Corb fought the urge to shake his head.

"We don't keep horses in cages, Mrs. Robbins. But no, he wasn't in a stall or corral. He was in his trailer."

"How'd he escape, then?" she continued.

"That is a very good question." Corb frowned. Leaving Britlyn leaning against a nearby stump, he walked towards the horse.

Huckleberry greeted his master by lowering his head and nickering. Corb patted his neck, then stroked his hand down his sides, inspecting the horse. Huck couldn't have fought his way out without a struggle, but he appeared completely unharmed.

Corb bit his lip, thinking. *Hadn't he locked the door behind him?*

"Is everything alright?" Britlyn called, nervously and a little too loudly.

Corb nodded, then quickly put his finger to his lips, warning her to be quiet. As he reached for Huck's lead, he remembered securing it to a tie loop inside the trailer. Yes, he'd quietly slipped past, careful to latch the door as he stepped off into the dirt.

"How *did* you get out, buddy?" he whispered, pulling Huck towards Britlyn's location. He withdrew his cell phone from his pocket once again.

SEARCHING FOR SERVICE, the screen informed him.

Corb glanced at the time. Lizzie wasn't due to meet him for another twenty minutes, but Britlyn needed a medical assessment; she reported that the girls were moving, but without knowing for sure what Amos had dosed her with, they couldn't know the possible effects. He needed to move quickly.

He pictured the red pickup, then wondered if Lizzie still kept a spare key in a magnetic box tucked under the lip of the bed on the driver's side. He could rush out of Anthem Hold and head towards town, meet law enforcement and EMTs en route, then hurry back to grab Lizzie. It would shave precious minutes.

Lizzie would exit her sister's house and walk the long, dirt path back to the entry gates, only to find her truck and her horse trailer missing.

She'd be livid, of course.

But she'd already been livid with him for nearly ten years. *What's another twenty minutes?*

He cleared his throat. "Mrs. Robbins, you're about to become a real Idahoan today."

"How do you figure?" she asked skeptically.

"You ever been on a horse?"

"Ha! Um, no," she answered. "They're terrifying."

"This here's Huckleberry," he introduced the animal. "And he's going to take us the rest of the way, alright?"

"No. No, I can't," she pleaded.

"Ain't nothing terrifying about ol' Huck," Corb insisted. "He's a big baby. A lover. Besides, I'm gonna be right behind you, okay?"

Britlyn blinked tears from her eyes.

"Unless you want to walk the rest of the way on that ankle," Corb pressed. "This is going to be the fastest way. Let me give you a boost."

After a moment, Britlyn nodded, and Corb took her good foot in his stacked palms, then hoisted her up. Britlyn grimaced as she swung her swollen ankle over the horse, then fearfully squeezed his ribs between her knees, clutching his mane in her hands. Corb followed behind, jumping on Huckleberry's bare back and snugging up against Britlyn.

"Good. Now, we're just a short ride away from where we need to be. We'll get to the truck, then we'll hit the road, then you'll be home safe before you even know it, alright?"

She let out a long exhale. "Okay."

"How're those babies doing, Mrs. Robbins?"

Britlyn swept circles over her belly with her hands, and Corb could feel her breathing slow as their movement soothed her.

"They're good, they're good," she answered.

"You know, if they were any bigger, you'd be riding sidesaddle. Like the Virgin Mary on a donkey," he chuckled.

She let out an easy laugh.

"Alright. Here we go."

* * *

As the horse trailer came into view, Corb could see the ramp extended out the back of the open rear doors.

He racked his brain, trying to piece things together.

Did Lizzie not latch them properly?

Did the tie come loose?

Did Huck somehow kick them open?

"Well, he just walked right out," Britlyn remarked, noticing the open trailer. "Maybe it wasn't shut all the way."

"You know, Mrs. Robbins, I bet you're exactly right," he responded. As he brought Huck to a halt and slid from the steed's back, he reached up to her with a smile. "Nothing to worry about."

She smiled back and allowed him to help her down from the horse, clearly comforted by his pleasant demeanor.

It was good — he needed her to be calm. But on the inside, Corb's apprehension was growing. He approached the trailer cautiously, scanning the enclosure for signs of foul play. It was empty, and the metal exterior bore only the typical scratches and dings he'd expect from normal use.

Corb swiveled his head back towards the entry gates, squinting to catch a glimpse of the gatekeeper. That asshole made it clear he was no fan of Lizzie's.

Maybe he let Huck out?

He turned back to Britlyn. "Let's get you in the truck," he insisted.

"I can do it. I just wanna get home," she pleaded. "As fast as we can."

"Alright, then. Should be unlocked. You think you can hobble on over to that side there while I get this beast loaded up?" he asked her.

She nodded, then began to limp towards the passenger door.

Taking his lead, Corb guided Huck up into the trailer, stepping alongside him until they'd reached the front. He tied the horse once again, looping his lead into a quick-release knot. Then, he secured the side door and finally latched the double doors at the back.

Corb rounded the trailer, resting his hands on the truck's bed. They'd bought the red Silverado used, figuring the few thousand miles on its engine was a small sacrifice for the huge amount it knocked off the brand-new price tag. Corb had been working at the jail as a detention deputy for years by then, and Lizzie had finally begun turning a profit boarding horses at the cabin. While they'd appreciated Uncle Jack loaning them his old farm truck when they needed to haul hay or horses, they needed something dependable for daily use. They scoured the classified ads in the local paper for months before Lizzie herself found the handsome truck, a 2006 model which still bore the broad nose and classic shape of the old body style. With a slight lift and tinted windows, the red rig was sharp. Even better, the large crew cab would accommodate a growing family when the time came.

She traded in her old Subaru, and they both enjoyed a good laugh on the porch that night at the sight of her new ride dwarfing his light-duty pickup. Later, they'd christened the back seat. It was an early spring evening, the first nice one of the year. With the windows down, the fresh, cool air had made its way into the cab and encircled them, potent with the scent of damp earth and wet, green grass finally freed from the icy grip of a long

Idaho winter. As he'd nuzzled into her neck, that bouquet mingled with the floral notes of her soft perfume.

Did she still wear it now?

Corb suddenly caught up with his runaway thoughts. He blinked them away, refocusing on the present moment.

The key.

He patted the truck, shaking his head. It was now fitted with a tonneau cover, which was rolled tightly shut over the bed. He began to pull it back, revealing an assortment of art supplies. It had been almost ten years — she was a different person, with a different career and a different life. A different mindset, a different outlook. He blamed himself for that.

And probably, he guessed, *a different hiding place for her spare key.*

Nonetheless, he reached under the cover, running his fingers under the lip of the truck's bed. To his surprise, in the far corner on the driver's side, he easily located the small, magnetic box.

Relieved, he rolled the cover closed again, then quickly pulled open the driver's door, hopping up into the seat.

* * *

Inside the truck, he pulled the door closed and began to reach down to adjust the seat, the present position of which had his knees jammed up into the steering wheel, a testament to Lizzie's shorter stature. He looked over at his passenger, who had apparently hoisted herself into the vehicle alright despite her sprained ankle.

Her dark brown eyes were wide with fear. Corb frowned, puzzled.

Before he had a chance to open his mouth, a raspy voice greeted him from the back seat: "Hello, Corbin."

He quickly spun around, and his heart began to thump violently against his ribs like a wild animal waking in a cage. In one calloused hand, Amos cupped Lizzie's mouth and chin tightly, clutching her head against the suspenders at his chest. In the other, he held a sleek handgun, a cool, steel piece with modern styling that clashed against the man's own plain and old-fashioned appearance. The muzzle was buried in the mass of blonde curls at her right temple, which was caked with blood.

"You motherfucker—" Corb fumed. He was interrupted by laughter, a dry chuckle that bolted from Amos's throat and filled the air with unease.

"Still a hothead, I see," Amos remarked. "Keep it in check, Detective. This here's loaded."

With every bit of will he possessed, Corb bit his tongue.

"Smart choice. Now, I see that you have trespassed onto my property and stolen something that belongs to me," Amos advised.

"It ain't 'capture the flag', Amos. You can't just sneak into a person's house and snatch 'em up. She's got a life of her own."

"That right? And what exactly is it you think you did to this one?" Amos asked, gesturing towards Lizzie with a nod. "Don't lecture me about staking a claim."

"That was different," Corb explained cautiously. "That was extracting her from a bad situation."

"You were in love with her," Amos argued. "And I'm banking on the fact you still are."

Corb met Lizzie's eyes. *It was true.* Even as a boy, he loved her dearly. But he'd only stolen her away from the sect after she showed him lashings so deep, he could still feel the ropy scars stretching over her skin several years later. The beatings alone were horrific, but then she'd detailed how her father would often crawl into the girls' shared bed – for warmth, he insisted. Then, he would wait until their mother fell asleep to enact whatever sordid fantasies he harbored with the two young girls. Though her mother slept in the same room, when she ultimately woke up and saw what was happening, she didn't save them. No, she simply rolled over and shut her eyes.

"Lizzie," he had told her candidly, "I don't even remember my Mom and Dad. But I'd rather have no parents at all than parents like yours." As she sobbed in his arms in the middle of the rusty, old boat, Corb came to the conclusion that he would be the one to save her instead. And he'd made good on the promise, even after they were apart.

Until now.

Corb took a deep breath.

"Whatever happened with Lizzie and I . . . was different," he explained to Amos. "We were kids. And you know how they treated her. How they treated a lot of you."

Amos glared at him, saying nothing.

Corb continued, attempting to soften the man's demeanor. "How they treated Adam. Or didn't treat him at all. I know you wanted more for him, too."

"You weren't wrong to take her away from here," Amos conceded. "You gave her a real shot at life. I can see that. But that's all I'm trying to do. To take us somewhere away from it all, somewhere with a fresh start."

"This is not the same, Amos — Mrs. Robbins isn't a teenage girl. She's married. She's pregnant, for Chrissakes. She needs medical care."

"And she'll have it. We have everything we need where we're going. Everything we could want," Amos assured him.

"What she wants is to go home," Corb informed him pointedly. "To get back to her family."

"I'm her family now!" Amos suddenly hissed. His breathing was ragged. As Amos's chest heaved, Corb noticed that his skin exhibited a grayish cast, and the whites of his eyes were a creamy yellow.

Corb thought of the letter opener and the blood coating the eight or so inches between its tip and hilt.

"That blade stuck deep, didn't it?" Corb concluded. "You're gonna go septic without proper treatment."

"We'll have treatment when we get there," Amos insisted.

"Shit, you may already be septic. . ."

"I said no," Amos grit his teeth angrily. He cocked the gun against Lizzie's head, and she closed her eyes tightly, trembling. "Time's up."

"Okay, alright!" Corb quickly interjected. "Alright. What do you want me to do?"

"I propose a trade," Amos tendered. "Your girl for mine."

"Done," Corb agreed.

"Are you kidding me?" Britlyn began to cry. "I trusted you!"

"You can still trust me," Corb promised. "I am going to get you home."

"Corb, don't!" Lizzie spurted out, breaking her mouth free of Amos's fingers. He repositioned his grip, muffling her continued protests.

Corb raised a hand. "He won't get far."

"Don't lie to them. I'll be taking the truck," Amos smugly informed him.

"Go ahead," Corb retorted. "But leave my horse."

Amos sneered. "You can keep your animal. You won't catch us."

Corb nodded, then carefully reached for the handle of the driver door. He walked Huck out, then quickly unhitched the trailer. Then, he returned to the cab.

Amos pushed Lizzie out the back door, still squeezing her skull between his sweaty grip on her hair and the muzzle of the pistol in his other hand.

"Throw your gun down," he instructed Corb. "Off to the side."

Corb complied, then showed his empty palms. "Your girl for mine, Amos. I've been easy on you. Now let her go."

Amos shoved Lizzie forward in the dirt, and she struggled to catch herself. Instead, she caught a face full of dust. Amos kept the gun trained on her, then inched backwards toward the truck.

"Point it at me, coward," Corb demanded. "She doesn't have anything to do with this."

Amos complied, raising the gun until Corb was staring down the barrel.

"This feel familiar to you?" Amos taunted him, gesturing towards his scars.

Corb laughed. "You think you're the only one who got dealt a shitty hand in this life? Standing behind that gun doesn't put you in charge. You're still just along for the ride."

"I could kill you right now," Amos threatened.

"Will it help, Amos? Go ahead, then. Leave the girls, take me, and kill me however you want."

Amos shifted uncomfortably. "You don't understand."

"Oh, I understand perfectly," Corb insisted. "So would she," he nodded at Lizzie. "Life fucked you, and you want to get even. But it doesn't justify this."

Amos scowled. Beads of sweat dripped from his brow into his eyes, yet he shivered in the hot sun.

"It isn't going to bring your brother back," Corb added cautiously.

Before he could reply, Amos abruptly lowered the gun as his arm collapsed under its weight. Quickly, he shuffled out of Corb's reach and into the truck. As he shut the driver door and began to accelerate, Corb rushed forward, squeezing Lizzie under the arms and pulling her to her feet.

"You idiot!" she began to shout, watching the truck drive away. The tears and sweat across her dusty skin streaked her face with trails of mud. "I told you not to do this! He'll kill her!" She swung at him.

Corb blocked her punch, then wrapped her tightly around the shoulders, keeping her flailing fists at bay.

"I don't think so," he replied. "He's in love with her. But he might have killed you." He nodded towards her head wound.

"So? You show up out of the blue and suddenly you care about my life? I don't need your fucking protection!" she continued, her voice grating with growing intensity.

"Hey," he soothed.

She struggled against him.

Corb pulled her closer, forcing her to raise her chin and look up into his dark, sage eyes.

"It's always been about protecting you, Lizzie," he confessed. "Even from me. Even if it meant I had to lose you."

With his explanation, her anger broke, and her arms fell to her sides. Corb released her shoulders, moving his hands up to cradle her head in his fingers. With his thumbs, he gently swept the mud from her cheeks. Lizzie sighed and reached towards him, hooking her fingers on his arm. She closed her eyes and pressed her face into his hand, brushing her lips against his palm.

Corb could feel the pulse at his wrist throb under her touch. This close, her familiar, floral smell was unmistakable and intense. *The same perfume.* It filled his nose and then imprinted on his brain, deciphering his distant, jumbled memories of her until they were clear and close once again.

"I have to go," he suddenly realized, breaking his trance.

Lizzie opened her eyes. "You'll never catch them."

He dropped his hands to her shoulders, offering a soft squeeze. Then, he hurried towards Huck. "I don't have to catch them," he called back over his shoulder. "I just have to stop them."

She looked around the lot, empty save for her vacant horse trailer. "And what the hell am I supposed to do?" she asked.

"Get to cell service and call Cam," he shouted as he pulled himself onto the horse. "Tell him to hurry."

SIXTEEN.

Accompanied by the reassuring rhythm of his horse's steady hoofbeats, Corb descended the mountainside. From that perch, the Palouse below him stretched out like a desert, its wispy wheat tips softened at this distance so that the rolling hills resembled dunes of sunlit sand. From Anthem Hold, the road corkscrewed down the mountain until it reached the fields and joined the main road that bisected them. In one direction, it then continued to the highway between Idaho and Washington. The other direction carried on towards the river.

Having roamed the terrain as a child, Corb knew from experience that Amos was right: he wouldn't catch him on a horse. No, without following the road, the area was too rocky and too steep to ride an animal safely and quickly enough to reach the bottom before Amos's vehicle could.

Instead, Corb cut diagonally across the hillside towards the neighboring property, a small ranch of sorts belonging to Randall "Rabble" Anderson. The Vietnam veteran had inherited the property from his father, and his father had from his own father before that. Aside from some Forest Service facilities, it was the only other part of the mountain that had been developed.

Rabble's property stretched from midmountain all the way down to the fields below, even including within its borders part of the river and a neighboring creek that ran through Lizzie's property. She and Corb had bought the ten-acre parcel from Rabble years ago — he'd saved all his earnings to cover the majority of the cost, then paid the remainder by baling hay and bailing Rabble out of jail. Corb was sure that, having feuded with the sect at Anthem Hold for all the decades of his life, Rabble was tickled pink to see Lizzie settled on his land, just close enough to the religious compound to rub it in their faces.

After he'd gotten to know Rabble a little better, he began to realize the real reason for the bargain on the property wasn't spite, it was sorrow: as a young man, Rabble had been married to a beautiful lady like Lizzie, with a spirit as tenacious as her blond curls. When she didn't want to share him with his demons, she left, and he'd lived alone on the ranch ever since. Now, he paid her reparations to Lizzie instead, helping her plow snow and frequently loaning her his farming equipment.

The Anderson Ranch was fenced with old posts and barbed wire, which was slack in places but still kept its owner's fifty or so cattle adequately contained. As Corb slowed to a trot just inside the "A" archway, the cows stopped chewing long enough to lazily raise their heads, then resumed their grazing. At the end of the dirt driveway, Rabble was shirtless on the porch of the two-story farmhouse, sucking on what looked like the remains of a joint and leaning against a white, wooden column where he proudly displayed a large, yellow rattlesnake flag. On the other side of the steps, he flew the traditional Old Glory.

Underneath the sparse white hair of his bony chest, what must have once been a crisp, black military tattoo was now faded and a livid gray, as if it were comprised not of ink, but veins. His abdomen and shoulders still exhibited a surprising amount of tone, and his tan skin had yet to accede to the pale, crepey demands of senescence. This used to surprise Corb, but he'd grown to believe that Rabble was somehow preserved by some divine combination of Vietnam-era tactical herbicides and his daily intake of rotgut liquor. He had a notorious penchant for two-dollar well whiskey and the twenty-something-year-old waitresses that wielded it; Corb had found the latter draped around the railings of Rabble's wraparound porch, recovering, on many a weekend morning. Yes, Rabble was most well-known for his wild Friday and Saturday night gatherings, raucous parties that usually involved at least one topless woman and a slew of Rabble's cronies drunkenly discharging firearms into the hillside to a soundtrack of honkytonk melodies.

As Corbin drew closer, Rabble took one last drag of the marijuana cigarette, then tucked it up towards his palm.

"This here's medicinal," he insisted with a smile, blowing the skunky smoke into the dry summer air.

"I'm sure it is," Corb rolled his eyes. "But I'm not worried about the weed, Rab."

"You want some?" Rabble offered.

Corb shook his head. "I need your help."

"Suit yourself. I don't work on Sabbath day," Rabble informed him.

"That would be tomorrow," Corb countered.

"Not for me. I'm Jewish," Rabble shrugged.

"Since when?" Corb scoffed.

"Since Saturday's a better day off." Rabble pulled out his joint again, puffing away.

"It has to do with your neighbors," Corb continued. "One of 'em got a screw loose and kidnapped some lady. Lizzie, too."

Rabble raised his eyebrows, standing upright. "Our Lizzie? Is she alright?"

"She is now," Corb reassured him.

Rabble exhaled with relief.

"But he's still got one hostage, and he's on the move," Corb added.

"If you ask me, they've all got a screw loose," Rabble grumbled, ambling down the stairs and scraping his joint in the dirt, snuffing its glowing tip. "What do you need from me?"

"You trust me?" Corb asked him pointedly.

Rabble smirked, crossing his arms. "Marginally. I mean, more than any other government agent."

"Good. Grab a horse," Corb instructed.

"Shit," Rabble ascended the steps, reaching just inside the front door to retrieve a hat and a pair of well-worn cowboy boots. "You got a plan, boy?"

"Think so," Corb nodded, looking down the grassy slope of the Anderson property. "You're not gonna like it. But I'm pretty sure it ends with my uncle buying you a new fence."

Rabble chuckled. "Count me in, then."

* * *

You've reached Lieutenant Camden McNulty. If this is an emergency, please call 911—

For the third time since being met with the voice mail greeting, Lizzie hung up the phone. She'd jogged the approximate mile down to the former Forest Service lookout, which was situated in a clearing off the edge of the steep hillside. She climbed the large rocks leading to its steps, then rested in the shade under the eaves while she attempted to reach Cam.

Taking a deep breath, she began to dial again, this time a different number.

"McNulty," the older man answered.

"Jack." Lizzie exhaled, relieved.

"Lizzie?" he checked, the concern in his voice mounting as he spoke the last syllable.

"It's me," she confirmed.

"Where are you? Is Corbin with you?"

"Not anymore. He went after Amos," she informed him. "I'm at Mineral Lookout. I ran down here from Anthem Hold as fast as I could."

"You found Amos?" Jack asked worriedly.

"He found us," Lizzie corrected. "Well, he found *me*, actually. Clocked me in the head with his pistol, then held me at gunpoint in my truck 'til Corb got back from his place with that missing lady."

"Oh, Lizzie. Are you alright?"

"I'm fine. She's not; Corb traded with Amos for me," she stated, failing to hide her vexation. "If anything happens to her—"

"Of course, he did. Amos is a lot more likely to hurt you," Jack interrupted, defending his nephew's reasoning. "And Corb's not going to let that happen."

"Can you find him?" As she spoke, Lizzie grew unsteady and leaned against the lookout's old, wraparound windows. She realized she was shaking.

"I can try. Amos still got your truck?"

"Yeah," she replied. "Asshole."

"And Corb?"

"He's on Huck. It looked like he was headed towards Rabble's, maybe."

"Okay. That's good, Lizzie." Jack had picked up on her rattled demeanor, and he was now speaking in a more soothing tone. "Help me out. Where's Amos going?"

"I don't know." She closed her eyes, and tears began to well behind them. "Far away. Another country."

"Canada, maybe?" Jack tried. "That ain't but a couple hours."

"No. Somewhere by the water. I think he's going to the airport," she managed to recall, trying to piece together their conversation while also struggling to forget the sensation of the handgun's muzzle tight against her temple. "A private jet, maybe."

"We've got someone at the airport already," Jack assured her. "They've gone through the hangars. There's nothing."

"Well, that's what he said. That he was going to the airport. I don't know." Lizzie let the tears stream down her cheeks.

"Were those his exact words?"

"Um," she cleared her throat. "Um. . ."

"I need you to think, Lizzie," Jack pressed.

"Okay," she agreed, breathing deeply again. "What he said was, 'we'll be airborne in ten minutes.' I figured, that's gotta be the airport."

"Ten minutes? You're sure he said ten minutes?"

"I'm sure," Lizzie responded.

"From Anthem Hold?"

"Uh-huh."

"He's not going to the airport. Airport's a half hour minimum, even if he's hauling ass. He's got a private plane stashed on that mountain somewhere," Jack concluded.

"Shit," Lizzie muttered, letting the possibility sink in. "He's in no shape to fly, Jack. And worse by the minute," she revealed. "Even if he gets off the ground. . ."

"We'll stop him before they take off," Jack pledged. "You stay put. Once I've got Corb in radio range, I'm sending him your way, alright?"

"Just keep him safe," she pleaded.

"Always. And Lizzie?" Jack added.

"Yeah?" she managed.

"It's good to hear your voice again."

* * *

As Amos descended the winding road, his hands naturally adjusted the truck's steering wheel to follow each bend. He imagined that learning to drive was a lot like learning to ride a bike; a skill that, once acquired, would never be forgotten.

He'd never learned to ride, of course, but he did know how to drive. On his Reflection, he had purchased his first vehicle, a light blue, compact truck with oxblood rust that had chewed its smooth edges until they were lacy and sharp. During that time period, it was a permissible purchase, and he'd used the vehicle to shuttle back and forth between his job at the fertilizer plant and the basement room he rented from an old lady in Moscow. The same day he bought it, he took the old pickup out onto the back roads, mastering steering, signaling, and stopping without the impediment and potential danger of other traffic. Since then, he had collected half a dozen other vehicles, from sexy convertibles to Euro-styled, compact SUVs, and stationed them at his various properties. He had yet to drive them, but like a child admiring a diecast car in his palm, he enjoyed having them, nonetheless.

What he was truly looking forward to, however, was purchasing a bicycle like the ones he and Adam used to talk about when they were kids. *A yellow bike*, Adam would excitedly whisper, *with lightning bolts on the frame, and great big tires!* Of course, it was just a dream — like most other technology, pedal power was prohibited by the sect, and the boys were restricted from riding. Amos recalled jealously watching his schoolmates, including the McNulty brothers, cruising around on two wheels. Some laughed as they passed the Anthem Hold children, who were clad in plain clothes and shoes and condemned to walking.

In Maldives, he would have a bike, he silently promised himself. And in a few years, he'd buy two little pink bikes, and he and the girls would glide through beachside towns, feeling the breeze in their hair and the smooth, pristine pavement below their tires. Britlyn would marvel at his patience as he guided their girls along, gently supporting their backs until they could balance all on their own.

He looked over at her now. Britlyn's eyelashes had disappeared into the surrounding puffy, purple lids, and her head hung as she watched the mountain slip past. She had given up sniveling, instead allowing the mixture of snot and tears to drip down her chin and soak her neckline. He looked away, repulsed not by her miserable appearance, but by her hasty resignation. After she'd discovered him in her office, he'd hoped she would embrace the situation, but at least her attempts to escape it were fierce. Now, that fiery spark was gone, replaced by a glassy vacancy in her eyes and limp hands that hung over her belly, rather than caressing it as before.

He should have been gladdened by her apparent acceptance, but instead, he felt mounting uncertainty.

Amos grit his teeth, mulling over the younger McNulty's words. *What if he was right? What if she didn't grow to love him?* Amos was met by a jumble of intrusive thoughts, each offering a violent but neat way to tie up loose ends. He'd thought of killing her when things previously went awry — why not just dispatch her after the girls' birth? Time and experience had shown him it was an efficient way to handle his business. He pictured the crusty, black remains of his childhood home. Once he set the trap, all he had to do was wait for the first cool night: someone lit a fire in the woodstove, and the rest took care of itself. By the time they located Amos and brought him to the scene, his parents' bodies had been whisked away, never to trouble him again.

But this was different, he admitted. In Amos's mind, they had chosen a death sentence when they handed one down to Adam, and they deserved what he gave them.

Britlyn suddenly sighed and leaned her head against the glass, closing her eyes. For a moment, with her petite frame, she resembled a child, and Amos felt a twinge of guilt. He couldn't punish her for simply failing to return his affections. . .*could he?*

As they rounded the next corner, the steering wheel shook in his hands.

Or else, his hands were shaking the steering wheel.

Amos reflected again on Corbin's warnings, this time focusing on the latter. *You're gonna go septic*, he had advised. Pain radiated through Amos's insides as he closed his fingers in a sweaty grip. He could make it. He was so close.

Suddenly, a dark object darted in front of him, and Amos hit the brakes, nearly losing consciousness from the shock of the seatbelt locking against his injured abdomen. Britlyn gasped, then cradled her womb worriedly.

"Are you alright?" he asked nervously, glancing over at her.

No — he couldn't kill this woman, he now realized.

"I think so," she answered. She was alert once again. "It didn't squeeze my belly."

Amos looked back towards the gravel road. Before him, a large, boxy body ran by on slender, black legs.

Then, another.

Soon, a seemingly unending stream of cattle had descended the grassy hillside and swarmed the area in front of the truck, blocking Amos's exit with their stampede down the mountain.

"Hang on," Amos cautioned his passenger. He pulled the gear shift into reverse.

As the car jerked backwards, the sound of an approaching siren began to echo through the valley below. Lights flashing, Camden McNulty surfaced in his police cruiser. In the passenger seat, Amos spotted the woman who had purchased his soap just hours earlier.

"Amos Sinclair," Cam announced over his P.A. system. "This is Lieutenant McNulty, Cattail Police. Stop the vehicle."

Amos continued in reverse, accelerating instead.

"PULL OVER," Cam insisted.

"Don't move," Amos instructed Britlyn. He briefly let off the gas. Then, with both hands, Amos lifted his gun and held it out the window, pointing it at the patrol car.

As the gun peeked out, Cam dropped the microphone.

Amos pulled the trigger.

"Get down!" Cam shouted, grabbing PJ's shoulder and yanking her upper half towards her lap. The first bullet penetrated the windshield, and the sound of shattering glass echoed inside the vehicle. The projectile whizzed past them, lodging in the molded plastic of the back seat. As they clenched their legs, Amos continued to fire. Cam watched PJ in fear as the bullets invaded the cab. With each soft whiff into the leather front seats, Cam worried one had found flesh. Shakily, he reached for his radio, then pressed the button with his thumb.

"This is Unit C17. Officers under fire," he relayed. "I repeat, officers under fire. We're pinned down in our vehicle at Mosquito Cutoff. Suspect's name is Amos Sinclair."

He paused to address PJ. "Did you see her?"

She nodded.

He resumed his distress call. "Do not engage. . .suspect has a hostage."

"C17, this is C21. Are you hit?" Corb's voice came in clearly over the radio.

"Negative, C21," Cam answered his brother. He listened closely, noticing the hissing sound emanating from his engine compartment. "But I think the car's toast."

For a moment, the cab was quiet, and Cam carefully peeked out over the dash. Steam poured from the radiator, partially obstructing his view.

"I think he's stuck between us and. . .cows," Cam updated him.

"It's the only way I could slow him down," Corb shared. "We cut 'em loose."

"Cowboy cop," Cam chuckled.

"Yee-haw. Also, we owe Rabble a fence."

"Nice thinking. But I don't know how long they'll hold him," Cam advised. "Those gunshots seem to be scattering the herd now."

"What're you doing over this way anyhow?" Corb realized. "Weren't you heading up to the Hold?"

"Chief sent us this way. Lizzie told him Amos had already left."

"Amos had her hostage. How's she doing?"

"She's at Mineral Lookout waiting on you. Chief says she's pretty shaken up, but she'll be okay. She's staying put," Cam informed him.

"What about you guys? Can you approach without agitating him?" Corb asked.

"He just emptied a clip into my fucking car. I'd say he's already on the edge," Cam advised. "Backup was right behind us. They were waiting on a SWAT vehicle from Coeur d'Alene."

"Good call. Chief know where he's going?"

"Somewhere on the water," Cam answered. "He thinks Amos has a plane stashed."

"Anywhere in particular?"

"Shit. . ." Cam watched as Amos threaded his way through the thinned herd. "He's poking through now. To the left. It looks like he's heading to the bridge."

"The bridge? He won't be able to cross with that dually," Corb reasoned.

"I'm banking on it," Cam revealed. "He'll have nowhere left to go."

"I'm 20 minutes from there. Where do you want me?" Corb asked, bringing Huckleberry to a steady trot.

"We'll hitch a ride with SWAT. You get to Lizzie. In case we don't intercept him, she might have more information about his plans."

"Got it," Corb confirmed. "I'll catch up to you."

"10-4," Cam responded. He took a deep breath, then turned his attention to PJ.

"It's gonna be alright," he promised.

She nodded stoically, continuing to hug her knees.

SEVENTEEN.

Amos shifted the truck into gear once again and began to crawl forward through the dissipating herd.

"There were people in that car!" Britlyn cried out. She swiveled her head towards the back window, watching the patrol vehicle for signs of movement.

"People trying to hurt us," Amos clarified.

"Hurt you, maybe," she said coldly. "They're trying to save me." Her lower lip began to quiver.

"Save you how, exactly?" Amos scoffed. "I am the one who is saving you. ME."

"From what?" she asked angrily.

"Your misogynistic, piece of shit husband, for one," Amos answered.

"Shawn's a good man," she defended him.

"If you knew what got him off you might disagree," Amos snorted, shaking his head.

"He fights against that stuff," she insisted. "He doesn't watch any of that."

"Maybe not the little kids. But the women? He really likes it when they're raped. Strangled. Beaten," he informed her. "Urinated on."

"Stop," she shook her head. "That's not true."

"Why would I lie? I just want you to see the truth, Brit. He can't handle your success. He can't compete with what you've built. . .he has to ride your coattails. And he hates you for it."

"You're lying." Britlyn crossed her arms.

"It's all so fake, isn't it? All these fake families, with their fake fucking values. I'm offering you something real. Anything you could ever dream of, anything the girls could ever dream of. The best medical care, the best educational opportunities — I can make it happen," Amos promised.

"Pfff," she frowned, looking out the window as they picked up speed. "You're just another sicko. Trying to fuck me."

"Oh, I've had plenty of opportunities to fuck you," he reminded her, his voice taking a frightening tone. He reached over and rested his hand on her thigh. "Haven't I?"

Britlyn looked back over at him, meeting his pale eyes. They were watery and wild.

"What then?" she trembled. "What do you want?"

"I want to love you," he explained. "For you to love me. That's all I've ever wanted."

Britlyn's breathing quickened, but she said nothing, choosing instead to look out over the dash.

After a moment, Amos withdrew his hand, focusing on the last stretch of road. At the bottom, a wooden, one-lane suspension bridge spanned the rippling river below. It was rickety and white, with its old cables stretched taut. Rather than cross, Amos stayed left, hugging the mountain and slowing the red truck's pace. As he crawled precariously down the narrow side road, Britlyn rolled her window down, warily watching the water spill through the canyon.

"You're gonna slide right down the bank!" she sputtered.

Amos ignored her, continuing to inch forward until the tires threatened to spin off the edge. He pulled as far left into the foliage as he could, leaving just enough space to exit the truck. He checked his rearview mirror as he shifted into park and turned off the ignition. They were out of sight of the bridge.

Almost in the clear.

Britlyn eyed the road ahead, which abruptly turned into a footpath, then wound down, over and around boulders until it reached the river's rocky edge.

"I can't make that," she said softly, gesturing to her swollen ankle.

Amos stretched a wavering hand towards her.

She shook her head.

"Neither can you," she warned him.

"We're not far," he promised. Even still, his other hand gripped the truck's frame tightly for support.

"If I fall. . ." she trailed off. She studied the rocky slope again.

"You'll be fine," Amos assured her. "Hurry. Take my hand."

"What about the girls?" she asked worriedly. "What if I fall and something happens to them? What if I lose them?"

Amos closed his eyes and his hand, squeezing it tightly into a fist. Then, he withdrew it.

"I won't risk hurting them. I won't do it," she insisted with growing resolve.

"Britlyn, I'm sorry," he began, reaching into his pocket.

"Wait! Please don't kill me!" she suddenly shouted, her eyes growing wide. She started to sob. "Please!"

He pulled the item from his pocket, then dropped it in her hand.

"I'm sorry this didn't turn out as planned," he finished. "You'll be a good mother."

"Are you. . .letting me go?" she asked, staring blankly at the set of keys. It sat heavy in her palm.

"Count backwards from a hundred," he ordered. "Loudly and slowly. If the truck fits, the bridge will take you the back way to town."

Amos winced as he pushed the door shut, then held tightly to the hood until he reached the front bumper. Releasing it, he staggered forward and down towards the shoreline. Each step threatened to claim his balance and send him toppling over.

As he'd hung on the driver's door, it had dawned on him that Britlyn was right. His help was of no use, and he was growing frailer with each passing second. But he could still make it alone; he was only a few hours from Seattle, where he had contacts for medical professionals and would be concealed amongst the city bustle while he recovered. Losing the girl was unfortunate, but the downgrade in criminal activity would also hopefully reduce the manpower behind the FBI's chase.

At the end of the rocky beach, he stepped in.

Though summer was in full swing, the water was cold, and it caught his attention as he waded in up to his waist. But the river here was calm, and even in his current state, Amos glided with relative ease through the nearly nonexistent current. He swam alongside the sharp cliffs until he found the familiar opening, then entered the cave. Tucked inside, with its sleek, folded wings and futuristic body, the seaplane was a welcome reminder of Amos's salvation from the shackles of his past life. No more dressing the part, or suffering through sermons, or stepping in cow shit. Amnesia could finally graduate from his virtual kingdom to his real one, where his heart's every desire was well within reach.

Though the swim was short, Amos had grown tired, and he clung to the floating dock for a moment while he caught his breath. He inched towards the ladder, then tried in vain to pull himself up. He'd visited the site a hundred times, though never in full clothing, and never so exhausted. His thick pants held the cold water like a sponge, and the heavy fabric felt like chains pulling him under. Panicking, he tried kicking his feet forward, desperately searching for a foothold in the darkness that was beginning to swallow him. His arms were growing weaker, and he could feel his fingers slipping off the metal poles.

Before he could succumb to the hungry river, a strong grip dug into his flannel shirt and around a suspender strap at his shoulder. The water let him go, and his dock materialized beneath him.

He wasn't alone, he realized.

Amos scrambled to his knees, finding his weapon in his waistband. He raised it towards the man's face, but paused before he could fire.

It was Chief McNulty.

* * *

"You," Amos softly spoke the realization.

"Mind getting the gun out of my face? I did just hoist you out," Jack said matter-of-factly.

"I remember you," Amos ignored him.

"And I remember you," Jack responded. "When I saw your brother. That must have been real hard for you. Especially at that age." Jack mentally checked off negotiation guidelines: *Listen actively. Demonstrate empathy. Build rapport.*

"What do you know?" Amos scowled, continuing to aim in Jack's direction. "Just another dead kid, right?"

"I understand why you think I'd feel that way," Jack responded. "But no. Not just another dead kid. Your father's comments really shed some light on the situation up there at Anthem Hold. On how bad things were."

"Still are," Amos corrected.

"Still are," Jack agreed. "And I've supported every bill to challenge that loophole. Shit, there's one on the table right now."

"It doesn't matter. It's too late for Adam," Amos choked up. "They made damn sure of that. They took him away from me!"

"I'm sorry," Jack offered.

"Throw them into the furnace of fire; in that place there will be weeping and gnashing of teeth," Amos quoted angrily. "They got what was coming to them."

"Whatever part you may have had in. . .what happened to your parents. . .is old history," Jack encouraged him. "First, the evidence from the fire wasn't well-preserved. And second, you were a juvenile."

"You think they deserved it, then?" Amos asked.

"I think," Jack carefully began. "You have options. It was an understandable outcome after what happened to you. How that would have affected you."

"We did everything together," Amos shared. Whatever warmth he had left had receded from his lips, which were now a troubling shade of blue and quivered as he spoke. "He was all I had. And I couldn't help him. I didn't know until you showed up. . ."

"You didn't know," Jack repeated, reassuring him.

"I could have done more," Amos scolded himself.

"I also lost someone," Jack revealed, holstering his firearm. "My own brother. I've spent a lot of time beating myself up, thinking those same feelings."

"How?" Amos asked. Amos lowered his own gun, though Jack wasn't sure if it was due to his progress or Amos's weakness. Amos pulled his legs towards him and leaned to one side, bracing himself on an arm.

"Drunk driving," Jack admitted. "Killed himself and his wife. Sure, we all said it was bad roads, but roads didn't have nothin' to do with it. I was there."

"That was an accident. That's different," Amos countered.

Jack shrugged. "Or maybe I could have done something more to avoid it. The difference is, I was an adult. You were just a kid. Kids don't carry that burden."

"Fine. But now what?" Amos inquired. "You're gonna throw me on death row anyhow."

"Where's the woman?" Jack asked.

Amos hunched further over his arm, fighting the urge to close his eyes. They fluttered towards the lawman. "In the truck."

"And where's the truck?"

Amos gestured with his gun in the bridge's general direction. "Just off the road. She's fine."

"See, then? Ain't no death penalty for kidnapping. Like I said earlier, you've got options," Jack reassured him. Showing his hands, he took a step towards Amos. "Let me help you up."

"I know my options," Amos suddenly hissed, stiffening his spine and sitting upright. "Stay back!"

Jack obeyed the request, stopping in his tracks.

"I'm not going to fucking prison, either way," Amos informed him. "I won't."

"You may not," Jack encouraged. "I imagine you're sitting on a wealth of information, the kind that makes you a valuable informant. And you'll be in the hospital for a while to think on that. You can meet with lawyers, discuss your position. . ."

"No," Amos refused.

"Whatever options you have," Jack lowered his voice. "They're gettin' slimmer by the minute. You need medical care. Right now."

Amos looked down at his hand with a look of surprise, as if his wiggling fingers belonged to someone else. "I was gonna be happy, you know," he managed a short laugh.

"No, you weren't," Jack said bluntly. "You know it, and I know it."

"What the fuck do you know?" Amos lashed out.

"You think 'cause you got a beautiful woman and some money, you're just gonna wake up to sunshine and rainbows? You're smart, Amos. I hear you dig into people's private lives, their search history and whatnot. And I bet it's a hell of a lot different than what they share with the world."

"What's your point?" Amos hissed.

"Nobody's fucking happy," Jack stated pointedly. "Grown-ups don't get to be happy. Not like a child is happy. Like a child *should be* happy. I'm sorry someone took that from you. And your brother. I truly am. But all you can do is make peace with yourself. Recognize those scars and learn to live with them." Jack spoke the words as if they were sacred to him.

Amos swallowed, trying to hide the heavy lump rising in his throat. Then, he felt a gurgling and noticed the rusty flavor of the saliva that trickled into his mouth. He tilted his head and spit, and a stream of blood flowed through his teeth.

He looked up at Jack. For a moment, fear glimmered in his eyes. It was quickly replaced by a disturbing stillness that turned Jack's stomach.

"Amos," he began. "Adam would want you to get treatment. He would want you to go to the hospital and to get well. You are his brother, too."

Amos shook his head. "Yeah. He was the only one who ever cared."

"That's not true," Jack disagreed. He began to draw closer once again. "Your community cares. I care. Since I met you in your kitchen, I've cared."

Amos cracked a smile, exhibiting a strange aura of relief. With his remaining strength, he raised his pistol to his head.

"Those boys are lucky to have you," he whispered.

"Amos," Jack pleaded. "Amos!"

Jack reflexively covered his ears as the deafening shot reverberated through the narrow cave, vibrating his bones.

* * *

Cam reached out the BearCat's rear door, then gripped PJ's hand, helping her up. She greeted the men inside, then sat on the bench beside Cam. In the already-full armored vehicle, space was limited, and the sides of their bodies pressed closely together.

"Tight squeeze," Cam apologized to her.

"It's alright," PJ replied quietly. Her voice lacked the confidence and conviction he'd come to expect.

"You hangin' in there?" he asked with an upbeat smile.

PJ nodded, but her expression suggested otherwise.

Cam turned towards her, gently resting a hand on her knee.

"You've never been shot at," he deduced.

"Not like that," PJ admitted. "He could have killed us."

"But he didn't," Cam pointed out.

"That's just like you. So nonchalant," PJ shook her head.

"You want to know how I keep calm?" he asked.

She met his eyes.

"I try not to focus on what could have been," Cam explained. "Instead, I just give my attention to what's right in front of me."

He gave her knee a squeeze. "You could have died. I could have died. But here we are. We got through it."

"You weren't scared at all," she smirked.

"Not true," he corrected her. "I was terrified. That's not how I wanted things to end, especially when we were just starting. . ."

Cam caught himself and closed his mouth.

"Starting to what?" she asked, resuming a livelier tone.

"When we were just starting to get to know each other," he finished.

"Hey, Romeo." The Kevlar-clad, muscular man across from Cam kicked him in the foot as he addressed him. Along with the vehicle, Coeur d'Alene had loaned Cattail PD two of their prickliest officers. From behind his wraparound Oakley sunglasses, the transplant squinted with disdain.

"I don't see no red truck," he managed through smacks of open-mouthed gum-chewing.

"It's here," Cam assured him, pulling his hand back from PJ. "There's no way he'd get across that bridge."

The SWAT vehicle parked in the roadway just before the crossing. Neither the BearCat's cameras nor the windows offered a glimpse of Lizzie's Silverado.

"You think he'd bail off the side of the mountain?" PJ asked.

"I think we'd have seen the signs," Cam responded. He furrowed his brows.

"I'm gonna hop out," he informed the unit.

"Me, too," PJ insisted.

Cam nodded.

"We'll cover you," a Cattail deputy responded. The SWAT officers joined in, readying their weapons.

Cam opened the hatch, then slid alongside the vehicle, surveying the hillside. Even without bearing any weight, the joints of the old bridge creaked in the hot sun. The faint rustling of leaves and cawing of nearby crows were softened by the water traveling through the gulley below.

"Anything?" PJ whispered.

He shook his head.

PJ raised her handgun, walking alongside the mountain towards a narrow side road. Suddenly, she stopped.

Cam cocked his head, and she motioned for him to walk towards her. Then, she raised a finger to her lips. As he drew closer, he heard the sound that had caught her attention.

"Seventeen," a woman's voice slowly called out.

"Sixteen."

PJ and Cam followed the road, and the voice became louder.

"Fifteen."

The officers began to pour out of the SWAT vehicle, following the duo down the hill.

"Fourteen."

Cam reached out, gripping PJ by the shoulder. "Wait," he instructed in a hushed tone. "There," he pointed.

Underneath a large tree, an overgrowth of bushes almost camouflaged the truck's bright, red paint. It was parked close to the mountain, as far down the road as it could travel without sliding off the edge.

"Thirteen."

Streaming out the open window, the counting continued.

"Britlyn Robbins?" PJ called out.

A tear-streaked face poked out of the truck. "Yes! Hello?" she cried excitedly.

"Britlyn, Cattail PD," Cam called. "We're coming to you."

He carefully surveyed the truck's cab as he approached. Aside from the woman, it appeared empty.

"The driver — where is he?" he asked.

"The water," she quickly revealed.

PJ shimmed around the side to the driver's door, then climbed in. "We're gonna back this up out of here," she assured Britlyn. "Until you can get out safely. Medical is waiting. You hurt?"

Britlyn shook her head. "He let me go," she replied, as if she still didn't believe it herself.

Corb tiptoed to the front of the truck, then helped direct PJ back up the hill toward the main road. After she parked, he turned towards the banks. In the mud between the boulders that led him down to the river's edge, he could see the flat, low-profile impressions of a man's Oxford shoes. Cam scanned the hillside and the water before him, looking for movement.

His thoughts were interrupted by the sound of a gun.

* * *

The unmistakable sound echoed across the water, sending Cam's heart into his throat and causing him to draw his own weapon in anticipation of a firefight. He swept the hillside and visible banks for the source, but aside from the flow of the Palouse River, there was no sign of movement.

"LT, you good?" The voice crackled over his radio, startling him.

"All good here," he confirmed. "You?"

"Yep," the deputy responded.

"And our vic?" Cam asked.

"Stable."

"You got eyes on that shooter?" Cam inquired, scanning the waterway again.

"Negative. Sounded like it came from somewhere closer to the water. Me an' C28 are gonna head your way."

"Keep your eyes open," Cam cautioned him. He released his thumb, then began another transmission.

"C21, where you at?"

"About to Mineral Lookout. I heard that blast, though. Need me to turn around?" Corb answered.

"No," Cam directed. "Get Lizzie. I don't want her going into shock in the middle of the damn woods."

"Lizzie's tough — she won't break. I'd be more worried she's gonna chase Amos down, too," Corb snorted.

"Well, get her secured, anyhow," Cam insisted. "You hear from the Chief?"

"Nothing," Corb answered flatly.

"I'll reach out. We may need to get a marine unit down here," Cam advised.

"Let me know what he says," Corb replied.

Cam walked closer to the water's edge. With each step, insects shot out from the smooth stones underfoot. The air was cooler down here, but the late afternoon sun was intense, and the bright reflections off the river made him squint his eyes even behind his polarized lenses. He brought his radio to his mouth again.

"Chief, this is C17. What's your position?"

Chief didn't respond.

"Chief, what's your status?" Cam tried again.

The silence that followed brought with it a wave of apprehension.

"Fuck it," Cam grumbled.

He holstered his radio, then sat on a nearby rock and began to remove his shoes. Cam needed to cross the water to get eyes on the beaches further down. The river here was calm and it would be an easy swim, though he preferred to do it without so many layers.

Next, he stripped off his sweaty, black socks.

Just as he got to his feet, the bow of an orange boat appeared from around the sharp bend. Cam's hand went to his gun, but then, he recognized the kayak as belonging to Uncle Jack. Under the brim of his hat, the Chief's face was solemn, and he thoughtfully and methodically stroked the water's surface with the blades of his paddle.

"Amos?" Cam asked.

Jack shook his head, continuing to maneuver the craft towards Cam. At the shoreline, he stopped. "GSW," he informed him. "Self-inflicted."

As Cam studied his uncle's pained expression, he felt a familiar empathy take hold.

Jack felt responsible, he realized. *Powerless.*

"You couldn't have stopped him," Cam comforted him once again.

Jack nodded, gritting his teeth behind tightly closed lips.

"Thanks, son," he managed to croak. For a moment, he let his head hang forward, focusing on the water swirling around him.

As two more of his officers came into view and began to descend towards them, Jack quickly regained his stoicism, softly clearing his throat. "Let's get a raft down here. Got a self-inflicted gunshot wound. His body is in the cove just up yonder," Jack gestured with his paddle. "How's the girl?"

"She's good, Chief. Corb's good, Lizzie's good, PJ's good. I'm good. Everyone's safe," Cam assured him.

"Yeah. Welp, I'm gonna get back to the scene," Jack advised. With that, he pushed away from shore and back upriver, slowly cutting through the waves that lapped at his kayak.

Cam put his socks and shoes back on, then reached for his radio. He needed to update Corb and Lizzie on the status of the investigation. Still, he couldn't quite find the words to say. For a moment, he paused with the device in his hand, watching the water.

It wasn't the first deceased suspect he had dealt with. Though he'd never killed a man, he'd been involved in enough incidents with fatalities to become familiar with death. He was there when Corb shot the absconding parolee on his porch many years ago. Since then, he'd witnessed a man blasted by a shotgun during a home invasion, an eluding motorist who was gunned down by police after weaponizing his car against officers, and a would-be rapist stabbed in the throat by a woman with a fistful of keys. All were on their worst behavior, and some would even say they were asking for trouble.

But even when it was the "bad guy" going down, it never felt good. Cam always wished for a different and less final ending; this was especially true for Amos, who had roamed the playground with Cam as a child.

He thumbed the button on his radio. "C21, this is C17. You reach the lookout?"

"Just now," Corb's voice came through the speaker.

"After you get Lizzie, I need you to do something for me," Cam informed him.

"Go ahead, C17," Corb answered.

"I'm gonna need you to call Nadine," Cam instructed.

"Officer involved shooting?" Corb asked.

"Negative. Just the suspect," Cam revealed.

Faint static buffered the silence between them.

"He's with his brother, then," Corb finally commented. "Even in death, not a bad place to be."

"Amen," Cam exhaled.

EIGHTEEN.

Bringing with him a cloud of dust, Corb arrived at Mineral Lookout in Rabble's UTV, an army-green Polaris Ranger with Mossy Oak seats. Parking the vehicle, he hopped out and trotted towards the structure. Lizzie must have heard him approach, as she was already descending the rickety, wooden steps.

"Hey," he greeted her.

"Hey," she replied. She gestured to the side-by-side behind him. "Huck okay?"

"Huck's fine, just needed a rest. I stabled him at Rabble's for the night."

Lizzie nodded, relieved. "How about that pregnant lady?"

"She's alright. And her girls, too. The hospital's gonna keep her overnight, but all is well," he answered.

"Thank God," she replied.

Corb inspected her with his eyes. "You okay?"

Lizzie took a deep breath. "Yeah, I think so. Just drained is all."

As she began to walk towards the Ranger, Corb detected a looseness in her legs, which she confirmed by catching her toe on a rock, stumbling slightly.

"Let me just give you a hand," he insisted, reaching around her. She leaned into him, her tired body welcoming the support. After a few steps, he eased her into the passenger seat. Lizzie laid her head back, resting it against the frame.

"I think I'm just dehydrated. . .I get low blood pressure sometimes, you know. Do you have a coconut water or anything?" she asked.

"Do *I* have a coconut water?" Corb chuckled as he climbed into the driver's side of the cab. He pointed to her cup holder. "Best I can do is a Gatorade."

Lizzie eagerly reached for the plastic bottle, taking a long swig of the salty, blue liquid. "That'll do."

"You can always pinch a dip if you need a pick-me-up," he offered jokingly, smiling just wide enough to expose the brown tobacco he was sucking.

"Gross. I'll pass," she rolled her eyes.

"Else Rabble's probably got some reefer rolled up in here somewhere," Corb jested again. He looked over at her, but her eyes were closed now, and she had pressed the sweating, cold sports drink against her forehead.

"I just wanna go home, Corb," she managed.

"I know. Almost," he promised apologetically. "We just have to swing by Nan's and grab my truck."

"Okay," Lizzie agreed.

"And then," he added, "we need to go down to the station. To get your statement."

"Fuck," she muttered. "The last thing I want is to be up on some goddamn witness stand and—"

"Ain't gonna be a trial, Lizzie," Corb softly interrupted her. "The case is closed."

Lizzie gripped the grab bar and sat up straight, returning her drink to the cupholder. He glanced over at her briefly, then pulled his gaze back to the road. Her expression echoed the same amalgam of relief and regret he could feel swelling inside himself.

They rode the rest of the way to town in silence.

* * *

Jack rhythmically plucked the tab of his Pepsi like a kalimba, each release of his finger sending hollow, tinny vibrations into the air inside the conference room. While he played, PJ's colleagues cleared the table and packed their things, leaving only sticky donut residue behind. PJ was in the Chief's office, tapping away at an email debriefing her unit back in Salt Lake City. Meanwhile, Cam and Corb were orchestrating the press conference planned out front, which was set to take place in mere minutes.

Ting, ting, ting. Jack continued his song.

A deputy paused in the doorway with a portable podium he had been rolling along. "Chief, you want this out front?"

Jack took a drink, then nodded.

The deputy continued to push down the hall.

Jack reflected on the events of the past few days. When Agent Robbins had called him up only 48 hours ago, he wasn't entirely sure where his investigation would lead. A blood-smeared room. The millionaire, social-platform princess missing from Cattail's ivory tower. An I.T. infiltration. For this small town, these were uncharted waters, but he had a duty to complete this complex undertaking, which required competent, capable officers from inside and outside his department. Then, rather than a body, Corb found their victim alive. A short while later, their suspect was dead, and Cattail was no longer at risk.

Jack's eyes darted to an excerpt from their code of ethics pasted on the adjacent wall:

I do solemnly swear to serve my community; to safeguard lives and property; to protect the innocent against deception, the weak against oppression or intimidation, and the peaceful against violence or disorder; and to respect the Constitutional rights of all people to liberty, equality and justice.

He had fulfilled his oath; so why did he feel so discontent?

Ting, ting, ting.

Corb suddenly entered the room, followed by his brother and PJ, who clutched her closed laptop under her arm.

"You ready, Chief?" he asked.

Jack finished his soda, then crumpled the can in his hand. He wasn't discontent — he was angry. He nodded.

Corb glanced down at his watch. "Let's go, then. Time to feed the animals."

* * *

Outside the Cattail Police Department, the diffuse, red light of the golden hour softened the dark jackets of the bustling crowd that had assembled. Since his first announcement, press coverage had grown, and every major news station now had a suit on site in Cattail, ready for this very moment.

Jack was grateful for the sun's glow, which offered him an excuse to keep his eyes covered behind his reflective lenses without the inference of bad manners. Leaving his nephews, PJ, and her colleagues standing behind him, he approached the wooden podium, the front of which was emblazoned with the department's seal. He cleared his throat, and all was silent but for the distant hum of evening traffic.

"Good evening. As many of you know, I'm Chief Jack McNulty of the Cattail Police Department. We are pleased to announce that, with the help of our law enforcement partners, we were able to locate Mrs. Britlyn Robbins this afternoon, and she is in stable condition, along with her unborn children. Moving forward, I've been advised that press inquiries should be taken up with Mrs. Robbins directly, or her legal team."

"Was it her blood?" one brave reporter piped up, impatiently.

"Why does she have a legal team? Is she suing your department?" another chimed in.

Jack raised a hand. "As I said, those are things you'll need to ask Mrs. Robbins herself. No more questions until it's over — or the conference will be cut short," he threatened.

The crowd fell silent again.

"In addition to Mrs. Robbins' safety, I am also pleased that we did not have any officers injured in the line of duty. These folks have dedicated all of their energy and resources to finding Mrs. Robbins alive, and sometimes that meant entering into uncertain and even dangerous situations. They exhibited exceptional bravery at the expense of their personal safety, and I am honored to work alongside them."

From the crowd, someone began to clap. It soon spread to those nearby, until the applause loudly reverberated off the glass behind the police. Jack glanced in the direction of the instigator and was not surprised to see Cayla loudly slapping her hands together, cheering for her father and brothers. She had pushed her glasses up onto her head, shamelessly allowing her tears to stream down her cheeks.

For a moment, when Amos pointed his gun in Jack's face, Jack had thought of baby Cayla. She was a radiant, happy child, and the light of his life. The sight of her now filled him with the strength he needed to finish his speech.

"And while I am also grateful that our initial assumption regarding this incident being an isolated threat was correct, and that our suspect — Amos Sinclair — is no longer at large, it is with great sorrow that I inform you he is deceased."

Reporters looked at each other, exchanging confused glances. Jack continued.

"For those of you who knew Amos Sinclair, you may also know he lost a twin brother to a childhood disease with a 90 percent survival rate. In some hospitals, 94 percent. This was largely due to what we call Idaho's 'faith-healing exception', which essentially allowed his parents to decline medical treatment in favor of prayer alone. As Chief, I was privy to the pain and suffering he endured at that time. It was apparent that this was a young man in need, who was going to be in need, of mental health services that he would not be allowed to seek."

Cam took a step forward, standing alongside his uncle in unity and support. Corb joined him.

"How exactly did you meet Amos Sinclair in your capacity as Chief?" a voice suddenly rang out from the crowd of reporters.

"I assisted our coroner at the time, Dr. Black, when he went to retrieve Amos's brother's body after he passed," Jack answered.

"How old was he?" the reporter followed up.

"Uh. . .twelve years old, I believe," Jack recalled, then resumed his prior statement. "While Amos is no longer here to diagnose, based on the kidnapping of Mrs.

Robbins and other facts of this case, it appears that the mental impact of his childhood trauma grew, unchecked, like a cancer of its own, until it had become a full-blown illness where he was no longer in touch with reality. In short, he became a danger to himself and others. Like his brother, I consider Amos Sinclair to be another casualty of this exception, which is affecting not only the children directly within its purview, but also the siblings and other loved ones left behind."

"So, you're saying that Amos Sinclair having some bad childhood. . .that's why he kidnapped Britlyn Robbins?" someone asked.

"If I knew *exactly* why folks committed crimes, I'd share that secret with you all and happily retire," Jack smirked. "But I will say that I think that played a large part in his actions. Trauma often does — that part's common knowledge. 'Adverse childhood experiences', it's called. Makes you a lot more likely to become both a victim and an offender."

After a moment of silence, a slender young woman with short, slick, brown hair and tawny skin raised her hand. Jack pointed at her and nodded.

"Thank you for your statement, Chief. With all due respect, I have to say, it is a bold position you're taking with regards to this 'faith-healing exception.' After the pandemic, aren't you afraid of forced immunizations and other ways the law would be abused if it were to be changed?" Her tone was polite and professional, and Jack realized he recognized her from one of the local stations.

"Yeah, I've thought about that. But this isn't about preventative measures, like vaccinations. Or whether you feed your kids homecooked meals versus drive-through garbage, or if they park their butts on the couch all day. It's just basic, diagnostic medical care for existing injuries and illnesses. And it's something that's currently denied to these children. I'm confident existing law could be narrowly tailored to meet this need. Thank you. Next question."

Another reporter spoke up.

"You talk about the law, but isn't it the law that gives parents the right to refuse that medical care in the first place? To make decisions concerning the care, custody, and control of his or her child, like the Supreme Court says?" This journalist, a slender man with an edgy haircut and tight-fitting suit, appeared to be from a much bigger city. His smile was blindingly white but clearly for show. "Who are you to say they should be denied that fundamental right?"

Jack could feel himself getting warm, and it wasn't just the setting sun.

"Sir, I'm a cop, not a lawyer. I can't tell you exactly what the Supreme Court said. But I do have the common sense to know that no parent with the ability to prevent their child's death should have the right to instead stand idly by," Jack asserted firmly.

"I think to some of your more devout neighbors, those are fighting words, Chief," the man continued. "And you're known as a religious man, as well. You don't think your statements here today directly contravene those freedoms?"

"Freedom? I don't think just sitting back and watching your kid die makes you free. Or favored by God. I can't speak for the rest of my department," Jack furrowed his brow, "but I think it makes you a monster."

NINETEEN.

Inside the police department, Chief McNulty paced the corridor, his footsteps echoing off the tile floor that stretched its length. Nadine had assisted in the retrieval of Amos's body, and he appreciated the peaceful, almost meditative manner with which she collected him and began that transport, even as anger rumbled amongst the other members of the PD on scene.

They were young and naive, Jack told himself, mentally forgiving them. And rightfully wrathful. He, too, had felt the stirrings of intense rage towards Amos, especially when he learned he'd fired upon Jack's own family.

Still, there was a sadness that he couldn't shake. Decades earlier, he'd left the boy's home, praying he would turn out all right. And in spite of Amos's parents' passing, Jack thought he had: he'd seen Amos at the Farmer's Market many a time while helping Cayla transport inventory to and from the McNulty property.

During each instance, Amos's smile appeared sincere, and he looked genuinely happy as he talked with customers about his wares. Even after the tragic events that befell him, Jack assumed he'd found harmony.

Perhaps it was he who was naive, Jack realized. He'd wanted Amos to be whole again, so he tricked himself into believing it was so. Maybe because he wished Amos wouldn't ache for his brother as Jack still did. Or maybe to salve Jack's own feelings of helplessness in dealing with Anthem Hold, which even now was still cloaked by the shield of a statutory exemption. He hoped the press conference had shed some light on things, even if it also resulted in heightened tensions between police and the local sect.

Screw 'em.

Exasperated, Jack shook his head, spinning on his heels and making another lap down the hall. This time, he turned into his office, finding Fritz fast asleep on the sherpa-covered foam pad he kept tucked in the corner. He kneeled at the dog's bedside, petting his soft, black fur in long, smooth strokes. Fritz opened his eyes briefly, then closed them in contentment, comforted by his master's hand. Jack felt a sense of comfort as well, and the tightness in his shoulders began to loosen.

"Ahem." From behind him, a voice sought his attention. Jack recognized it, and he tried in vain to hide his contempt as he turned to face the man.

"Agent Robbins," Jack started, observing the banker's box in the man's arms. It was full of his personal effects. "Going somewhere?"

"Oh, you know. . .ISP wants to continue my leave a little, just until they tie up the loose ends," Shawn explained.

Jack managed a tight smile. Both men knew it was due to Shawn's ignorance of internet security measures — as well as moral concerns stemming from the extremely violent pornography comprising his personal collection — that had prolonged his administrative suspension.

"Well, good luck to you," he nodded.

"Thanks, Chief. Guess your boys pulled it off, after all," Shawn responded.

"I told you they'd come through," Jack replied. "They always do."

Shawn smirked. "Yeah. Well, I heard it could have been a lot sooner. You guys had her, then lost her —"

"During a fluid situation with more than one hostage, at that point. I stand by Detective McNulty's decision," Jack stated firmly.

"I know your nephew's girl made things personal for you, too," Shawn continued.

"Careful," Jack cautioned him, rising to his feet.

"I hear you raised her up yourself, practically," Shawn pressed.

Jack's smile dropped. "Best you get on home, Agent Robbins. Have a good night," he said curtly.

"For sure. It shouldn't be a late one for you, either — at least this asshole had the good sense to save the taxpayers' money and just kill himself," Shawn sneered.

Jack crossed the room quickly. Picking up on his master's aggravation, Fritz followed suit, his hair bristling. He let out a low growl.

With his dog at his side, Jack stood over Shawn, who shrunk away towards the door. In a rare occurrence for the even-tempered man, Jack's shout rung through the halls:

"Get the fuck out of my office!"

* * *

Cam and PJ exchanged glances as the Chief's voice bellowed down the hall. Cam ran to the door and opened it, poking his head out of the conference room. Despite cradling his belongings, Shawn did not appear disconcerted. Instead, he haughtily sauntered past, averting his eyes as he passed the two officers.

Cam frowned at the man, crossing his arms.

"Your ears work?" he asked.

"Ye-p," Shawn responded smugly, loudly popping the "P" with his lips, as if the word were two syllables.

"Then pick up the pace," Cam followed up, slowly walking towards him. "You heard the Chief."

Shawn scowled but quickened his steps, scurrying out of the PD.

Behind Cam, PJ appeared in the doorway. "Can't wait to see what's in store for him," she noted out loud.

"He's on admin leave for the foreseeable future, at least," he replied. "And I imagine he'll be decommissioned from the Task Force permanently. You guys going to charge him?"

"Maybe. That laptop was the gateway to a ton of stolen evidence and classified information. Arguably, his complete disregard for security protocols could rise to the level of willfully enabling that information to become available," she surmised.

"Hmm," Cam pondered. "Well, it sounds like he'll be out of our hair for a while, anyhow."

"And out of town," PJ added. "On the way to the hospital, Britlyn mentioned moving back to Seattle."

"Can't say I blame her," Cam opined. "I wouldn't want to be surrounded by reminders of my own abduction. Especially with two babies on the way. Besides, it's not like they ever really adjusted to the community."

"Seems that way," PJ agreed.

Cam strolled back into the room and pulled on a ball cap.

"So, with all the promotions you're gonna get for finding Amnesia, do you think you'll be in the market for a multi-million-dollar, vintage farmhouse?" he teased.

"Not exactly," she laughed. "That's not my aesthetic, anyhow. All that white paint and chippy furniture. . .it's too cutesy. How about you?"

"My trailer's just fine," he insisted. "Perfectly styled. I've got the 'Live, Laugh, Love' sign and everything."

"You're joking," she smiled.

"I'm actually not," he laughed. "It was there when I bought the RV, and I just never found the time to take it down. It has pink carpet, too. Come see if you don't believe me."

They locked stares, and her cheeks flushed.

"Are you inviting me over, Lieutenant McNulty?" she said slyly.

"I suppose I am," he answered. "That's pretty forward of me, isn't it? I told you I'd keep a lid on it, I apologize..."

"You got any beer?" she added with a smile, putting her hands on her hips.

"I do," he confirmed, returning a grin. "Real beer, even. Not that watered-down stuff you all drink in Utah."

"Well, count me in," she nodded.

Cam withdrew his keys from his pocket. "Let's go."

"In your car?" PJ asked, raising her eyebrows.

"Yeah, my car," Cam answered. Then, it hit him: "Shit. . .*my car*." He pictured the steam pouring out from under the bullet-peppered hood. He thought for a moment, then walked down the hall.

PJ followed him to the administration area, where he unlocked a cabinet containing a pegboard for holding keys. Most were checked out, but two remained.

Cam glanced at his watch. "Can't take the car; Sabato starts his shift in just a couple hours." He plucked a tubular key from an uppermost hook. "You like motorcycles?"

"Oh, I don't know. . ." she began nervously.

"Otherwise, we're asking Uncle Jack for a ride," he mentioned.

"No, no," she urged, waving her hands. "Count me out of that awkwardness. The bike will be fine."

Cam chuckled and pocketed the key. "Speaking of Uncle Jack, I'm gonna check in with him real quick. Then we'll hit the road."

* * *

Cam found the Chief seated behind his desk. He was still patting Fritz, though this time the dog had rested its head on his knee.

"Is he gone yet?" Uncle Jack asked, annoyed.

Cam nodded. "He's gone."

"Jiminy Christmas. It's about damn time," Uncle Jack exhaled.

"PJ thinks they're getting out of town, too," Cam informed him.

"Boohoo," Uncle Jack remarked sarcastically. "I like the girl alright. But I won't miss that snake in the grass."

"Me either," Cam agreed, leaning into the door frame. For a moment, it was silent.

"How you holding up?" Cam finally asked.

"Oh, you know. It's not the first time I've seen a person die. Or a suicide, even," Uncle Jack downplayed the situation. "Comes with the job."

Suddenly, Corb shimmied past Cam's body and into the room. Fritz perked his ears, then left his master for the promise of a pet from a fresh pair of hands. Corb scratched the happy dog's neck scruff, then kneeled beside him, brushing the length of his back with his palm.

"Yep. Things get pretty fucked up sometimes," Corb added abrasively.

Irritated, Cam glared at his brother, then addressed his uncle again. "Well, if you want to talk about it. . ." he trailed off.

"Thank you," Uncle Jack acknowledged. "I'll be alright. I just wish things had turned out different for Amos, is all."

"Some cuts are too deep," Cam observed. "It takes a lot of special attention to heal something like that. Some good people in your corner. Trust me."

"Ain't that the truth," Uncle Jack responded, reflecting on his own trials before Sandy helped him to his feet. "And he didn't have anyone," he lamented.

"Well, I'm out," Corb abruptly announced, getting to his feet. "I'll leave you ladies to your touchy-feelies."

"You're an asshole," Cam pointed out.

"I know," Corb winked.

"Corbin, wait," Uncle Jack stopped him. "How's Lizzie?"

"She's good," Corb replied. "Amos knocked her out cold with his pistol, but she doesn't seem to have any lingering symptoms. Mostly just upset. He threatened her niece and nephew, apparently. Got her all worked up."

"You gonna get her home safe?" Uncle Jack asked.

"Of course," Corb assured him. "I can't believe I even got her into this. I put her in harm's way."

Jack bit his lip. "You know, this is not official approval of your. . .methods. . .but I don't think Amos snatching Lizzie up was anything you could have prevented. Not that far from his property. Not really."

"Well, it won't ever happen again. So long I've got blood in my veins," Corb pledged.

"Who's touchy-feely now?" Cam teased him.

"Fuck you," Corb scoffed, waving goodbye as he strolled out the door. Uncle Jack rolled his eyes.

Cam waited for his brother to leave, then resumed their earlier conversation. "Anyhow, I'm here if you need me."

Rising from his chair, Uncle Jack crossed the room and put a hand on his nephew's shoulder. He smiled. "You did good, Camden. The both of you," he praised him.

Cam patted his uncle's hand. "Thanks. Anyhow, my car's shot to shit, so I'm taking the bike."

"Got it," Uncle Jack nodded. "Tell Agent James goodnight for me. Don't forget, she has an early flight to catch."

"What? I don't. . .she isn't. . ." Cam stammered. Uncle Jack's eyes twinkled in amusement.

As his cheeks reddened, Cam shut his mouth.

"I'll see you tomorrow," he finally managed.

"Goodnight," Uncle Jack smiled.

* * *

After the press dissipated, Corb met with both Robs, updated computer records, and called Coroner Klein. He scoured Lizzie's truck for any remaining evidence, then completed the forms relating to its release. Tomorrow, he'd have someone bring it out to her. Tonight, he would personally ensure she got home safe.

Outside the station, Corb slid into the driver's seat of his truck, a champagne-gold GMC Sierra so caked with dust, the metallic paint was rendered dull, and both license plates were illegible.

Lizzie stirred, then looked over at him. Her blue eyes were heavy and bloodshot.

"Go back to sleep," Corb insisted. "You need the rest."

"You guys all finished up?" she ignored him.

"Cattail PD is. At least for this case. The Feds have some work still — they pulled a ton of evidence out of his house. The hidden portion, in particular."

"What about Amos himself?"

"Dr. Klein has him," he answered. "Our coroner."

"For the autopsy?"

"Yeah," he replied. "She's gotta document how he died."

"From being stabbed, right?" she asked.

Corb kept his eyes on the road, pondering her question. He said nothing.

"He killed himself," she inferred.

"Dr. Klein says he would have succumbed to his injuries, anyhow," Corb finally answered. "She was shocked he was still alive. 'He'd have been in a tremendous amount of pain.' That's what she said."

"Well, he did it to himself. He tried to take her from her home. . .that's just plain, old self-defense," Lizzie reasoned.

"Indeed, it is," Corb smirked. "Investigator Lizzie closes the case."

She rolled her eyes.

"I bet your uncle took that pretty hard," she sighed.

"Seems that way. I didn't even know he knew Amos," Corb replied.

"Oh yeah, he's known him since we were kids. Amos was still clinging to Adam when they came to take his body. Jack had to talk to him about it all."

Corb looked over at her dumbly.

"He had to help him say goodbye to his brother," Lizzie continued. "Amos started crying and asking questions, then Jack told him us kids should have been going to the doctor this whole time. His parents flipped out and it became a big thing for the church. They really took it out on Amos."

"Yeah," Corb muttered. "Dr. Klein said that, too. Lots of scars and broken bones and shit from when he was a kid. Some of it healed. Some healed wrong." He thought of the scars Lizzie wore. Though fainter with time, he was sure they'd never fade entirely.

"Did Jack not tell you how he knew Amos?" she asked.

"More likely, I just wasn't listening," Corb sheepishly admitted. "I didn't realize it went past tagging along to pick up the kid's body. I was just giving them hell for being crybabies about the whole thing, but now I feel like a dick."

"No, that doesn't sound like you," Lizzie responded sarcastically.

"I'll make it up to him," Corb vowed, passing the last stoplight on the way out of town.

"Don't dwell on it," Lizzie softened her tone. "He knows you have a good heart."

"Do I now?" Corb snorted.

"Yep. It's your head that's a fucking mess," she teased.

He smiled, and his scars stretched towards his ears. She studied them, recalling the moment she'd first seen the gory pits that the bullet left in his cheeks.

"Those healed up nice," she remarked. "You can hardly see them with the scruff. Does it feel any different?"

Corb passed the McNulty property, driving the last stretch towards Lizzie's. "My face is numb a lot of the time," he revealed. "I used to shave around them — while they were still healing, you know — and I wouldn't even know that I'd cut myself until I got blood all over the place."

Lizzie reached toward him, stroking his jaw with her finger.

"Can you feel this?" she whispered.

"Yeah. I can feel that," he replied softly. Her touch sent electric tingles throughout his body and goosebumps down the back of his neck.

As he turned into her long driveway, she continued to run her fingertips over his face. When they reached the cabin, Corb turned the key backwards in the ignition, and the truck's engine stopped with a shudder. Then, all was quiet inside the cab.

Corb swallowed, then exited the driver's side towards the passenger door, which he opened. Holding Lizzie close, he helped her up her front steps. As they reached the porch, he released his grip, standing back while she opened the screen and fumbled with her keys, their jingle accenting the sound of nearby chirping crickets. Even in the middle of her country plot, hidden deep in the valley, Lizzie was too seasoned and cynical to enjoy the blissful ignorance of an unlocked door. She twisted the knob, cracking open the entry. Then, she turned back to face Corb, resting a palm against his chest. His heart pounded against her hand, and she began to close her fingers around his shirt, which was damp with sweat and flecked with mud. She pulled him towards her.

But Corb planted his heels, resting his hand over hers and squeezing it.

"If you wanted to stay. . ." she began, her chest quickly rising and falling with her quickening breaths.

"Lizzie," he weakly protested. "Come on. I don't. . ."

She closed her eyes tightly and shook her head.

"Don't you say that, Corb. Everything about you is telling me you do."

She squirmed out of his grip, running her hand down his abdomen, which was taut under his shirt. Before she reached his belt buckle, he took a step back.

"It's not that I don't want to. It's just not that simple. It's not. . .a good idea," he explained.

"You can sleep on the floor," she tried.

"Shit, you know I wouldn't be sleeping on the floor. We can't," he stood his ground.

Lizzie opened her eyes. "But why?" she pleaded.

"I don't know," he answered quietly.

She took a deep breath. "Like I said, Corb," she tapped her temple, "you're just one big mess up here."

He nodded. "You have no idea."

"I wish you'd let me in," she whispered. "I care about you."

"Yeah. I know you do," he admitted. "I care about you, too. God knows I do. I don't know what my fucking problem is." In the orange glow of the porch light, his eyes were glossy. "I'm sorry."

Lizzie shook her head with resignation. "No; you have nothing to be sorry for. You saved my life."

He shrugged.

"For the second time," she pointed out. "And I could see that today. I felt like I was visiting Rachel in a prison. And Amos? Look how he turned out. Who knows how I would have ended up if I stayed at Anthem Hold."

"Don't think about that," he said firmly. "Forget that place. Look at your paintings! These galleries. . .you're really doing it. Your dream. You keep the focus on that."

"Yeah, it's good. I'm getting there," she admitted. "I just don't know how I can repay you."

"Repay me?" he huffed. "Even if I wasn't your friend, I'm a cop. You don't need to repay me."

"Not my own personal cop," she argued.

"It's like I said before. . .I will keep you safe. Always. I promised you."

For a moment, only the crickets' songs and the nearby trickle of water filled the air.

"Then let me paint something for you," she insisted. "To thank you."

Corb smiled.

"I was thinking, maybe a painting of Huckleberry? A war horse after today," she grinned.

"I'd like that," he agreed. "I'll stick it up in the barn with all the others."

Lizzie rolled her eyes. "Very funny."

He winked.

"Someday, Corb, you won't live in the barn. You'll get your mind right," she encouraged him. "You'll realize that you deserve love. And when that day comes, maybe we can try this again."

A decade of scorn had fallen away. Its replacement, hope, was a flickering flame, an uncertainty that illuminated his every fear, and every unrealized disappointment, and every imminent anxiety. He wasn't sure he knew how to hope anymore.

Corb leaned forward, gently kissing Lizzie's cheek. Her skin was warm under his lips, and it prompted adrenaline to course through his body.

If he wanted to go, he thought, *he'd better do it now.*

As he descended the stairs to his truck, Lizzie turned back towards her front door and took a step inside. She cursed herself for the hastiness with which she'd let him affect her. Years ago, she had promised her healing heart a more guarded approach. More restraint. Not this wide-eyed, gullible eagerness that had, once again, resulted in Corb holding all the power to make the final decision, leaving her lonely.

"Hey, Lizzie, wait a second," Corb called out to her. He nervously tapped his fingers on the hood of his truck. "Do you wanna catch up sometime, maybe? I hear Sam's gonna play another set at Spud's before he leaves town."

Lizzie emerged from the shadows of the doorway, and the porch light illuminated her soft smile. "I'd like that," she replied.

Corb nodded. "I'll call you," he promised.

Lizzie retreated into the cabin, quickly locating her afghan blanket and pulling it over her shoulders. She hurried to the front window.

From there, she watched as Corb's taillights disappeared down the dirt road.

* * *

Under Corb's weight, the ladder to the loft welcomed him back with wooden noises that softly squeaked from each rung. Even before he decided to dwell in the barn, he'd climbed the ladder many times: as a boy, he had run from his uncle's house and hidden from homework and farm chores here. Then, he'd chosen the site to smuggle Lizzie away when she was at her most vulnerable. Later, when Nan permitted her to stay in a spare room inside the main house, he would still sneak over and meet

Lizzie up here in the loft, where they would fall together into some nest of hay.

Now, the hay loft was home. At the top, skylights nestled in the peaks offered a glimpse of the stars that sparkled against the indigo summer sky. With his toes, Corb pulled at his heels, slipping out of his brown leather boots and kicking them aside. Ignoring a nearby lamp, he made his way through the near darkness to the full-size bed at the far end of the makeshift studio apartment, pulling his badge from his neck and throwing it onto the handmade, knotted quilt he'd had since he was just a boy. He knelt down, momentarily burying his face in the blanket and inhaling the fabric's comforting scent.

After a few seconds, Corb sat up and reached into his nightstand, one of two old, oak ice boxes that had been gifted to him by his Nan. Past a small, velvet ring box, he identified by feel a shapely glass bottle and wrapped his fingers around its neck, withdrawing it from the cabinet. With the other hand, he plucked a crystal tumbler from a stone coaster on the table's surface. Corb had spared the vessel, another heirloom, from a boring life as a water glass, imprisoned in Nan's hutch until the most special of occasions. Instead, it enjoyed nightly use.

The cork stopper dislodged with a gentle tug from the bottle, which vibrated with a tone like a low bell. Corb began to pour, grappling with the urge to fill his glass completely.

Amos had cocked his gun in Corb's face, and Corb laughed down the barrel. But then, the question presented itself again:

Did he want to die — or did he not?

This time, he hadn't thought of his father pitched from the unforgiving bend in the road and into the darkness. Instead, Lizzie came to mind. He thought of the soft creases in her face that had silently formed during the time they lost. Her familiar voice that morning and again tonight, begging him to let his guard down.

He wanted to live.

Sitting on the edge of the bed, he looked towards the prairie. He hadn't a window, but it was no matter.

He could see the horses prancing. Galloping in the golden fields. Shaking silky manes and pawing at the earth, they joined together to run in thunderous splendor.

His small collection of oil paintings glistened in the moonlight and reflected it back towards him, and the whiskey danced like fire in his hands. Corb took a drink.

ABOUT THE AUTHOR

Camellia Cann lives in picturesque North Idaho with her family. A former public defender, in 2022, she put her criminal defense career on hold to dedicate herself to raising her two wild children as a full-time mom. With the support of her wonderful husband, she decided to use the increased time at home to also pursue her  childhood aspiration of becoming a writer. She loves cooking, starting new DIY projects, fine wine (okay, mediocre wine, too), and spending time in the sun during the short — but sweet — Idaho summertime.

Camellia is currently working on the next book in the McNulty Brothers series. It is expected to be released in 2024.

"Thank you for your purchase. If you enjoyed A FAITHFUL FOLLOWING, please consider leaving a review — it only takes a few seconds, and it really helps indie authors like me!"

- Camellia Cann

ATTRIBUTIONS

Photos used in cover art:

- Rob Wingate on Unsplash,
  https://unsplash.com/@robwingate

- Mateus Campos Felipe on Unsplash,
  https://unsplash.com/@matcfelipe

Faith healing and COVID statistics:

- https://www.ktvb.com/article/news/health/coronavirus
  /teen-idaho-covid-19-child-death/277-14f45b94-ad56-
  4c71-ad60-6c93c15b53d0

- https://healthandwelfare.idaho.gov/dhw-voice/covid-
  19-related-deaths-idaho-arent-just-among-oldest-and-
  sickest

- https://www.kmvt.com/2022/01/13/panel-wants-
  legislation-introduced-address-faith-healing-issue/

www.ingramcontent.com/pod-product-compliance
Lightning Source LLC
Chambersburg PA
CBHW021702260626

47154CB00023B/2107